THE BILLIONAIRE'S PROPOSAL

EMERY CRUZ

CONTENTS

CHAPTER 1

Claire

I'm done.

I did it, no matter the obstacles and all the long hours when I thought I would give up. I am so done. A giddiness fills me, and I tamp down the urge to squeal.

I am done! With a smile I can't hide, I click the submit button and let my exam answers speed through the ether to the instructor. She will probably grade them tonight, and after that, I will officially be the latest fashion design graduate from the International Fashion Academy in Paris. Not only that, but I'll be able to appreciate that extra line of fancy calligraphy on my diploma, too, a side note of my extra studies being completed.

I've busted my butt for years to maintain good grades for my bachelor's in fashion design, but I went the extra distance to complete the university's bridal program on top of it. And it's coming to a close at last. All those days of studying, all those nights of perfecting projects. Those will be nothing but distant memories.

"Finished?" the instructor asks as I head toward the door.

I nod and smile wider, so much so that my cheeks start to ache. "Yes. Yes, I am." I couldn't be prouder of myself, but it's not the time to dally and share more than a hug with her as she wishes me well. Taking the last exams for my classes was only one thing on my list today. The tasks I've got lined up for this afternoon are just as important and pressing.

I leave the room with lifted spirits, high on the success of simply getting to this point. My heart has always been in design, and my passion has never wavered from the exciting blank canvas of designing bridal gowns. Some of the courses I took weren't as fun, but I trudged through them all to reach this point. No one enjoys electives and the other junk that supposedly makes an education more well-rounded, but those days are over. I won't have to put up with annoying classmates. No more early test times. No more logging in to check if assignments have been graded with the steady stress of aiming for perfection. I won't miss being a student, but as I hurry down the hall to exit the large, old building in the heart of Paris, I'm happy I've put myself through it.

Now, I'll have the credentials to back myself up. I won't just be another girl who likes to look at pretty dresses and boast that she could make them. I can prove that I've studied it extensively and met the approval of other trusted designers. And if I have any chance of making my real dream come true and one day, have my own wedding gown shop, this is the first hurdle cleared.

Get my degree: check.

Get married so I can have access to my trust fund and use the billions waiting for me there as a capital investment to make it happen...That's next.

Without giving myself a chance to catch my breath from the whirlwind of emotions, I hurry home to hop in the shower to get ready for my wedding. It won't be one of my dreams. Not even close. In just forty minutes, I'll be eloping with my boyfriend, and that's close enough.

It's a roller coaster of high emotions that fuel me to hustle. After the anxiety and suspense of preparing for and taking my final exams, the happiness of finishing them should have filled my soul. I can't take a break now, though. I'll congratulate myself later. As I rush through a shower, I push aside the need to relax. I can't sit down and truly feel at ease until I've seen this appointment through.

Thinking of my marriage as an appointment seemed cold, but I was limited in my choices. My mother has attempted to dominate my choices pertaining to my future, and this is the one way I could wrest some control back in my favor. It's pretty simple, really. I can only obtain the money my father left me once I'm married, and since I've never seen eye to eye about the men my mother wants me to be aligned with, setting up a time and date to marry Owen at the courthouse is the wisest idea I've entertained yet.

Owen Talbot is the sort of man any woman would be lucky to get hitched to. "Mrs. Owen Talbot." I test out the name again as I grab the hanger from my closet for my outfit. "Mrs. Claire Talbot."

I can't help the grimace in my reflection as I pull my smart white Chanel dress on. It's not a gown, but a skirt, one-third of the pantsuit-like ensemble that will work for today. I don't need anything fancy since we're doing this with a business approach, just at the courthouse like it's a transaction of names and titles.

After I put my blouse on, then shrug my arms through the sleeves of the chic jacket, I try it on again.

"Mrs. Claire Talbot." I wince again. It sounds as awful as I feel. I'm sure I'll get used to it one day, but it's not this one. I'm full of nerves, and the only way I can combat them is to think again that this is my only solution for getting my mom off my back.

This whole thing is my idea, so I've got no right second-guessing anything now.

"Mrs. Talbot." That's not any better, but I can't afford to waste another minute in front of the mirror like this. I'll be late to get to the courthouse, and when my phone rings, I sigh and answer on speakerphone so I can multitask to touch up my makeup as I speak to my cousin.

"Hi, Dalton."

"Hey, Claire. How'd the last classes go?" His deep voice fills the room, reminding me how empty it is, and I wish he could be here. I always feel less alone when we chat. He is the only family I've ever embraced. My mom is impossible to tolerate. I have no siblings, nor does he. Dalton is the only connection I can ever count on, and it touches a small part of my heart to know he has me and my tests on his mind.

"Fine. They went perfectly fine."

He chuckles. "Of course, you'd say that."

"Because I studied my ass off to be able to say that."

"No doubt about it, overachiever. I hope Aubrey and I can fly out and come to your graduation next week."

I roll my eyes as I touch up my lipstick. I'd love to see him and meet his girlfriend, but not like that. Since I told Dalton about my plans to elope with Owen, my cousin has been against it. Even his best friend, Caleb, who's like another brother I didn't have, advised me to reconsider marrying Owen like this.

I dismissed their concerns since they've both met the loves of their lives in the last year. Dalton means well, but he sees everything through rose-tinted glasses right now, so an elopement might sound unromantic to him. He's so fortunate to have the freedom to be romantic and do as he pleases, though. I do not.

"Dalton, this is France. They don't have big, elaborate graduation ceremonies like they do in the States."

"Well, we'd love to come and celebrate regardless."

I shake my head.

"And maybe talk you out of eloping..."

"Not gonna happen," I argue airily. "Because in a half hour, it'll be done and over with."

He huffs. "Done and over with? That's no way to view your wedding."

Says you. He just doesn't get it, but it's impractical of me to expect him to.

"I'm going to be late, Dalt." I reach for my phone and hurry out the door.

He sighs. "All right. I'll call you later, okay?"

"Yep." I hang up quickly and leave my apartment. I don't have time to hear him out. Neither of us has time for me to explain my reasoning. And I'll miss this appointment if I try to do either of those.

I reach the courthouse soon enough, but I'm the only one there.

No worries. I check the time, nodding to reassure myself that it's cool. Owen has ten minutes yet. He's punctual to everything, but maybe he's taking a while to get here because it's such a big day. For him.

I'm so hooked on thinking this is just another way to do business, but as I pace, I remind myself that things aren't as bleak as Dalton might worry. I *do* like Owen. He's a great guy. We've had fun dating. Since I suggested eloping, he's been excited about it. We're both young, and while he's already graduated and working in finance, I've only just completed my studies. I know he's enjoying the optimism of having his whole future right before him, there for him to grasp and enjoy.

Another glance at the clock shows that eighty-six back-and-forth paces equals eleven minutes. Still no Owen. With one minute past the hour, that's officially late for him, and that doesn't make sense.

I pull out my phone and swipe past the notification reminder of my mother's voicemail I had yet to find the patience to listen to. Calling Owen, I resume pacing.

"Hello, you've reached the voicemail of—"

I hang up, not in the mood to leave a message about getting here as soon as possible. Already, a thread of worry sneaks under my skin. He's never late. Is that a sign?

I shake my head and take a seat to wait.

Maybe I forgot about a rescheduled appointment he had to take.

Or he might be nervous.

While Owen is punctual, he can be clueless with directions. I bet he thought we were going to a different courthouse.

Multiple excuses filter through my mind, but I refuse to nag and scold him to get here. I've never been the kind of girl to chase down a guy. After my mother's high-handed approach to my life, the last thing I ever want to do is dictate another's actions.

So, I wait.

And wait.

And I wait some more.

Once the minute hand has made a complete circuit around the clock, I sigh and get up. I refuse to run after Owen and drag him here, but his no-show is telling. He's either ghosting me or unable to make it, and I won't know which if I sit here alone any longer.

Dejected and disappointed, I head home. Today's been such a trip of ups and downs, but now a sinking confusion fills me. My stomach twists and my heart starts to throb. Stress is taking its toll on me. I worked myself up, cramming for my last test, and now it feels like too many unknowns linger in my mind, and I fear what answers I might find at home.

If he's even there. If Owen can't find the determination to elope at the courthouse, maybe he's ready to give up on me altogether. With that dreadful thought, I take the steps up to the flat I share with him. I'm tense. My muscles ache, and when I catch myself grinding my teeth, I try my hardest to loosen my jaw and focus on simply breathing as steadily as I can. Going into the exam room this morning hadn't caused this intense fear. As I open the door to the apartment, I hold my breath and wonder if my last-ditch attempt to get my mother out of my life will fail.

Owen stands there. He looks up as I enter the apartment and close the door behind me.

Without a word, he stares at me from the doorway to the bedroom, pausing from shoving his things in a bag.

He's packing. Leaving with no intention to be at my side as my husband.

Dammit.

CHAPTER 2

Claire

"What the hell are you doing?" I set my purse down and draw a deep breath, trying my hardest not to sound like a bitch. My tone is hard despite my best attempts, but I can't rein in the temper that flares at the sight of Owen packing to leave.

"We agreed. We agreed to elope," I remind him as I approach, furious when all he can do is continue to grab things and shove them into a bag. He's so hurried and rigid that he's not pausing to fold anything anymore, just flying through his drawers to remove his clothes and stash them in the bag on the bed.

"We agreed, yeah. Sure. I agreed to elope because you were just so in love with me." He snorts a laugh and shakes his head. "In love. What a bunch of bullshit."

I gape at him until anger takes over me. "How dare you! You're calling me a liar? Accusing me of not wanting to marry you?" I stab my finger at my chest. "I was just there at the courthouse. I showed up while you didn't bother."

"No." He pushes the bag flap down. "No. How dare *you* try to trick me like this." He points to his phone lying on the comforter. "I got a call from your mother."

Oh, shit. My stomach tenses again.

"She found out about our plans to elope. Which was so interesting. Because when I asked if you would like to wait until she could come, you insisted she was too busy on vacation. She wasn't, Claire. She was just at home, stunned to discover your plans to elope. She said she hadn't heard a word about this. None!"

Fine. He caught me in a lie there, but that doesn't matter. It shouldn't matter. If he really wanted to marry me before speaking with my mother, the little technicality about if I told her or not shouldn't make a difference. Of course, I didn't tell my mother about this.

"She called me, asking where I got the idea I should marry you when you belonged with someone else."

I cover my face, feeling like my world is imploding. I plop onto the chair and groan. "I'm not." She would make it sound so awful. "I don't *belong* to anyone." Then I lift my face and narrow my eyes at him. "Actually, I thought that I would 'belong' to you, since we were supposed to elope, and I'd be your wife by now."

He shakes his head, scowling. "I see how it is. I know what you were trying to do. She offered me a freaking bribe, Claire. When I told her we wanted to get married because we were in love, she laughed. She laughed! Like it was such a crazy idea."

I wince, hating that his pride is coming to the forefront.

"So she offered to pay me off if I didn't show up and marry you. What kind of a woman does that?" He resumes packing even faster than before. "At first, I was offended. Then I worried about how she could do that to her daughter, but then she explained."

I'm sure.

"She told me that you could only want to marry me—and so quickly—just to get her to leave you alone."

"And I won't get sympathy from you on that front, then?" I retort.

"It's not mine to give. I don't have time to get between whatever drama you have with your mom. I'm not going to be a scapegoat or an easy out for you. I told you that I would elope because I thought you loved me. That you wanted a life with me."

I stand up. "I do!"

"Which is it?" He turns and crosses his arms to glower at me. "You want a life with me to get out of putting up with whatever your mom has in mind for you? Or you want to marry me out of love?"

I blink quickly, put on the spot. "I love you, Owen." I say the words confidently but deep down, I can't ignore the sensation that I'm not being entirely honest.

He notices. I stalled too long to reply because he snarls and turns back to his bag. "You don't. She's right. She's right about this. You only wanted the convenience of marrying me just so you could be married and get your trust fund. It wasn't about love. It's about money and getting what you want."

"That's not true."

"It is. Don't lie to me. I know how eager you are to open up a dress shop. And you'd only be able to start that with a lot more money than what I've earned yet."

I reach for him as he zips the bag. "Owen. Stop. You can't believe her over me."

"Don't tell me what to believe. It's shocking how easily it all makes sense. You only want to use me as an excuse to escape being forced with someone your mother approves of. Someone wealthy and influential. Someone she approves of. Not just a guy working in finance with no impressive family name."

He wrenches out of my grasp, picking up his bag, and heading toward the door.

"You're just as stuck up as she is, only concerned about your life and what you want to do. And that's nothing but work on dresses and make a name for yourself in design."

I follow him out of the bedroom, enraged that he's stooping so low as to accuse me of such things. After a call with my mother, I shouldn't be shocked. She's always been uncannily skilled at making others turn against me. She's a master of manipulation and an expert in persuasion. If he wants to complain about a woman who's determined to get her way, he's spoken to the reigning champion of it.

"You're a selfish workaholic, Claire." He stops at the door with one hand on the knob and the other clutching the handle of his bag. His glower is hot and serious. He's no longer the boyfriend I tried to love. He's just a pissed-off man who's closing his mind to anything I might say to defend myself and my actions. "I tried to look past that for too long. I thought *I* would be the one with the long hours and demanding career expectations. Not you. It's just taking me this long to accept it's true. You're married to your chosen career, and I refuse to be runner-up for your attention. And I'll be damned if I get married just so you can get the money you want to become even more of a workaholic."

He twists the knob and steps into the hall. After one last withering glare, he looks me over, then turns on his heel to leave as he slams the door shut.

For a long moment, I'm so numb and shocked I can do nothing but stare at the door. The panel of wood offers no solace. It doesn't give me any advice or comforting words. Yet, I lock my gaze on it, stunned into a stupor.

I'd been so confused why Owen would stand me up, but now I know.

I'd been so stubborn to resist the idea that he might not want to marry me, but that Band-Aid has been ripped off, leaving me staggering toward a realization that even my last-resort option is imploding before my eyes.

A swift sense of loathing fills me. I cannot beat the crushing feeling of defeat that swallows me as I consider the fact that my mother has won again. She chased Owen off.

Now, what am I supposed to do?

I scrape my hair back from my face as I slowly turn and face the empty apartment.

Owen was right. When I asked him if he wanted to elope, I did so with the hope that it would be the final nail in the coffin of my mother's control. He guessed correctly. I did have my eye on him because he wasn't another rich guy from a good family of her approval. I was so enthusiastic to pull this off because I figured it would force her hand. That with my married status, she would no longer have an excuse for not handing over my trust fund. I wasn't trying to get that money for the sake of having it. I only wished to have *some* money to start working toward my dreams.

She foiled me. I couldn't guess how she'd gotten ahold of Owen, to begin with, but I had to deal with the fallout.

"What can I do now?" I whisper aloud in the home that had never felt like one.

I have a job loosely lined up for the fall, an apprentice sort of arrangement that one of my instructors offered to be able to put real-life work experience on my portfolio instead of relying on only my education. I've been under the illusion that it would work out just like that. Marry Owen and have my funds released by the time I would be done with that designer position at someone else's shop. I would've been ready to open my place and take off.

Now, I'm stuck. Again. That job in the fall will take me nowhere if I don't have the resources to start up my own place.

I suck in a sharp breath as panic descends upon me. "I can't stay here." I'm not even sure if I have the desire to accept that apprentice position. Because what good would it do now? I didn't want to start a career as someone's assistant or backup. My dreams were too damn big to be constrained like that.

My phone rings, further snapping me out of the trance-like reverie of having my plans ruined.

I furrow my brow as I look at the screen. Two hours ago, I was in a hurry to end my call with him, but now, as I feel untethered and lost, I can't answer quick enough.

"Dalton?"

He sighs heavily. "Hey, Claire. I'm not crazy about how you did it, but I want to be the first to offer you congratulations."

I sniffle.

"Is it as overwhelming as you envisioned it might be?" He chuckled lightly. "It can't be easy going from single to hitched that spontaneously."

"I'm not."

He snorted. "You're not overwhelmed? Well, of course not. You take life by the horns and—"

No. I never did. I never will. Unless my mother is stopped, I'll never have a chance to do anything with my life. "I'm not married. Owen..."

Tears cut me off from explaining that my short-term fiancé not only stood me up but also broke up with me. Big, fat tears leak from my eyes, accompanying gut-wrenching sobs that feel like a horrible ab workout I didn't sign up for.

"Claire?" Dalton has never been a man of many words, and it's a blessing now. As I break down completely, capable of only gasping around my cries, I stutter through the only explanation I can manage. He doesn't badger me for answers or rush to offer stupid words of comfort. He listens to a cacophony of sobs and tears. Sniffles and hiccups, too. I'm a mess, and I express it with raw pain.

I don't know how he can understand, but I try to give him the details I'm able to process so far. Owen not showing up. My mother calling him. Owen leaving me for good. My mother still lording over my funds.

"I don't know what to do now, Dalton." He's aware of my goals to open a shop, and he's grown up with me, treated to a front-row seat of the level of manipulation my mother is capable of. "I have this apprenticeship in the fall, but what's the point?"

"No. Claire, no. Don't give up."

I sob harder, hating these hot tears. "Then what?" I shout, not meaning to yell at him but needing to vent this swirl of anger and desperation for a way out. "Then what can I do?" I'll never quit, but the temptation to throw that option out there feels so logical after my mother thwarted me again.

"Come to Colorado."

"To the boonies?" I huff, wiping at my face.

"Maybe you could come out here for a while. I've got business ventures going on, working with Caleb. I bought this house last year, but I haven't done anything with the guest cabin on the property yet."

"That's your idea? Come hide in the wilderness?"

"No. You have no reason to hide from anything. In fact, this is perfect."

"My life falling apart is perfect?"

He grunts. "Your life isn't falling apart. You just finished school. If anything, your life is just starting."

It doesn't feel like it.

"Caleb is getting married, remember?"

I know he can't be telling me this in some twisted, sick sense of rubbing salt in the wound, but I glare at the wall. "Yeah. I know."

"Lauren is having a hell of a time finding a wedding dress. According to Aubrey, she's getting downright frantic, fretting about it. I bet you could design something that would work."

I blink, letting his proposal settle through the haze of crying. Now, this perks me up. Design a dress for a woman who can't find what she wants? That's a puzzle I would love to solve, while I ignore the bigger riddle of what to do with my future.

True to his nature, Dalton stays quiet. He doesn't need to campaign any further after planting that seed for me to stew on.

I gaze out the window, seeing the Paris cityscape as a distant image. It's not the area I love and want to be part of right now. I'm not a fan of bugs and wild animals, but maybe my cousin has a point here. Perhaps a change of scenery is just the thing I need.

I bet the reception is bad out there, too. That alone—not having easy access for my mother's calls—sounds like utopia.

I never imagined visiting the West, not that far, up on a mountain, but now it sounds like just the place to find my footing.

"How soon can I come?"

CHAPTER 3

Claire

A week isn't a long time, but it feels like I've been waiting an eternity to come to Colorado. After spending years in Paris, I've had to disassemble it within days. I'm not sure yet if I'll return for that apprenticeship position after I spend time in Colorado. There is no way in hell I'll want to stay there, of all places. I'm not an average, outdoor-loving kind of girl. Considering a future way out there in the middle of the mountains is crazy talk, but I'm game to try it for a while.

I'm not certain what my state of mind will be with this change of scenery. I'm hoping I can relax without the pressure to date or even meet any men. I'm really counting on the crappy reception Dalton complains about. The inability to be reached sounds like a blessing, so I'm looking forward to zero calls or emails from my mother. But most of all, the allure of designing Lauren's gown consumes me. I'm excited. I'm focused. Even on the flight to Denver, I'm imagining ideas and shifting through options of what I could present to her. That's why I'm losing interest in that job offer. I don't have to make a decision on it yet, but I realized Lauren would kind of be a job. She won't be a client, not at all. I won't accept a single cent from her because she's Caleb's fiancée. He's like family, so she will be, too.

Besides, I muse as the flight attendant checks up and down the aisle that everyone is prepared for landing, *I can't actually make her a dress.* I'm assuming that Dalton will tell her I can design something for her, and I can—on paper. But I have nothing to *make* a gown for her. I'm coming to stay with them temporarily, and all I'm bringing are suitcases of my clothes and shoes. I have no sewing machine, no bolts of fabric, or dress forms to create any garment. Still, just talking about her dress and helping her find something is the next best thing.

We touch down in Denver, and I quickly secure my bags off the luggage carousel. Dalton texted me earlier to explain that he wouldn't be free to pick me up, but Aubrey is available. So is Lauren, I realize when I see not one but two excited ladies waving at me.

The shorter woman with black waves is definitely Aubrey. Dalton sent me a picture of them last year when she agreed to move in with him. She's even easier to identify because she's holding up a sign written in black marker that says *Welcome Claire Bear*, Dalton's teasing pet name for me because I was obsessed with my Care Bear stuffed animals when I was younger.

Taller and blonde, Lauren holds up a twin sign. She lowers it when I wave at them, and I wonder how they spotted me.

"Well, that was easy!" Lauren giggles as I approach. "You *do* look like a model."

Aubrey rolls her eyes. "What? You were planning on guessing every model-like woman was her?" She smiles at me. "Welcome, Claire." She furrows her brow. "You are, Claire, right? Not some soon-to-be traumatized stranger who's going to call airport security on us for hitting on you?"

I stifle a laugh. They're amusing already. "I'm Claire." I hold my hand out for a shake. "Nice to meet you, Aubrey."

She wrinkles her nose at my hand and instead lunges in for a side hug. Maybe she wanted a full hug, but my carry-on remains between us.

"I'm so excited you're here!" Aubrey exclaims. "Dalton has told me so much about you, but that's not the same as actually getting a chance to hang out with you."

Lauren doesn't wait for her turn. She flanks me on the other side, tugging me her way for a hug as well. "Caleb, too. He's mentioned you so often I feel like you should've been here with us all this time."

Wow. I hadn't been sure what kind of welcome I'd receive. Because both women are with the two men I consider my brothers, I knew they would be welcoming to some extent. This gushing, super-easy acceptance is hard for me to get used to, though. They might have heard of me, but I'm still a stranger.

Smushed between them and still holding my bag, I'm at a loss for how to react or reply. I can't hug them back. My arms are trapped at my sides, but even if they weren't, I wasn't prepared for this. Most of the women I know are mere acquaintances. Classmates at the university came and went, and I kept them at a distance so I could dive into my studies and avoid college drama. Colleagues and instructors were more like necessary stepping stones for me to file away for future reference. And further back, I lacked friends as a child, too. The one time I attempted to befriend someone purely for the sake of a friendship, not a transaction of popularity or anything else of a gain, my mother sent her away, deeming her too inferior for someone of my financial status.

I like to think I'm simply career-driven and focused on my goals, but facing these too-bubbly women emphasizes the fact that I really don't have any true girlfriends in my life. I bet if I did, I would know what to do and say as they release me and step back.

A slapped-on smile has to be a start, I suppose, because they grin right back at me.

"Well, don't just stand there," Aubrey tells Lauren and nudges her with her hip. "Grab a bag, and let's go before the truck is towed."

Lauren giggles as she reaches for a suitcase handle. "Marian would never forgive us if we lost her new truck."

I blink, stumped at so many things. Aubrey can just tell her what to do, as though Lauren is her hired help? And Lauren isn't offended? More than that, the women sincerely intend to help me with my luggage instead of asking for someone to do it for us. Dalton told me that the women were best friends, but their easy camaraderie is so foreign that I can't follow. It can't be a French versus American difference, but something else.

Am I really stuck up like Owen thinks?

"Ready?" Aubrey asks, tilting her head to the side.

I nod, banishing my thoughts as I follow the women. "I really appreciate you coming to pick me up."

"Ah, no problem," Lauren says.

"Sorry if we embarrassed you with the sign." Aubrey sighs. "It was Dalton's idea."

"Caleb thought it would be funny," Lauren adds.

The sign was fine. It's my struggle to know how to act around them that's tripping me up. "That sounds like them," I say instead.

"Maybe it would have been better if Dalton and Caleb were here to pick you up," Lauren said, "but we were just so excited to have another woman around that we couldn't wait!"

I don't know how to reply to that, so I stick with what I'm familiar with. Business, or more to the point, dresses. "And I'm excited to help you, too," I tell them, eyeing Lauren. "I can't wait to get right to work discussing your gown."

"My gown?" She furrows her brow. "Oh! My wedding dress."

"We'll have lots of time for that," Aubrey says. "We'll let you settled in first."

I don't know how.

"Yeah, we want to get to know all about the exciting cousin from Paris!" Lauren gushes.

Me? Exciting? Yeah, right. But they try to unearth me as a figure of grand interest. On the drive to Dalton's property, the women pepper me with questions almost to the point it feels like an interrogation. They keep it fun and silly, though, lighthearted enough that I don't think about Owen, my dreams, or even Paris once.

By the time they reach the cabin and drop me off, I'm halfway warmed up to them, wishing I wasn't so tired and jetlagged that we could spend a little more time together. It's morning, though, and I've been on a plane all night. Jetlag catches up to me, and I find myself yawning nonstop as I wave at the girls as they head back to the truck they borrowed from Marian.

"Remember, Dalton's made plans for us to meet up later in the evening. You'll get your first chance to eat one of Marian's famous dinners!" Aubrey calls back to me at the door.

Dinner sounds so far away, but I know it'll be here before I know it. A nap is critical. I never believed in staying up to adjust to time differences. I love my sleep. I need my beauty and brain sleep, so I go to the largest bedroom and crash.

Or I try to. Sleep simply doesn't come, and when construction noises start up outside, it's impossible to relax at all.

"I know you've got your business ventures," I grouse as I stare at the ceiling, "but I didn't realize you meant they were happening on your land!"

My headphones don't block the sounds. Slipping in my earbuds doesn't cut it, either.

I try to find a Zen place and ignore the distant distraction, but it just does not work.

Fed up, cranky, and about to snap, I growl as I get to my feet. I go to the sliding glass doors and wrench them open. They're stiff to move, but with some elbow grease, I manage a wide enough gap to step through. Mindful of the wet wood, I walk across the deck and wave both arms to capture the attention of the construction crew at a cabin adjacent to mine.

No one notices. Not a single damn man can see me jumping, waving my arms, and shouting. My throat is raw from shouting. Clearly, *their* ear protection is foolproof. Their noisy tools don't help me either.

There's nothing left for me to do but stomp over there and beg them to have some consideration.

"Hey!' I shout grumpily at the first burly man I come across. He doesn't turn off the drill, just peers up at me with raised brows.

"I'm talking to you!"

"What?" He scrunches his face, showing his struggle to hear me without considering shutting off his tool.

"For the love of..." I turn to see another man approaching. "Hey!"

He's younger, and with every step that brings him closer, I see more of his handsome features. Tall, muscled, tanned, and with a sexy, smug smile.

He faces me, towering over me, and slips his sunglasses up to reveal striking green eyes that suggest he's highly amused.

Still, I can't help but lose my train of thought. I came over here to say something, but locking my eyes on this hunk, I clap my mouth shut and frown.

He runs his hand through his thick brown hair, and as he smiles deeper, showing me a dimple, he rakes his gaze up and down me, from my heels to my bed hair.

That does it. I will *not* let this construction idiot ogle me like that, like I'm some freak show interrupting his day. I don't care how hot he is. I refuse to acknowledge how...aware of him that I am at first glance. And I don't want to remember that these guys must be here doing their job for my cousin.

"How can I help you?"

Dammit, even his voice is sexy. Deep and husky.

I set my hands on my hips and breathe in deeply, gearing up to light into him. "I just got off a plane from Paris, and I can't sleep with you all carrying on like this!"

He smirks, pissing me off even more, so I point at his face, making sure he hears me and knows I'm not anything to ignore.

"I've had a couple of really shitty, hellish weeks, so if you could keep it down out here, that would be great."

Because I'm about to reach my breaking point, and I'm tired of staying strong to keep it together.

He extends his hand to me. "How about we start over with some manners this time?"

I look down at his calloused, dirt-covered hand and feel my lip curl in a scowl.

"I'm Sawyer Cameron. How can I help you?"

CHAPTER 4

Sawyer

I face off with the short, petite woman and hold back a smirk. She thinks she can come out here all full of fire and tell me to stop working? Snap her fingers and get her way? I know her type. I can tell just by looking at her that she's one of those uppity, big-city rich women who thinks the world revolves around her.

I watched her pick her way over here. Tommy pointed out that the guest at the luxury cabin was waving her arms. At first, he thought she was trying to capture someone's attention for the sake of having it. Women could be like that. This little blondie wouldn't be the first I've come across, wanting to have men's eyes on her for the thrill of knowing she was hot enough to turn heads.

Because she was. As she climbed down the wet steps at her cabin, then stumbled over the rocky dirt and clumps of mud between her lodging and the road we were putting in, she damn near teetered over and fell no fewer than a dozen times. I could give her credit for determination. Instead of stopping to preserve her fancy, pretty heels that made the trip far more treacherous than it normally might be otherwise, she charged ahead, not turning back until she could give us a piece of her mind.

I watched as she shouted at big old Barry, too, but he was tone-deaf to defiant women. He likely put up with enough crap from his three teenage daughters to want to hear this woman bitching at him while he was on the clock.

I took my time in approaching her, figuring she might cool down once she was no longer in danger of slipping or tripping on her walk here.

But no.

I stand before her for a moment, doing my best not to stare at her and make her any madder. She noticed when I lost control. My curiosity won out and yeah, I looked my fill. From her mud-crusted heels, up those shapely legs, past her trim waist, over her generous rack, and all the way up to her curly short hair, I took her in and sized her up. My diagnosis? She was hot, easily one of the most beautiful women I have ever seen, and with that defiant lift of her chin and the sizzling anger in her eyes, one of the boldest.

"I don't care who you are," she sasses back. "But you have to quiet down out here."

I lick my lips and cross my arms. "Is that so?"

"Yes!" She stomps one foot and windmills one arm to avoid falling.

I bite my lip. If I laugh, steam will rise from her head.

"And who might you be?" I ask cockily. I'm awfully intrigued to know who she is, especially since Dalton hasn't told me that he's planning on having a guest at that cabin yet.

Hayes used to have a lock on most of the construction work up this way, but Dalton never cared for my competitor, opting to hire me for the work he needed done. I'm supervising the installation of a new road this way, making it easier for the luxury cabins out here to be flipped for Dalton to rent. This spitfire's cabin happens to be closest to where we are currently working on the project. It's a shame she'll have to put up with our noise and dust during her stay, but that's on Dalton, not me. The man has millions, if not billions, so I can't understand why he would find a guest prematurely.

"I'm Claire Rennard." Her chin tips up higher yet, and I want to smile wider at her attitude. What, she thinks she can look down her nose at me? She's a full head shorter!

"And you, Mr. Sawyer—"

She points that finger at me, and I catch it. "Mr. Cameron. Sawyer Cameron," I clarify.

She didn't take my hand to shake in the simplest version of polite manners, but now I regret offering to touch her at all. She's sizzling in every way, burning me up with the feel of her wicked glare and the smooth, warm, softness of her skin. She has the silky kind of skin that needs to be caressed, kissed, and treasured, and I can't help but notice the contrast of my filthy hand in her soft one.

She's delicate, I can tell, but her sass suggests the opposite.

You're one of those walking contradictions, aren't you?

"And you," she complains as she yanks her hand back to form a fist to put at her hip again, "need to quiet it down."

"I can't just stop a day's work because you want a morning nap."

She growls. "I'm not telling you to stop. Just keep it down."

I lean in, getting mesmerized by her golden eyes streaked with brown. "We can't exactly do this quietly."

Her lips curl again, and she huffs.

"Take it up with Dalton," I advise as she slits her eyes at me, honing her fury in a finely sharpened dagger.

"I will."

I grin, curious how the man will react to this hotheaded complaint. He has no business telling a guest they can stay this close to the worksite without expecting noise.

As this woman turns, she doesn't disappoint. She twirls around abruptly, likely eager to show me she'll storm elsewhere to get her way, but she moves so quickly that she almost falls over—again. Her arms shoot up in the air, and her mouth falls open in a gasp. With wide eyes, she tips to the side, but I'm quicker. I grip her elbow, catching her before she can face-plant. Once more, I'm seared. A simple touch is all it takes to make me burn inside, and when her cheeks go pink, I'm guessing she's feeling the same damn streak of electrical zing that I am.

That or a mighty hit of embarrassment.

She jerks her arm free and glowers again, probably wishing her evil eyes could smite me on the spot.

Mad, sassy, and cranky. It doesn't matter which. She's beautiful no matter what. I would be quick to say she's gorgeous if not for that big ol' chip on her shoulder.

"Hey, since you're apparently the boss," I tease, "you can keep an eye on my crew today."

Among the hoots and hollers that rise up from my men at the taunt, I watch her walk away, teetering with her arms out due to the constant threat of tripping.

Unbelievable.

Barry sets his drill down and furrows his brow at me. "Why's a guest at that cabin when Dalt knows we ain't done with this part yet?"

I shake my head. "I'm not sure." But I'll be meeting up with him in an hour to talk about all the projects, and I plan to ask him about this development.

Now that the billionaire real estate mogul is done with the city and has moved here to live with his girlfriend, Aubrey, he's got his hands full with similar projects here. His main focus is restoring the old hotels and ski resorts abandoned all over Summit County. It's a solid source of work for me, but first, he's prioritizing my crews completing residential work on his land. Once we're done building this new road through his acreage, we'll be able to connect it to a trio of luxury cabins nearby that are in the works as well.

"So, I met the one and only sexy Ms. Rennard earlier when she wanted to bitch about me for ruining her chances of a nap..." I say after I've brought him up to speed about where my crews are at.

He sighs and shakes his head. "She called me already. I'm sorry, Sawyer. My cousin's behavior is inexcusable."

Cousin? Shit, maybe I should leave out that part about her being sexy then.

"She needed a place to stay."

As if she can't afford one, right?

"And she's been through a lot."

What, not getting her way every time she made a demand?

He shrugs, furrowing his brow as he looks off in the distance. The man has never been one to offer a ton of words, so the fact he's sharing this much is odd, almost like a word vomit.

"I can't make excuses for her, but I am sorry she went off on you."

I grin and lift my hands. "Hey, no worries. I can handle a sassy woman."

His smile seems off, like he can't make sense of what I said. "Sassy? Barry said she was acting like a diva who wanted to throttle you."

"Sort of."

"She's something like a little sister to me and Caleb, but that doesn't mean she's got any right to act like that."

"How long will she be here?" I scratch the back of my neck, hating that he added that part. A little sister? I wasn't exactly best friends with this guy, but that sounded an awfully lot like something a man couldn't ignore in the bro code.

Dalton telling me that Claire is like a little sister means I can't be harsh with her. She's under his protection. I can tell. It also implies hands-off, no matter what.

"I'm not sure," he admits, and I can't decide how to interpret that. Disappointment fills me with the prospect that she might not stick around at all. Because sassy or not, a friend's sibling or not, I am too damned curious about her already.

CHAPTER 5

Claire

Later that evening, I climb into Dalton's truck. I didn't get much sleep, more like none, no thanks to the hot construction worker, but my stomach is growling. Tired or not, I'm impatient to see what is so special about this woman's dinners.

"Brace yourself," Aubrey warns when I'm sure we're close. It's not a long drive, but every minute that passes feels long.

"For what?" I ask.

"Meadow Lane," she quips from the front seat.

A massive jolt nearly sends me flying back toward the window. I grab the armrest and hold my breath. It makes no sense when Dalton continues to drive up the road. "Did the tire fall off?" I ask.

Aubrey giggles. "No. It's just the road."

"Worst road in all of Colorado," Dalton gripes. He takes Aubrey's hand, though, and I smile. Seeing him be so sweet with her warms my heart. If I could ever think about finding and holding on to love, I'd want it to be something like what he has with her. Lasting and deep.

"Hey, if it wasn't for this road, I wouldn't have hated you so much," she reminds him.

"And then we wouldn't have fought enough to get so close."

I blink. "That sounds kind of backward to me." Another hard jolt rocks the sturdy truck, and I slant in the opposite direction as he zooms around a twist in the road.

"But it worked for us," Aubrey says as she leans close to him to kiss his cheek.

"Pothole," Dalton announces before he holds her close.

"They'll never fix this road," she grouses as she sits facing forward again.

He grunts. "Caleb and I are already trying to rally for it."

After more potholes, large cracks, and so many curves I lose count of them, we pull up at a large yellow house. We step out of the truck, and I smile as Aubrey tells me about how Lauren found this place. One of her bigger projects was painting the place this canary color, and I have to agree that it suits it. It's lovely with the setting sun. In the fall, it probably blends in a bit with the leaves changing colors, and then in the winter and spring, it must be a peppy, bright hue to herald the coming return of summer against the drab gray of coldness.

Lauren is no less charming this time as she welcomes me into the big house.

Caleb hugs me and presses a kiss to the top of my head. "Welcome to the Goldfinch," he says warmly.

"What is that smell?" I inhale deeply, about to drool at the scents of freshly baked something. I just spent years in the heart of Paris. There was no shortage of bakeries around my apartment I shared with Owen, but nothing there smelled as lovely as the goods being prepared in here somewhere.

"Marian's magic," Aubrey says with just as deep of an inhale as I did. "Oooh. I love this casserole. She makes these little apple biscuits to go with it, and it is *divine*."

An older woman with long, graying hair comes through the hall, beaming at us all. "Oh, you boys are right. She *does* look like a model!"

Lauren and Aubrey giggle, and I give in to the urge to smile. "I do not," I protest.

"So glamorous." She steps closer, taking my hand to squeeze. It's not a shake, but still, kind of comes across as one. Having her hand on mine doesn't make butterflies take off in my stomach like when Sawyer gripped my finger earlier. A slight blush threatens to warm my cheeks as I think back to it. *Why didn't I let go? Why did I let him hold on to me like that for so long?* I hated how stuck I got on the feel of his rough hand on me, like a taboo threat that was too exciting to stop.

"I'm Marian," she introduces herself, "and I'm so happy to have you here. The boys have talked about you so often, I feel like you were destined to show up."

"Why?" Caleb asks as he leads us into the dining room. "Because her life is kind of rocky?"

I cut him a stern look. I don't need a reminder of why I'm practically hiding here. Lauren jabs her elbow in his side.

"Where are your manners?" she scolds.

"He's not wrong," Dalton says. "We all ended up here when we needed a change of scenery." He gives me a sympathetic look as he holds a chair out for Aubrey.

"Marian," an older man says as he pops his head around the doorway, "that backsplash is done for today." He grins and winks. "I'll see you tomorrow."

I do a double-take, almost missing my chair as I sit. I'm new here, but he looks so familiar that I need to glance at him again.

"Thank you, Jason," Marian says as she waves at him.

After he leaves, I glance around the table, wondering why everyone's giving Marian such sly looks. She doesn't pay them any attention, and I feel too much like a stranger to be so rude as to ask what's going on.

"He totally has a crush on you!" Lauren finally blurts out as we pass dishes around.

Still, Marian doesn't react, not looking up at her and acknowledging her comment. "More chicken, Aubrey?"

"Marian and Jason," Aubrey sings, "sitting in a tree. K-I-S—"

The B&B owner smirks at her. "The only tree Jason and I would fit in was the one that fell down near the house last summer. Stop that nonsense." She's not scolding. It looks like she's fighting a losing battle not to smile.

"It is interesting, though," Caleb says, "that Jason is hanging around fixing so many things so soon after we had the place remodeled last year."

"He's finding something wrong everywhere he looks," Dalton teases. "Almost like he wants an excuse to be here."

Marian still doesn't react. She's either the coolest cucumber ever, or there's nothing to what they're hinting at.

"Maybe the person who did the remodeling did a lousy job," I say, eager to back up this sweet older woman.

She cackles, laughing.

"You won't hear an argument from me," Dalton grumbles. "Hayes was an ass."

Caleb chuckles as Marian beams at me. "No. Jason *is* looking for excuses to hang around." She winks. "I'm just playing hard to get. But thank you for being on my side."

Lauren and Aubrey give her a hard time about being coy with Jason, and even I struggle to keep a straight face. "Why does he look so familiar?" I ask when the chatter calms down.

"Jason?" Dalton asks. "Well, since you met Sawyer earlier..."

Guilt gnaws at me. I regret being so curt with him, but I was so damn tired!

"Sawyer is Jason's half-brother," he answers.

Aubrey nods. "He's got another brother, too, Kevin. He teaches at the same school that I work at."

Marian raises her brows at me. "You've already met Sawyer?"

Dalton snorts a laugh.

"Yes, yes, I have," I reply.

Marian smiles. "We don't often have too many crews working around here. But with these two determined to renovate the whole state, it seems we've got a bevy of business coming our way."

Lauren rubs her hands together. "The bed-and-breakfast will be booming in no time."

"Maybe I won't need to rely on the advertisement to get my reservations," Marian says.

"For this food?" I ask as I take my second helping. "No. If you advertise this, you'll never run out of customers."

"No, how couples who meet here stay together."

I give her a quizzical look. "What do you mean?"

"Lauren met Caleb here. Then Dalton met Aubrey here."

As one, they turn their heads to me. I roll my eyes and shake my head. "No matchmaking on my agenda. Give up on my love life before you even think about it."

I have.

Marian's smile is polite, and when she immediately asks me about my so-called lux life in Paris, I'm grateful. She's sharp, witty, and too observant in noticing that I didn't want any attention on that matter. I need the easy out, and talking about the years I spent in Paris is a much more preferable topic than why I shouldn't hope for a lasting love like the others have found here.

"It sounds like the adventure of a lifetime," Aubrey says. "Studying abroad?" She sighs as Lauren brings out dessert. "I stayed in LA for college because of the scholarships that got me there, but I wish I could have seen more of the world."

"It's no different than an education anywhere else." Being in Paris sounds like a vacation, but it wasn't. I chose it not only because it is such a fashion center, but also because I needed that distance from my mother. "And that *is* what I went for. After all the hours of studying and working on projects, I didn't have much time to party or explore."

"You've always been so dedicated to your interests," Caleb agrees.

"More like her *one* interest," Dalton corrects. "It's always been fashion."

"Not fashion," I reply. Before they can do that model nonsense again, I add, "I'm interested in *designing* fashion."

"All work and no play?" Marian teases gently. "You're a workaholic?"

I sigh, trying my best not to let her use of that word hit me like it did when Owen said it. He'd shouted it like a cruel accusation. Marian is too kind to be like him, and I can't envision her ever calling anyone stuck-up either. It irks me, though, that having a steadfast commitment to making a career can have such a negative connotation, especially as a woman. My mother has and will never lift a finger to do anything that would be construed as work. She's lazy and entitled, with only one goal of maintaining and holding the wealth my father granted her when he was alive. He passed away when I was a teen, and it didn't matter—whether my mother was married or widowed, she was still an old-fashioned elitist, deeming a career a waste of time better left for the inferior plebs of the world.

"It takes one to know one," Marian adds. "This place is my work, and no matter how much I let Caleb and Lauren help, it will always be my dream job."

I grin, loving how easily she gets it. I'm not a workaholic, and neither is she. We simply want to never quit on our dreams.

I counted on coming here to relax and hide from my mom the best I could, but I hadn't anticipated how much I could benefit from finding a mother in Marian here, too.

On the topic of working, though, I smile at Lauren. "And I can't wait to get started on your dress."

"You'll do it? You'll really make me a dress?" Her eyes widen with excitement.

"I can design it." I sigh. "But I don't have the tools and materials to it make one here."

Caleb grunts. "Uh, yeah, you will."

"Fabric? Threads? A form?" I huff. "A sewing machine?" I shake my head. "I know *you* can do what you want with your money, but it's not so easy to set up all of that so quickly here."

Dalton chuckles. "Just you watch."

Caleb takes Lauren's hand. "She *will* have a gown she wants for this wedding. Cuz it's gonna be her last."

"At any rate, Lauren," I tell her as I wait for the jealousy to fade over how much love they have for each other, "could you come over soon to start the design process?"

She agrees, and soon enough, we wrap up dinner and head home.

Caleb and Lauren simply walk over to the big house next door to the B&B, and Dalton drives me and Aubrey back to his property. Within minutes, Aubrey's conks out, too sleepy from the big homecooked meal, I bet.

"Claire?"

I perk up at his voice. "Hmm?"

"Maybe you can go easy on Sawyer, huh?"

I roll my eyes. "He called you to tattle?"

He chuckles. "We're all adults here. No tattling necessary. We were discussing projects and he expressed confusion about why I was renting out that cabin when I knew work was going on. So I explained that you're not an ordinary guest but family."

"Whatever. I don't plan on running into him anymore." And I already ordered the heaviest-duty headphones I could find online.

"He's just doing his job. Keep that in mind the next time you happen to see him."

I narrow my eyes at his smirking reflection in the mirror. I'm not sure I want to know the reason for that amused expression. *Just what did Sawyer say to him about me?*

I shake my head and turn back to the passenger window.

It doesn't matter what his first impression of me is.

He's not worth my curiosity.

Regardless of how strong it is.

CHAPTER 6

Claire

I enjoy my coffee on the deck, but it's already looking to be a hot day. Last night at dinner, everyone was joking about how last summer was just so hot. Unusually hot, and this season seems just as warm. Paris could be uncomfortable at times, but I didn't explore. I didn't set out to vacation in France because I was so busy with my studies and working ahead on projects. The university was cool with the industrial air conditioning, but otherwise, I never noticed how sweltering it could be there.

Just as well that I'm not going on any hikes or anything. I only brought my coffee out here to avoid the sound of the squeaky fan in the living room. I have to add it to the list of other pesky items in the cabin. I know he's letting me stay here to get out of my mother's sight, so I hate to complain for the sake of not being treated to a five-star stay. He's doing this as a favor, and I don't want to sound ungrateful.

Before the sun can really rise and bake me anymore, I head inside. Jetlag still bothers me, but I have something important to look forward to today, something more rewarding than noticing the little odds and ends that stand out at this cabin or lamenting the warmth that's preventing me from sitting out on the deck with my coffee.

Lauren's coming over today, and I can't wait. The chance to sink my teeth into a design excites me, and soon, I fall into a spell of impatience, wanting her to be here already. She arrives before too long, though, and I show her in.

"Hi, Claire!" She comes with me into the living room, where I left a notebook open on the coffee table. I can't help but feel like a student, eager to please and ready to dive into what I studied so long and hard for.

"Thanks so much for offering to help me with this," she says as she sits on the couch. "You cannot believe how challenging this is for me."

"Because of the distance?" I ask. It feels like we're in the middle of nowhere up in these mountains, but so much is online now, not in a studio or shop. That's part of the magic, though, being immersed with the options of gowns. Maybe it just doesn't feel the same being so remote up here.

"Well, yes. That, too."

That too? She said it like that would be an afterthought, not a main point. *What else?*

"It's just something I haven't done, and I'm overwhelmed with all the options."

I pause and let that sink in. Lauren was engaged before, so I'm not sure how to interpret that comment. She probably means an assistant or wedding planner handled it all, and this is her first time taking over the process on her own. That's got to be it.

"I hear you about the options. So many to consider, but that's what I'm here for."

She's like a blank canvas, and she can't have any idea how much this matters to me.

For the next several hours, I focus on figuring out what her dream dress would look like. I don't think about my mother, or Owen, or that apprenticeship where someone else would be in charge. I'm the boss of this design, and I have no room to think about anything else.

We cover lengths and styles. I show her design samples of different dresses. Seated together on the couch, she can lean over and see on my tablet what I'm referencing. She asks about fabrics, and I ask her about what vibe she wants. She tells me what her hard passes are, and I suggest what I think would look good with her body shape.

"Please tell me it won't have shoulder pads." She glances at me sideways with a smirk.

"Shoulder pads?" I slap my pen to my notebook and raise my brows. Sure, she's funny when she wants to be, but I didn't realize she's this kind of comical. "You want to request no shoulder pads?"

She nods, serious, with wide eyes staring back at me.

"Why..." I shake my head. "Why would you even think I would consider *shoulder pads*?" I can't help but cringe at the mere idea of a cushion on her shoulders. Not only are they sorely out of style as a trend that should never allow to rise from the dead, but they would look terrible on her, specifically with her slender frame.

She sighs. "I just wanted to make sure to mention it."

Blinking a few times, I try to guess again if she's joking. "No. No shoulder pads, Lauren." I almost want to shudder at the idea of them.

She perks up and sits straighter, happier after clearing away that detail. "You don't know how much this means to me."

Because I have the common sense to say no to shoulder pads?

"Before you arrived, I woke up every morning with a little sense of dread. That I wouldn't figure this out or even know how to navigate dresses and picking one thing versus the other. You're making it so seamless and simple. So relaxing. And now, I'm actually *excited* about what my dream dress will look like! How long would it take for you to make the dress, whichever style we go with?"

I smile. Has she forgotten what I said last night? "I didn't bring much with me, Lauren. For one, I don't have my sewing machine. I don't have much fabric to show you, and this isn't a well-equipped studio and workspace to create the dress of your dreams." I smile, but inside, I hate that I can't. Talking about what she might like is infectious, and I wish I could count on the experience of handling this myself. Of feeling the satiny smooth materials and shaping it to her size. It just won't be the same to design and envision her gown and let someone else try to bring it to justice, but that's just how it'll have to be.

Lauren smiles and shakes her head. "But Caleb will spare no expense," she reminds me. "I'm aware you've known him for a long time, so I can't imagine how you would think Caleb wouldn't spring for making this happen."

I couldn't. I really couldn't think of that ease of having money like she likely assumes I can. Billions are waiting for me, but I've never once considered myself wealthy. My mother holds those accounts, and she is the "gatekeeper" of my finances. I've only been able to tap a little bit for living expenses, and those were expected to show that I was a Rennard, that I was from a prestigious name. I didn't have the simple capital to open my own dress shop, let alone sourcing the materials and things I would need to make Lauren her dress here.

"He wants you to make my dress," she explains bluntly. "Whatever you need, we'll make it happen."

Those words are music to my ears. My mother might never let me have the funds to work as I've always wanted to, but my cousin's best friend isn't as stingy. He's clearly over the moon about his fiancée, too, and I know he means it when he says he'll get her whatever she wants.

"Look at it this way: you have no budget, Claire. You have full rein to make this dress happen."

I glance around the living room, picturing a dress form, a sewing machine, and another workstation with lighting, letting the magic of her words seep in. "Really?"

"Oh, *yeah*. Really. I've never cared too much about fashion. I never could."

I furrow my brow at that odd statement.

"But I can tell you definitely know your stuff. Even your sketches show so much talent!" She points at my notebook.

"Well, I have a good idea of what I'm working with." That's not true. I have no *things* to work on yet, but I believe her and Caleb, and I will have fabrics soon. "I have a solid grasp on what you'd like," I amend.

I stack up my notebooks when she says she needs to finish an errand for Marian before it's too late, but before she leaves, she grows quiet, watching me like she's debating to say something.

"I heard you were going to elope," she finally says softly.

I hide a cringe. "Yes. Yes, I was." I sense that she's got a story, too. Her comments about not picking her dress make me wonder why, and it seems that closeness and curiosity goes both ways between us.

Lauren is sweet and considerate, I can tell by her words and mannerisms, but delving into the topic of my failed elopement isn't small talk. That's deeper. I've never had a close friend to confide in, and while a big part of me wants to think Lauren could be such a friend, I'm hesitant to open up that much and be too comfortable to share it all. In the end, I'm doing this for money. I'm *working* for her, so already, that connection of a service being rendered has tainted how true our friendship could be.

I only came here to be too busy and slightly unreachable from my mother, but I'll have to face her and return to Paris eventually.

She pats my hand as she stands, interpreting my lack of a further answer correctly. I don't want to talk about it, and she respects that.

After I see her out, a restlessness fills me. Lauren doesn't seem as outgoing as Aubrey. From the little I've seen of the two friends, I've picked up on that. Still, having Lauren here in the capacity as someone who could be a friend, not a client, made the cabin seem less lonely.

To escape the reminder that I have no one to rely on for company or companionship, I head outside. With the sweeping vistas and wide-open scenery here on the mountainside, I should feel smaller. Like one speck of a person in such a vast, large world, but it helps.

Or *he* helps to stave off some of this loneliness. Sawyer is hard at work down below, and when I get as comfortable as I can on the deck that overlooks the area where he's working, I'm reminded that I'm not entirely isolated after all. It's a small thing, but I'll take it.

With a sweating glass of ice water, I do my best to ignore the heat of the sun. My headphones block out the annoying noise of their equipment, and with them as background noise and company, I find it quite workable when I'm no longer alone or restless. Between the fabric sample book I do have and the notes from talking with Lauren, I'm soon lost in sketching more in my book, scheming options of what I could do when I get the materials to work with and make her dream dress a reality.

The only problem I discover is that Sawyer is also feeling the heat. He's so sweaty he's working shirtless, and it's becoming harder and harder to ignore him. My curiosity intensifies, and the temptation to stare is more difficult to ignore.

He's just doing his job. Dalton's words from last night trickle through my mind, and I try to double down on doing *mine*. Each time the cocky man catches me looking, I frown and focus again on my sketch-es.

It's a losing battle, but I can't bring myself to go inside and deprive myself of seeing him out there. I don't know if it's the age-old magnetism of seeing something attractive and struggling to look away, or the deeper desire not to feel so alone in this cabin with so many faults and odd flaws.

Either way, I'll do my best to avoid thinking about exactly why I can't keep my eyes on my own task. It's one thing to admit to being curious about Sawyer, but it's something else entirely to confess that he's too hard to ignore.

CHAPTER 7

Sawyer

My father remarried when my older half-brother, Jason, was twenty-one. A year later, I was born, then a year after that, Kevin was born. When Dad passed away, it would've seemed logical to split his construction company into threes, but Kevin was already in school to be a teacher, and he had no desire for the industry anyway. As such, Jason and I each received half of Dad's company while Kevin got a smaller inheritance not connected to his company. Jason retired a few years back, giving me his shares, and with all of it, I've turned it into an even larger mega-construction company. Work has been good. Jobs have been steady with the ups and downs of the economy. I could retire from working with my hands and showing up with my crews every day, but I'm not ready to go sit behind a desk day in and day out. I'm not sure that lifestyle would ever be for me. I'd miss out on the glorious sunshine and beautiful outdoors.

And, per the last three days working on Dalton's property, I would have missed out on one certain sexy girl from Paris who can't keep her eyes off me.

It looks like she's recovering well from her jetlag, because despite the distance between her up on that deck and me down here with my crew, I can see how fresh and rested she is. For such a fancy woman always dressing to the nines, even way out here in the wilds, she doesn't wear much makeup. Perhaps I've been doing my fair share of checking her out, too, if I could notice how free of cosmetics her face is. I'd own up to it if anyone were to ask. My crew has been giving me shit for glancing at her as it is. More than once, Barry caught me peeking in Claire's direction. Other than shrugging and smiling, I haven't said much about it.

How could I not notice her? Her narrowed gaze on me felt like a hotter ray of heat than the sunshine blaring down. I don't know if it's just a case of sixth sense and knowing someone is watching me or what. I've dealt with that plenty. Working in the residential construction field, I've had to complete numerous jobs in homes or near them, where people can hawk over me and my crew. Out here, though, I figured it would be less visited.

And she's not even supposed to be here. Since Dalton told me the little he had about his cousin who, was more like a baby sister, I've wondered what her story is. What could be so bad in her life that she would want to stay out here before this end of the property was truly ready for guests?

It's not simply a sixth-sense feeling of being watched, though. It's the way she's looking at me that makes it hard to look away. In the few seconds when I meet her gaze, before I can smile knowingly and catch her red-handed for ogling me, she'll stare with so much raw lust that I have to refrain from growling. Then, when she meets my gaze and realizes she's caught again, she'll scowl. That expression only eggs me on, so I've taken to upping the ante of this challenge. I don't normally take my shirt off when I'm working a job. Yeah, it's hot, but sometimes having at least one layer on helps for the sake of comfort and protection from the elements.

I should feel bad about teasing her, but I figure she's able to go inside instead of hanging outside for a glimpse. That's her own doing, and I can't say I hate how she's noticed *me*, not the rest of my crew. I relied on the manual labor of the job to keep me in shape, but hell, Tim over there is a meathead at the gym and busting his ass in the field. She has plenty of us to watch out here, but I can't ignore how it's only me who's captured her eye.

When Friday rolls around, though, I'm glad to call it a week. As fun as it is to entice Claire to look at me, I'm beat. I stick around to help the guys wrap up the project for the day. Since I'm the one in charge, I take my time to ensure the job site is left to my expectations. The guys trail toward their trucks to leave, but I remain to check on just a few more things. Leaving a key in a piece of equipment is a mistake I'll never repeat. A few years ago, a worker forgot a key for the tractor, and a teenager decided to have fun. No one is around out here, but still, I won't take my chances and check that everything is locked up and disabled.

Satisfied that everything is secure, I go to my truck and open the door. An ice-cold beer is calling my name at home, and I can't wait to shower. Before I can, though, strange footsteps sound behind me. I pause, one foot in the truck, and turn to see Claire. She's wobbling through the gravel. That's the cause for the scraping, unsteady pattern of noise. In heels again, she walks down toward me.

Dammit. She's going to break her freaking neck walking around in those shoes. Doesn't she have any common sense?

She lifts her face and makes eye contact. Another scowl, but not as severe. I'm the only one here, so she's got to be coming for me.

I sigh and turn away from my truck, retreating to meet her before she really does lose her balance and scrape up that pretty skin. The denim cutoffs look cute, but they're not worn in at all. And her blouse is so crisp and white it's too, clinically clean to fit in with the scene.

"Looking for someone?" I ask, both in teasing and seriousness. We're both aware of how she's been making a habit of watching me work, but I have no clue why she's seeking me out.

"You."

I want to smile at how bold and honest she is.

"I'm..." She stops at the back of my truck, brushing off her arms as though daring the dust that might have landed there. "I'm..."

I lean against the truck bed. "I don't have all day."

She frowns. "I'm having trouble with some of the outlets in the cabin." She crosses her arms and sighs after she gets those words out, clearly not happy about her situation.

I shrug. "So? Call Dalton." *That's what he gets for letting her stay somewhere not renovated.*

"I don't want to bother him."

I snort. "Well, damn. Should I feel honored that you have no qualms about bothering me?"

"You're already here." She tightens her arms and tips her chin up.

"So, I'm convenient."

She narrows her eyes as she exhales through her nose.

Why is it so fun to rile her up? Is it because she doesn't back down? I've never been shy about facing a challenge.

"Are you just telling me about the outlets, or are you asking for my 'convenient' help?"

"Why would I walk all this way out here just to tell you about it?" she snaps.

I wait her out, biting my lip not to comment on just how she walked down here to me. *Did she wait until everyone else was gone to talk to me alone?*

"I'm asking for your help," she clarifies.

"Then...ask."

Her eyes go wider with annoyance, and I refrain from grinning. She could stand a lesson in manners.

"Will you please help me?" Her tone is defeated, but I give her credit for following through.

I grin and lift my arm, indicating for her to lead the way. With my arm up, I feel the soreness in my muscles, though, and I wonder how long her issue will take. Scratch that idea for a shower. I want to soak in a tub.

I follow her up to the luxury cabin Dalton told her she could stay in. Behind her, I have every chance to check out her ass and legs in those itty bitty shorts, but I don't. I spend too much time spotting her in case she falls, wobbly as ever in those heels.

"None of these work," she says once we enter. She points at one wall of the living room, and I pull out my conductivity tester from my toolbelt. Here, on the wooden floor, her heels click against the even surface, and I sneak a glance at her slender legs.

"You shouldn't walk with those heels on the road we're building. You'll hurt yourself." I squat down, bringing myself to eye level with her knee as I test an outlet.

"I don't own anything but heels."

I drop my gaze to her ankle, then check out her polished nails. *I can tell.*

"I need to check the circuit box."

She leads me to the stairs, pointing at the basement where it is.

"I can find it," I tell her, not wanting her to risk climbing down these steps in those shoes.

I quickly see the wiring issue and head back upstairs. She's coming from the bedroom as I return. In her hand are stark-white designer shoes. "I do have these, but they're hideous."

I roll my eyes and chuckle. "No, don't wear those."

She tosses them to the sofa as she follows me, practically hovering, as I go back to the first faulty outlet and unscrew it from the wall. "Yeah," she scoffs, "they're pretty ugly."

"No. I meant don't wear those if you're going to come down and bug me because they're flat with no tread. Better yet, don't bug me, and you won't have to worry about breaking your ankles or getting your fancy shoes dirty."

She smirks, leaning close and ignoring what I said. "What's that for?"

"To test the electricity," I explain.

"What do you think is wrong?"

I shake my head. "I *know* what's wrong."

"Is that metal prong supposed to be like that?"

I sigh, holding back a growl at this spontaneous episode of twenty questions. I don't mind teaching someone something. I enjoy spreading knowledge. But with her body heat so close to mine and her sweet floral scent invading my nose, I feel filthy—not just because of how much she's luring me to get closer even though I know I shouldn't, but also because of the reason why I definitely don't belong with her. I feel so opposite her and almost unworthy with my rugged, dirt-caked clothes. I've been reminded of how I don't fit with a pretty woman like her. I've been reminded of how not everyone can see the real me past my blue-collar exterior. And I should know better than to wish for something like that with this hot blonde from Paris.

I never learn. Women, snooty women at least, see men like me as nothing more than eye candy, something to appreciate and fantasize about from afar. Never up close.

I answer her questions, and she continues to hover and pepper me with more. As I muse about the contrasts between us, I try to distract myself with a closer look around the room. Sewing patterns cover the coffee table, and piles of fabric cut in squares lay on the couch.

When I'm finished with repairing the rusty parts of the closed circuit, I show her how it's all working by plugging in a lamp. She must have wanted to use it by this chair over here to draw under brighter light. The sketchbook that lies open on the side table catches my eye. If she were to wear a gown like that...*Hot.*

"These are, uh, really good."

She arches her brow at where I point.

"Very detailed," I add so I don't sound so stupid. What would I know about dresses other than how sexy they might look on a woman. That and how quickly I could take it off them. Still, the detail, shading, and pencil work are not that of a hobbyist.

"You're really talented." I glance up to catch her vulnerable expression. For once, she's not scowling or smirking. It's a softer look of surprise that she quickly shutters.

"That doesn't mean much from a guy who swings a hammer all day," she replies.

I pull my lower lip between my teeth, fighting the urge to smile. I'm not shocked she thought that. We are different. But I admire that she said it out loud. I can't figure out why, but I kind of like that she's mean. That she gives as good as she gets, yet I can't shake the suspicion that something else is going on with her than that defiance.

I sigh and step back, reaching into my wallet for my business card. I leave it on the kitchen counter as I pass through and head out, not needing her to see me to the door.

"Call me if anything else goes wrong, all right?"

I exit before waiting for her reply. Because if I stay in there for a moment longer, alone with her and intrigued about how she doesn't back down, I'm afraid I'll want to find more buttons to push.

And I'm not sure what to do if she lets me.

CHAPTER 8

Claire

I came to Colorado because Dalton said the change of scenery would be good after Owen broke up with me. The reception proves not to be as horrible as I thought it would be, but I still ignore my mother's calls and emails. Since Lauren asked me to work on her dress design, I haven't entertained the possibility that I could be idle. I've been anything but. Having an actual "client" sparks me to work even harder than I did when I was preparing to graduate in Paris. Those long nights and days full of studying were just that, studying. Doing the real thing for a real person and not a simulation or assignment makes it different.

Every day, I wake up excited to return to where I left off the day before. Video calls help me check with Lauren, and it seems the bug bit her, too. She's growing more curious and excited about her dress. With her busy decorating and designing the interiors of the motels she and Caleb are flipping, Face Timing her is the fastest and easiest way for her to stay in the loop with where I'm at. It's convenient for me, too, to check if I'm getting warmer with what she is envisioning.

Convenient. I roll my eyes as I stitch another sample of the floral embroidery I think Lauren would like. Sawyer threw that word at me, accusing me of asking him for help with those outlets because he was convenient. Yes, he was. Sawyer was convenient in the sense that he was nearby and likely knowledgeable about basic electrical work. But the way he retorted with that question, he seemed to be making a bigger dig at himself. Like he'd previously been reduced to a label of convenience, rather than something else. In those few minutes when he fixed the wires, he showed me that he was also patient and smart. Then, when he complimented me about the sketches he happened to see in my book, he proved he had a compassionate side, too.

Stop thinking about him. I set the piece of embroidery down in my lap and flex my fingers. I've been at this for too long, and even though I'm seated under the high-powered light Caleb purchased for me as part of the materials and resources I need to make Lauren's dress, I am not doing myself any favors hunching over and overdoing it with the same repetitive hand motions of sewing. This is just a sample piece, and when I make the actual dress, my fingers and wrists will really be in for it if I can't find a suitable sewing machine.

Adding that to the list. Or moving it further up. I have so many to-do checklists I need a master list to keep track of them. One is for weird little things in this cabin that I can't stand. The leaky sink. That squeaky fan blade. The weird way the washer won't kick on. Another list is for things I need to find to make Lauren's dress a reality. More pencils would help, too.

It doesn't matter if it's practicing sample embroidery or redrawing options for Lauren, I'm meticulous about perfecting a vision for her to consider. So many details need to be considered, and it's a good place to pour all of my energy.

Or too much of it. Just as I weigh the pros and cons of taking a break or looking up where I could get a massage to relieve the tension in my neck and hands, a knock sounds on the door.

I'm hopeful it's Sawyer, but as I stand, I push the idea away. Since he called me out on watching him, and even worse, teasing that I was coming down the drive to bug him, I've been going out of my way to not even be visible.

He's shown up with his crew every day, but I refuse to go sit on the deck. He's been out there, hot and so sweaty under the sun with his shirt off, but I will not approach him and give him another chance of saying I "bug" him.

I sat out there because I was lonely. I still am, but I have Lauren's dress to focus on, so the solitude doesn't get to me as much.

It's not him, though, and seeing Aubrey at the door, I wonder if he really meant it. If he really didn't want me to bug him anymore. The only saving grace that I can cling to is the fact he left his business card. When he left, he told me to let him know if I needed any help. That didn't sound like *stay away and don't bug me*. I'm confused about what he wants with me now. After getting my hopes up that it would be him at the door, curious why I wasn't watching him anymore, I hated to think he wasn't interested in anything with me.

No. That's ideal. I don't need him in my life.

"Hello, workaholic!" Aubrey greets me cheerfully and sarcastically in the same breath. "I've been summoned to get you out of the house for a bit. Lauren's right."

"About what?"

She giggles and shakes her head. "That you're trying to become a hermit in here. Come on. We're going out to the Breck."

"Oh, no. No thanks. I'm working on Lauren's design and—"

She tugs my wrist when I lift it to jerk my thumb at the seat I vacated. "Nope, I'm not hearing it. You need to get out, and I'm not taking no for an answer."

Pushy, aren't you?

An hour later, though, when we stroll along the sidewalk with Lauren, I'm glad Aubrey convinced—or browbeat—me into coming with them. Hanging out with friends simply for the sake of spending time together seems so foreign. I never went shopping idly. I either expected to let an assistant handle purchases for me, or I was limited with what I could spend from the allowance my mother permitted me out of the family account. Never before have I had a chance to simply chat and window shop with women my age, who are not only my peers but individuals who aren't employees, friends of the family who matter for the sake of appearances, or colleagues to impress. Lauren and Aubrey have a solid friendship that includes me. They don't make me feel like a third wheel and exclude me since they've been friends for so long. Instead, they ask me questions and seek my ideas about items.

In the one fabric shop we stop at, Lauren listens to me with rapt attention as I explain the differences of what she could have for her dress. The shop is bare bones compared to what I could find in a larger city, very limited compared to Paris's offerings, but I have a start here.

"But can you find the others?" Lauren asks.

"Sure. I will just need to order it elsewhere." I hold up a bit of white material. "But this is a start." After I select the items for purchase, I feel giddy with the high of actually doing this. All these things won't go toward a grade, toward a project for my instructor's approval, but a client, a real bride.

"And this machine will work?" Aubrey asks as I finalize the purchase of a sewing machine.

"It will work for now," I reply, but I don't mention to them that it means I'll be doing a lot of hand embroidery myself. "It'll have to do for now until I can figure out something better."

I set aside the fabric samples the shop owner offered to me. Lauren has been flipping through it, but nothing is catching her eye. "This looks nice, but I feel like I'm just saying that because it's convenient. Because it's here, and I haven't seen everything you have in mind."

I nod, shoving aside another thought of Sawyer because of that one word. He's too hot to be convenient. Too tall and broad, oozing masculinity and power when he's busy working. The way he said it that day, it sounded like he'd been called convenient in a negative way, and I can't shake that nagging thought from my mind.

Who would ever reduce him to a convenience? He makes me so curious and irritated, that he seems the opposite of anything convenient or trivial. But I've got to stop thinking about him. If I'm not careful, I'm bound to mention him out of the blue.

I can tell that Lauren and Aubrey are including me as another friend, but I'm nowhere near the stage of talking about men with them. Flustered with this inability to stop thinking about Sawyer, I latch on to the first thing that comes to mind.

"Where is the wedding taking place?" I ask Lauren. "I know you said it would be indoors, but I'm curious where." *Because designing winter-appropriate outerwear to go with your dress sounds like a fun challenge, too!*

"Oh, let's show her!" Aubrey says.

They drive to the gorgeous venue. It's an older structure near Vale, and I can't help but feel like I've been transported to a mountainside castle.

Lauren walks me through her plans. From the outdoors, to where she'll get dressed and ready, all the way through the ceremony and the reception on site.

I love weddings. I always have and always will. Since I was a child, I've enjoyed the magic of the events. My mother has tarnished my personal dreams of marrying someone out of love. The simple fact that *I* suggested to Owen that we should elope was proof of my hopes being lost. I was really reaching, stooping so low to give up and consider eloping, and with a man who didn't have my heart. But what else could I do? So long as my mother held my trust fund over my head, I couldn't marry out of love. I would never forgive myself for marrying someone she wanted me to just for the sake of being able to get my money and open my bridal shop. At the same time, I also would regret marrying a man out of love and never being able to pursue my dreams.

Despite my issues, I don't begrudge the idea of weddings. As we walk through the venue, I give Lauren tips for decorations and small details that she'll appreciate. She jots down ideas as we explore, and I try not to skimp on anything that comes to mind for what would make the venue pop. I suggest flower arrangements and where they should go. Crystal and china, and what mistakes with linens to avoid. Lights and décor that would work with the seating setup she has in mind.

By the end of the tour, my heart is full. Lauren is beaming, clearly more enthusiastic about her big day. When she gives Aubrey a teasing smirk, though, I have to smile along. "And what will you do for your big wedding?"

Aubrey rolls her eyes. She blushes as she waves her friend off. "Oh, stop. Dalton needs to quit dragging his feet and pop the question first."

"Any hints he's getting ready to?" I ask. I know my cousin is smitten with her, but after his last attempt to propose, I can see why he's taking it slow and not rushing into anything.

Aubrey shrugs, but she can't tame that blush.

Later that afternoon, after they've returned me to the cabin where the bathroom lights still won't stay on reliably, I try to relax with a hot shower. I need to be careful with my posture when I'm sitting and sketching so much. My search for a massage turned out to be a dud. I don't want to find a rental car to drive all the way out just for a massage when Dalton's been so nice about letting me stay here. Still, I need something to get rid of this tension. I rub the back of my neck after I dry off, but as I exit the tub, I realize my calves are sore, too.

From walking over gravel in my heels. I roll my eyes at my reflection.

Outside, the sound of tires grinding up the drive alerts me to a visitor. I furrow my brow. Again? I swear Aubrey said she would be busy grading papers this afternoon. It's a Saturday, so no one would have a reason to be around here.

Not even Sawyer. I growl as I tighten my robe around my waist, go to the door, and step out on the front porch. "Stop thinking about him," I mutter as I reach the railing to peer down below.

Easier said than done. His truck is pulling up here at my cabin, and a minute later, after he parks, the sexy man walks up the steps to the porch I'm peering down from.

My heart races as he comes close, and curiosity keeps my mind running a mile a minute as I try to figure out why he might be here. I have yet to call him for any more repairs even though so many of them are adding up on my mental list.

I hold my breath, realizing I'm in my robe as he looks me up and down slowly. Just when I think I might melt at his smoldering gaze, he hands me a bag.

"What's this?" I ask as I take it.

He leans his elbow on the railing and tips his chin at the bag. "Look."

Inside is a shoe box. I arch a brow as I open it. He bought me a pair of the most hideous shoes ever manufactured. They're white and gray with utilitarian treads. They look sturdy, but so damn dumb.

I shake my head. "Why?"

"I didn't want to watch you stumble around every time you find an excuse to talk to me." He winks, and I feel my cheeks turn red.

"Every time? It was just the once," I argue.

But inside, I want to squeal with what this means.

One, that Sawyer Cameron seems to be busy with thoughts about me all weekend, just like the way he's a persistent thought on my mind.

More intriguing, though, is the second fact—that he's looking forward to me finding another excuse to be near him again.

Chapter 9

Claire

My eyes are about to cross with all the hours I've been spending on these designs, but it's a labor of love, and I get more excited to keep going. I live and breathe to see this dress meeting Lauren's desires, and this afternoon feels like a true test.

I open the door to Lauren and Aubrey. We just saw each other a few days ago when we went to Breckinridge and strolled the streets to shop. Today, they're both giddy and impatient to get inside. With them is Marian, and I laugh at how eager she is to visit. She's delighted to be involved with the wedding planning, gushing over Lauren, and thrilled to be included.

"I'm just so dang excited!" she exclaims after she takes a seat. She chose the armchair, directly across from the sofa, facing me. She pats her hands on her thighs, almost like a drumroll. I try not to feel put on the spot.

"You're bouncing like one of my third-graders before snack time!" Aubrey jokes. She's no better, wide-eyed with anticipation and also facing me. I'm presenting Lauren with the sketches I've come up with so far. I have several pieces of hand-stitched embroidery to show her as well, so she can see the visuals I'm keeping in mind.

"I can't wait to see what you've come up with," Marian tells me. "I've waited so long for this!"

"What, since the day you met me?" Lauren jokes.

Marian scoffs. "I know whatever Claire has designed will be far superior to that mess you wore that day!"

I smile at the trio as I gather my sketchbooks and tablet. Drawings are best when done on paper, in my honest opinion. Nothing beats the sound of a pencil scraping over the sheet and leaving behind art. On my tablet, though, where I've conveyed what I drew by hand, I can easily manipulate more options in the designing program I'm most familiar with.

"Do I want to know?" I tease.

Aubrey shakes her head and shudders. "No. You don't."

"I'm just glad you arrived that day at all," Marian tells Lauren.

It's clear how much she dotes on her. Even if Dalton hadn't told me the basics of their background, it's easy to see that Marian has all but adopted Lauren and Aubrey. They are the daughters she never had. And Marian is the mother they've always needed.

I draw in a deep breath, applying that parallel to myself. The mother I need is someone other than the one I was born to. A woman who would be excited for my wedding and future happiness, not selfishly worried about the financial repercussions of losing control of a trust fund.

"So." I clear my throat and shove aside the emotions. "This is the first option."

For hours, I share the three main designs I've made from what Lauren has told me. I measured her quickly the first time we chatted, but that was just eyeballing her height and size. Depending on which of the three designs she goes with today, I can fine-tune it, tailoring it to her size.

"I'm not sure..." Lauren grimaces, stuck with a volleying focus among all three. "I love them all!"

Aubrey giggles. "I'm sure Caleb can afford all three."

She shakes her head. "No. That's ridiculous. I only need one dress, but I can't pick one over the other."

"What if I combine everything you like from each option into one dress?" I suggest.

She widens her eyes as she gapes at me. "You could do that?" she whispers.

I nod. "This is your dress, Lauren. You can do whatever you want."

She blinks quickly, then sniffles. I feel like I've unlocked a tearful level of this game, and my first instinct is to go still. Lauren is so level-headed and calm, and this is an unexpected turn.

Did I say the wrong thing? Does she want more guidance? Am I making it sound like I don't care? I don't have a chance to properly freak out or worry that I've failed my first client.

She takes my hand and squeezes hard, like she needs to ground herself. "You have no idea what this means to me."

Marian hugs her, stroking her hair. "Lauren didn't get to pick her dress for the previous...non-wedding. Before she came here, no one would have ever told her what you just said."

Aubrey nods, smirking. "Yeah. Her parents were trying to force her to marry he-who-shall-not-be-named."

"Voldemort?"

Lauren laughs, sniffling. "No. Jeremy, my former fiancé. Before I ran from the altar the first time, my parents and Jeremy decided everything. I had no control over the wedding. The day, the dress, none of it."

"Did you say the first time?" I ask incredulously.

She nods as Marian continues. "Lauren ran from her father's vineyard, leaving Jeremy at the altar."

Aubrey raises her hand. "Thanks to my genius diversion." She winks at Lauren.

"I got on a bus and ended up here," Lauren says.

Marian cringes. "In that ugly, horrible prom dress of a wedding gown."

I point at her. "Is that where the shoulder pads came from?"

Lauren shakes her head as Marian goes on. "Then Caleb showed up, and they fell for each other. But then that scumbag, Jeremy, came back and threatened me and Caleb if Lauren didn't marry him."

"Oh, no." I squeeze Lauren's hand.

"So I went back so I could marry him, then divorce him, and go back to Caleb, but Caleb ended up showing up and rescuing me." Lauren smiles.

"He crashed the wedding," Aubrey holds her hand up again, "with my help again, thank you very much, and they're living happily ever after."

"I didn't get to pick the second dress, either," Lauren tells me. "I didn't want to marry Jeremy, but it felt so much worse being totally controlled and having no say in my dress. It was a confining hopelessness, so going through this design process is a huge deal."

"The second one is the one that would give you nightmares," Aubrey says. "Shoulder pads."

"So many layers," Marian adds. "Like a cloud of gloom."

I raise my brows.

"I still say we should burn it," Marian says with a shrug.

"No," Lauren argues. "The smoke from it might release a hex."

"Where is it now?" I ask.

"Buried in a garbage bag with the first dress," Marian says.

"Which would just hex the land, right?" Aubrey jokes.

I giggle. "If you and Caleb came here and fell in love," I tell Lauren, "and Aubrey and Dalton did the same, I think this place is a good-luck charm more than anything."

"What about you?" Marian asks.

"What about me?"

"Doesn't that just mean it's your turn?" Lauren says.

I shake my head, determined not to even think of Sawyer. "I'm glad I can help, Lauren. You remind me why I love bridal design so much." It means everything to me to give her this sense of control and freedom.

After Lauren and I list the things she wants to incorporate into one final dress, Aubrey points at the shoes I left near the door. "I was just talking to Dalton about getting that pair. My other shoes are beat. The tread is almost worn to the sole from all the hiking we do here."

I glance up from my book. "Oh. Sawyer dropped them off."

"Sawyer, huh?" Marian asks.

I look up in time to see Aubrey and Lauren exchange glances. Marian seems alert. "Yeah. Sawyer."

"Is something going on between you two?" Aubrey asks.

I grunt a laugh. "Because he dropped off shoes?"

"Those aren't cheap," Marian says.

Now, I look like a materialistic snob. "They do seem sturdy," I admit.

"They are," Aubrey says.

"So it's not so much that he bought you shoes," Lauren says, "but that he wanted you to have sturdy footwear."

That, or he can be quick to suggest I don't bother him anymore. I can't tell which it is. He wants me to have better access to bug him or to stay away?

"They're just shoes."

"Are you sure?" Aubrey asks.

I feel awkward, pressured to defend myself about anything happening with anyone. Instead of responding, I fall back to an old staple I used in Paris constantly. I avoided the discussion by pretending to be slightly offended.

"I think I would know if something was going on between me and Sawyer." My tone is bitchier than I want it to be because, in reality, it feels good to have girlfriends who would be enthusiastic about a guy like Sawyer being interested in me. It's a night and day difference to my "friendships" over the years, all the acquaintances I merely put up with, those people who only wanted to be near me because of my wealth and status.

If any of those so-called friends learned that a construction worker was giving me attention, they'd ridicule me. If my *mother* was aware a blue-collar man with dirty, work-roughened hands like Sawyer was making me feel all these butterflies in my stomach, she'd throw a fit.

Lauren and Aubrey are not judging him as anyone inferior, and I wish I could embrace that laid-back mentality as easily as they have.

Later that night, long after the three women left, I can't shake him from my thoughts. I decide to take a hot bath and forgot about it for a while. I change out of my clothes and put on my robe but head back to take one last look at the sketch.

It's no longer a matter of *if* something could be going on between me and Sawyer but a matter of if I *want* something to be happening there.

Stop. Thinking. About. Him. I sigh and shake my head, wishing I could clear out these errant thoughts about him just as quickly.

Tapping my pencil against the edge of the sketch, I wonder if this is it. If I've finally finished the sketch for Lauren. It's taking me longer than it might otherwise, likely because of how often I keep thinking back to Sawyer, but it looks complete.

"But I need to find better fabric samples first." It won't do to show her the final sketch and not have something for her to feel, too. As I pull my tablet closer to research where I might find a better shop or supplier, a loud cranking and grinding noise erupts from the basement.

"Oh, shit." I scurry toward the couch, eager to get off the floor, as though the vibrations could seep through the floor. I swear I hear scurrying sounds, and as my heart races, I imagine all kinds of vermin and beasts lurking down there.

I call Dalton, hating that I'll sound so whiny and desperate, but it's late. He doesn't answer.

I whimper again when the noise resumes. Without hesitating, I run to the kitchen and grab Sawyer's business card.

I toy with it, flicking the corner of the paper as I wait in suspense for the sound to come back. Maybe it's gone. Maybe it's—

The cranking thumps louder, and I hold my breath as I call Sawyer.

He did say to call if I needed help...

CHAPTER 10

Sawyer

I have to wonder what she needs this time. Claire just called me, and with the desperation in her tone, I know she's looking for another rescue from a slight issue with the cabin. Something about a sound in the basement, but I'm not too worried. When I was there to check the circuit box and repaired that wiring, I gave the underbelly of the cabin a quick look. No obvious holes for vermin to come in. No strange cracks or leaks that stood out. I've never needed to dabble with home-inspection services, but since I was there, I gave it a quick look.

I yawn as I get in my truck to drive over, curious, to say the least, but not worried. I imagine she'll be tracking each minute it takes for me to arrive, and even though I warned her that I was about twenty minutes away at my home, she's going to be one of those impatient people who obsess about the timing and hold a slight minute over as a grievance forever.

I should be amused about it all. Whatever is making those noises is probably nothing worrisome, but to a city girl like her who's never had to deal with any maintenance or repairs of anything at all, it probably seems like the world is ending for her. It's just another way I can see the differences between us. A woman used to living further from civilization wouldn't freak out like this. A small-town woman could rationalize that something needed to be looked at in the morning. But not Claire. She didn't insist that I come right away, but she asked. Nicely. And I'm just enough of a sucker to want to give in when she's begging and pleading, so clearly needing me.

My younger brother, Kevin, used to give me so much crap about having a hero complex. He'd tease that I wanted to save everyone and deliver on every promise made. That being a "simple" minded man who works with his hands, that's all I would ever have going for me. When he made those jabs and insulted me like that, it was when my high school girlfriend tried to two-time us. She was with me but broke up with me to hit on him. Then, when she grew bored of him, she'd end it with him and wanted me back. If I hadn't been so young and stupid, I wouldn't have entertained any of it, but I was just that, young and stupid, and Kevin's words hurt just like he knew they would.

I could just see it now. Kevin would see me hurrying to Claire's cabin because I wouldn't know how to impress her in any other way than to "save" her. It was bullshit, but the thought struck me as I pulled up to her cabin and approached her door.

Why was I rushing to help her?

Why did I have to be so aware of her when I know she's my opposite?

I don't have a chance to knock on the door. She must have been looking out for me, because by the time I step onto her porch, the door flies open.

And there she is.

Damn, girl.

Last time, when I gave her those shoes, she wore a thick, plush white robe. Tonight, she gives me a peek at something else. In a short, silky robe, she taunts me to wonder if she is wearing a stitch of anything beneath it.

I draw in another deep breath, raking my gaze over her from her curly hair, down the robe she clutches together, all the way along those toned legs, to her bare feet. Hot pink polish glints from her nails, reflecting the light from the lamps.

"Claire." I nod in acknowledgment, hopeful the next time I speak that it won't sound so breathless.

She furrows her brow and licks her lips. "I think it's a bear."

She says it so gravely, so soberly, it's comical. I want to laugh. It's waiting right at the tip of my tongue, bubbling up my throat, but I settle for a smirk and roll my eyes instead.

"It's a bear," she insists, reaching forward to grab my wrist and tug me into the cabin.

I lurch forward, having just enough time to reach back for the doorknob to shut the door after me. I highly doubt a bear is in her basement. I saw no sign of one getting in there the other day. Unless Yogi

Bear rented an excavator to drill his way down there in a tunnel, she is more likely to receive a bear visitor by leaving her front door wide open.

That push and pull makes me stumble forward, and I reach out and grab her arm. The shoes I bought for her are right there on the floor just inside, near the entrance. She hasn't worn them. They remain as clean and brand-new as they were the day I delivered them. A small part of me worries that I was an idiot. That I never should have considered buying such a stupid, practical thing for a high-maintenance woman like her. I knew she probably wouldn't use them. I haven't seen her set foot outside for days. Unlike when she was spying on me and watching me from afar, my act of gifting her shoes made her do a one-eighty and stop looking for me at all. Which means *I'm* the one seeking her out.

I learned my lesson long ago. I won't chase another woman with expensive tastes again. But here I am, falling against her with her haste to get me inside. If she were hurrying me in for something naughty, I wouldn't be opposed to that. But she's not. Her eyes are still wide with panic, frantic to usher me toward the imaginary bear.

That annoying need to please and deliver takes over me, so when I find my footing, almost caging her to the wall, I want to soften and comfort her. Against my better judgment, I want to soothe her and solve her worries.

"It'll be okay, Claire."

She swallows, darting her gaze all over my face. I don't know what she's searching for, but for once, I want her to see that I'm not here to rile her up. Not this time.

"What does it sound like?" I ask. I ball my free hand into a fist to stop from reaching up and brushing her hair back, and I can't bear to think of releasing her upper arm. She sucks in a deep breath and parts her lips, darting her stare from my lips to my eyes. She's still uneasy about this sound that she's panicked about, but I might be distracting her with a hard hit of attraction, too.

"It's a cranky sound."

"A cranky bear."

She scowls. "A cranking noise. Then a grinding one."

I shake my head. "Not following."

After she licks her lips, she makes the noises. Her mimicking what she heard is so comical, and I smile.

Do you have any clue how adorably sexy you are?

"It's a bear."

I shake my head. It sounds like a gear stuck somewhere. "You stay here, and I'll take a look."

She nods, only now seeming to realize I've been holding her upper arm. I release her and step back, needing the clarity of distance from her.

I go downstairs and notice a fainter clicking sound coming from behind the utility door. I glance down at myself, loathing that I'm not wearing my usual worn work clothes, but I sigh and open the door to see what work needs to be done.

Just like I suspected, the blower on the furnace is the culprit, and with a little bit of finagling, I fix the issue and retreat from the slim area. I can only imagine what she'll think when she sees me covered in dirt and grime in her space.

She cringes, looking me up and down when I go back upstairs. "Find the bear?"

"Nope. Just the blower on the furnace acting like a punk." I narrow my eyes as I lift my shirt to wipe my brow. A squeal reaches my ears, but I don't miss how her eyes linger on my abs before I drop my shirt. "What's that?

She lifts her face, blinking quickly. "What?"

I will never tire of catching her looking at me like she wants me for dessert. "That squeal."

She points up. "The fan."

I huff and shake my head. From here, I see the slow drip of the sink in the kitchen. Between the plops of water and the fan blade, she must be going nuts. "Anything else I can do here?"

It's a loaded question, and while I have something wicked in mind, I'm sincerely asking about repairs.

She crooks her finger, beckoning me to follow her toward the bedroom, and I wonder if she read me correctly, or incorrectly, I suppose. I'm quiet as she takes me on a pathetic tour of maintenance past due. Wobbly showerhead in the master bath. The door to her room doesn't shut properly. A draft in every window. I sigh, making a list on a piece of scrap paper.

When we end up in the living room again, I tell her the truth. "I met Dalton right after he bought this property. It used to be owned by a big vacation rental company. They were called luxury cabins, like Airbnbs. While they look nice and modern, they weren't built well."

"I can tell." She crosses her arms, glaring at the squeaky fan overhead.

"I can see if my brother Jason has time to work on this."

She brightens, making this late night all worth the while. "The one who has a crush on Marian at the Goldfinch."

I chuckle. I want to be here to see more of those smiles. "Yeah, but I can handle this instead, actually." I'm all for spending more time with Claire and hanging out. She shouldn't be in my thoughts, but I can't shove her out of my mind.

"I'll come over tomorrow and start on some of those things."

She follows me to the door, and I can't help but wish I could ask if she'll still be wearing that robe then.

"Thanks, by the way," she says softly as she toes the shoes at the door.

I follow the tap of her hot pink toenails on the white of the sneakers, then I drag my gaze up along her leg, wishing my hands—and mind—weren't so filthy that I can't touch her.

I sigh. "Anytime."

As I leave, I wonder when I became a glutton for punishment. Putting myself in the position to be near such a high-maintenance woman so far out of my league is nothing but asking for trouble.

CHAPTER 11

Claire

I wasn't sure if Sawyer would actually show up to work on the cabin. He seemed off last night. Or maybe it was just me. I was panicky, assuming that noise meant a bear was in the basement. In hindsight, I can see that I was overreacting. But when he showed up and seemed so concerned, I felt vulnerable and needy, eager to melt against him and let him solve all of my problems. And when he looked at me with that hungry stare, practically disrobing me with his gaze, I started to forget why leaving the realm of curiosity to fall face-first into desire was a bad idea.

He hesitated, too, telling me Jason could come by and offering to handle my repairs himself. I want to assume he was simply willing to spend more time with me, but as what? For a hope of seeing me in another robe? And if so, is that such a good idea?

Hooking up with a man is the very last thing I need to do. It would be nothing but a rebound, seeking physical comfort and wanting to scratch an itch after Owen's breaking up with me. And there's nothing wrong with that. I just know it's not a remedy for anything, and my life is in need of a lot of fixing.

Considering a fling with someone like Sawyer was even more of a reach. In his rugged work clothes and those filthy smiles that suggest such wicked delight, he's the opposite of anyone I could really bring into my life. He couldn't stay in my bed. He wouldn't fit in with the circles my mother expects me to linger in. Sawyer is the opposite of everything I should want to have in my life. Knowing he's so forbidden lends him a mysterious, sexier air, but it also derails me from even contemplating anything more than a guest-and-contractor arrangement.

I can't choose a man to make mine forever in the name of love. When Lauren, Aubrey, and Marian were talking about me yesterday, I fought to keep the truth quiet. I couldn't explain how my mother has ruined my hope of settling down with a man for the sake of my heart.

And I can't hide here and entertain flings with someone like Sawyer, either. It would get me nowhere, and knowing a true future is impossible makes the entire effort of seeking happiness seem like nothing but a waste of time.

Fortunately, I don't have ample time to sit and dwell about the rut I'm stuck in. Nor can I afford the freedom to marvel at the way Sawyer does show up. He gets straight to work, beginning with the leaking kitchen sink. Instead of ogling me again and tempting me to think about his hands on me—wearing jeans and a plain t-shirt helps there—he's diving into loosening and switching out pipes and pieces. Unlike the work he completed on making that new road for Dalton, Sawyer's not overly loud and obnoxious within my space.

He becomes a fixture, a familiar face and presence, and just knowing he's here and cares enough to carve out the time in his busy work schedule to fit in this cabin's repairs comforts me. The laundry list of things I pointed out last night weren't life or death. I didn't take Dalton's offer to stay here with the guess it would be equal to a five-star hotel experience. But it will give me peace of mind to know some steps are being taken to make this place more tolerable. At least that fan's squeakiness. That sound was unbearable.

With Lauren's decisions yesterday, I'm more honed in to what I'll likely need to make her dress dreams come true. Now that I know how much it matters to her that she picks her own dress, I feel more pressure on my shoulders to make it absolutely perfect. Which means this day is turning out to be a wild goose chase of locating all the materials I'll need. Searching online is a tedious process, but I start to feel hope when I realize a few shops in Denver should be able to help me out. I still don't have a rental, but I can get one. The drive isn't something I'll look forward to. After so many years in Paris, I've fallen out of the habit of driving in America—not that I ever had much experience with it at all. Mother insisted on drivers, claiming the act of operating a car herself was beneath her.

I roll my eyes. "Wonder what the drive time…" I mutter aloud as I type on my laptop.

"Drive time?" Sawyer pipes in from the kitchen. The island where the sink is located stands in the middle of the room, giving me a full view of his progress. "Where are you going?"

"Near Denver." Mostly. Some of the places are scattered around there.

"You're looking at an hour, hour and a half for the drive."

I huff. More than that. I still need a better sewing machine that can handle this job. "Plus all the time spent there." When I was younger, I used to have a better sense of wanderlust. Not anymore.

"Interested in some sightseeing?" he guesses.

I frown, pausing from my search. "No." I shake my head, curious what Dalton told him about me. "This isn't exactly a vacation for me." Getting a change of scenery sounds like a vacation, but focusing on making Lauren's dream dress isn't.

"It's not?"

"Nope." I start looking for places to stay nearest the bigger store I'll have to stop at. No way am I driving all the way to Denver, then hurrying back after a lot of time on my feet shopping. "I just finished my class for my BFA in Paris before I came here."

"BF what now?"

I smile. "Basically, a bachelor's of fashion arts. I also took the required coursework for their bridal design program."

He grins, glancing up at me. "So that's what all those sketches were about."

I nod. I wonder what he thought they were for when he saw them the other day. I haven't forgotten that he said they were detailed and spoke of my talent. While I know his level of critique is far different than what my clients could say, I appreciate his kind words.

"And what does a fashion designer do way out here in the mountains?" he asks. "If your calling is in a fancy shop in Paris…"

"I'm here to design Lauren's dress, but my calling isn't just in someone's shop."

"No?" He raises his brows as he tightens the faucet again. "Where would you work then?"

I stare for a moment too long at his forearms as he tightens the wrench around the metal.

"Claire?" he asks when I don't reply, jarring me from staring.

"A few boutiques were interested in my portfolios before graduation. One has given me a chance to complete an apprenticeship with her at her shop. It's supposed to begin this fall."

"That's great. Having an apprenticeship is a great way to secure work experience on your résumé."

That was my exact thinking. "Or not."

"What do you mean?"

"Designing Lauren's dress *is* work experience outside my education. But I'm not sure I'm completely confident in my ability to do this apprenticeship or to work for anyone else. My dream has always been to open my own bridal shop. To offer my own gowns."

"Then why don't you?"

As soon as his question hits my ears, I clam up. I tense and hold my breath, unprepared to answer. The reply should be straightforward.

I'm not opening my own bridal shop because I lack the capital resources to do so. I don't have the money I feel like I should, and the only way I can get it is to jump through the hoops my mother insists on. I have money of my own. I inherited it after my father died, but I cannot access a single penny of it until my mother approves it. The only way I see that happening is if I marry a man she chooses, and that will end with nothing but hell for everyone involved.

Telling someone like Sawyer doesn't feel right. He's got to be unfamiliar with trust fund drama like this, and having to explain my mother's motivations will likely make this easy companionship awkward. I don't want his pity, and I know he can't help me or save me from this situation. I have a hunch he would be a good listener, but it's easier to skirt around the whole subject about my mother and the money she's holding over my head.

"One day, I will," I tell him instead, wishing it could be true.

My deepest desire is to unlock it all. I can't figure out how she changed the stipulations of the fund to work against me, but she's got it secured and unreachable. Even Dalton is limited on finding out the details, that's how tight she is about the money from my father. Besides, I never had the guts to tell him about it. My cousin is a smart man who can make things happen, but I hadn't felt the hard force of my predicament until now. For years, I shoved that worry to the back of my mind, knowing I had to get through school first. Now that school is done, though, this dilemma consumes me. I can't dismiss it or put it off any longer, and I wonder if it would help or hurt if I open up to Dalton about it. He's no miracle worker, but maybe he'll have some ideas of how I can handle my mother and the way she lords over the trust fund that should be mine.

I can't consider giving in to my mother. That's not an option, even though I feel powerless. I simply can't stomach forfeiting my goal of having my shop. Of being able to give women like Lauren a chance to make their dreams come true on the most important day of their lives.

Sawyer doesn't push after that, and when he gets a call from someone on his crew who's working elsewhere for the day, I tune him out and focus on mapping out how I can get what I need as soon as possible. I never had to hunt for materials at school, and I'm learning just how challenging this phase is in the real world.

"I'm done for the day," Sawyer announces, pulling me out of my searching and negative musing.

I glance at the clock and realize the entire afternoon has flown by. Stretching my back, I nod at him.

"I've got to meet a few guys in town. We're getting drinks." He gathers his tools, preparing to go.

I stand, following him as he heads toward the door, envious for a brief moment that he's so secure in his life and with his friends that he never has to worry about having someone to kick back with.

At the door, he faces me with a small smile. "Want to come?"

His words sound so simple, but they punch me with a brutal force of excitement. Do I? Hell, yes. But the opposite leaves my lips. "No, I better keep working on finding materials."

I could kick myself. I'm not sure why I turned him down. It's second nature to reject invitations. For so long, I made sure to have no life because school was my life. Now, though...

Why did I say that? Because he's getting too close? Because it's harder to remember why I should resist him?

I hate the feeling of regret that washes over me. Just because I've got no business starting a fling with him doesn't mean I can't cling to the tiny shreds of friendship he's offering, does it?

Before I can change my mind, he dips his chin and opens the door. "I'll pop in every once in a while, as my schedule allows. You know, to continue bringing this cabin up-to-date."

"Thanks." I hold the door and watch him go, torn with the idea of missing him already.

He's not mine to have or miss. But what I wish I could have with him scares me even more because I know better than to dare to think with my heart and wish for anything lasting.

CHAPTER 12

Claire

"I can't wait," Lauren tells me as she leaves the cabin. She takes my hands again and squeezes them tight. Her eyes are glossy with unshed tears, and I hold back on the pity. This woman doesn't need my pity for the reminder of why choosing her final design for her dress is such an emotional experience. Of course, it's a memorable moment. What she needs now is my encouragement and determination to make it happen.

And I will. Somehow.

"Me too, girl. Me too." I'm absolutely itching to get my hands on some proper fabric. New bolts of material to test the feeling of it and examine the thread. More samples of lacework. Different styles of beads and adornments. It's been so long since I've held anything. Sketching and imagining a design on paper is only half of the experience to get to the phase where the real magic can begin.

I'm overdue to plunge into a project, and I'm eager to make it happen.

After Lauren leaves, I do my best to prepare for how the creation of this dress will take over all my hours. It's going to commandeer this living room, too, but not yet. Too many pieces of furniture stand in the way. I need to figure out better lighting options. I also need to check how I can move that longer table from the dining room to the area over by the front door. Light is critical, and I already know I'll need another heavy-duty work lamp.

Brace yourself, Caleb. The spending is only beginning.

I spend hours organizing and rearranging the living room to warp it into a decent workshop. I didn't realize I've been here long enough to let clutter accumulate, and that's the first thing I need to get rid of. Then there are all of the materials I've been starting to collect. Fabric samples that don't cut it. Trays with spools of thread. Containers of pins. And the form! I can finally drag out the mannequins I ordered. Marian dropped them off since they were sent to the Goldfinch, and she was eager to deliver them because she was so excited for Lauren's dress to be made. I ordered three: a full-size, one to the waist, and then another that is cut off at the bust. Each will be used in different stages, and I debate which should go where. It shouldn't be this hard to make room for my equipment, but I struggle to make up my mind.

After lunch, I spend time dusting as well. Moving all these pieces of furniture around reveals all the nooks and crannies that have collected dust, and that's unacceptable. I need this space as clean as can be, so with my earbuds in my ears, blasting music so I can really get into the cleaning spirit, I almost miss someone knocking on the front door.

Sawyer!

He said he'd pop in when he could, but I hadn't counted on that happening so soon. I hurry to the door and open it, smiling wide. I look like a mess. A headband barely keeps my hair out of my eyes, and I'm wearing a decent coating of dust, but it's not the sexy contractor who's getting a glimpse of me so disheveled. It's Dalton.

"Oh." I slump, resting my weight on my feet as he raises his brows. "It's just you."

"Expecting someone else?"

I open the door wider to let him in. "No," I lie. "I was simply wondering who it might be."

"Uh-huh." He strolls through the living room, taking in all my progress. I'm almost there with setting up the space as I'd like it to be, but it's overall a mess.

"What is going on here?" He picks up a sketchbook and flips through the pages.

"Rearranging to make space."

"I see that."

I smile, taking note of how far I've come. "Lauren has finalized her dress design, so now the fun part can begin."

"Just one dress, right?" He chuckles, pointing at the trio of dress forms.

"Yeah, just the one. Although it might be a good idea to design a matching outerwear to go with it." I grab my notebook and scrawl more notes. The women mentioned it when we explored the venue, but it wouldn't be too much of a hassle to incorporate a simple shawl or jacket to match her dress. Just in case.

"What brings you by?" I'm not bothered that he's visiting, but I can't make sense of it. There's no way he's merely here to ask about my work.

He continues to walk around the setup I've begun. "I just spoke with my mother."

I go still, keeping the tip of the pen on the paper mid-note as I look up at him. "Oh?"

Dalton doesn't have a great relationship with his parents. My aunt and uncle are not very loving, and the family seems estranged more than anything. He sure doesn't have the same concerns as I do with my mother. His wealth is at his disposal.

But this news is alarming. His mother is my mom's sister. His mom doesn't like mine, but I'm nervous about what they could be thinking or saying. Is my time here already over? It's not fair if I have to end this break from her already.

"She mentioned that Adelaide has been trying to get a hold of you." He perches on the armrest and crosses his arms. "I'm aware of how spotty reception can be out here, but it's not so bad that you're off the grid completely."

Unfortunately.

I purse my lips, waiting for more bad news. He must sense the turmoil I'm trying to keep in because he sighs before adding, "I didn't tell her you were here. It sounds like Adelaide is calling around in Paris, even reaching out to your instructors and well-known classmates."

"I didn't tell anyone where I was going." I lock my gaze on him, daring him to admit he's betrayed this secrecy.

"Nor did I. I didn't tell my mother. And even if she knew where you were, I doubt she would tell Adelaide, to keep it from her out of spite."

Our family is so messed up.

"What's going on, Claire? I'm aware you and Adelaide have never gotten along. It's never been easy with my parents either, but we're not terse and apart like you and Adelaide." He gets up to move toward the couch I've slumped onto. "I'm aware she's controlling. Always has been, even when your father was alive. So color me curious, cousin. What's going on?"

I lick my lips, wondering if I should dare to tell him.

"Why are you so against speaking with her? Why does any mention of her make you curl up in yourself like she's a predator who's chasing you down?"

I swallow and hope he'll believe me. I think I can count on him to side with me, though. "She wants me to get married."

He lifts his brows. "Is that why you wanted to elope with Owen so badly?"

"Partly. I wanted to elope to get her off my back about needing to marry. She's never supported my dreams of working at all, much less with something so 'frivolous' like a bridal shop."

He furrows his brow, listening and waiting patiently for more.

"She wants me to marry someone of her choosing. Someone who meets her expectations. And also to ensure I won't have the freedom to do anything with my trust fund."

"The trust fund your father left you? The one you've been living on since his death?"

I shake my head. "My mother only gives me an allowance. She has a death grip on my funds that he set up for me."

"How? It's *yours*. It's in your name."

I shrug. "She's manipulated it somehow so that I would only receive it after I'm married, but she's determined to choose who I'm able to marry."

Grunting an angry bark of laughter, he shakes his head and stands. "I don't think that's legal."

"Oh, like a Rennard won't have a mighty legal team to rely on."

He sobers, almost deadpanning at me. "Never mind them. I'll look into it. Caleb's lawyers and mine. We'll investigate this bullshit, Claire. I mean, why not add it to the mix..."

"What do you mean?" I ask, too pragmatic and defeated to let his promise make a difference in my mind. I'm not being stubborn or in denial. I believe very much so that Caleb and Dalton likely want to help me. But this is my mother they're talking about. His last words are cryptic, and I focus on them. "What do you mean about adding something to the mix?"

"Caleb and I are already concentrating on a similar matter. Another trust fund issue, and a certain man who's going to pay dearly for messing with our women. But don't worry. We'll look into this with Adelaide."

I stand, tired of the topic that I've long since accepted as my unchangeable fate. There is simply no beating my mother. As I wave him off, I return to sorting out the items on the table. "I've got far more pressing issues at the moment."

"Like what? Other than finding so many issues with this cabin that you need to hire Sawyer." He chuckles. "Sorry about that. I'd only just gotten the keys to this place, and you needed to bolt from Paris."

I nod. "And now, I need to find a way to get to Denver and secure the fabric samples I need Lauren to review."

"You want to get a rental?" he asks as a familiar knock sounds on the door. This time, I know it's Sawyer. He always knocks with four raps of his knuckle. I let Dalton answer the door and welcome him in.

"Hey, just the man I was hoping to catch up with," Sawyer says, taking a moment to tip his chin up at me in a greeting.

My tablet dings with an email notification, and I hurry back to it, hopeful it's one of the shops in Denver replying about my inquiries about their stock.

Dalton and Sawyer linger near the door, dropping into an instant conversation about projects.

"The road is done," Sawyer says, and I roll my eyes.

A road? It's a long, pressed gravel driveway that reaches to the far end of Dalton's massive property.

"And we'll start doing the demo on the old cabins way back there next week."

"Perfect," Dalton replies.

"I just have to run to Denver and pick up a different trailer, so I'll be gone dealing with that, but after I'm back, the crew will be on it."

Dalton snaps his fingers and points at me. "There we go. I see a solution to at least one of your problems."

Oh, no. I tense, already guessing what he'll say.

"You can go to Denver with Sawyer since he's heading that way."

My stomach tightens. It's not anxiety but a funky sense of butterflies taking flight and causing tension.

Riding with Sawyer for how long of a drive? It's one thing to be here at the cabin while he works on repairs, and I labor away with sourcing the things for Lauren's dress. We can tiptoe toward being familiar with each other with the fallbacks of our work as a handy distraction.

But stuck in a truck with him, going out of town?

I glance over at Sawyer and find those gorgeous eyes looking right back at me. I look down at his lips for a second before I force myself to look back at my tablet.

I can't tell if I'm dreading it, unsure if I can resist the way my curiosity is blooming into full-fledged attraction, or if I can't wait for a chance to spend more time with him.

CHAPTER 13

Sawyer

Before I can plan to go to Denver, I need to check in with Jason. So, two days after Dalton proposed that awesome idea of Claire riding with me, I head to the Goldfinch, where he's working.

Honestly, if Dalton didn't suggest his cousin should hitch a ride in my truck, I would've offered myself. When she mentioned looking up the drive time details, it was on the tip of my tongue to tell her I could take her there. The man saved me from having to put myself out there and ask instead.

As I drive along the crappy road up to the B&B, I wonder how far along my older half-brother is on the flooring install in Marian's kitchen. Even though Jason retired a few years ago and gave me his part of the company our dad left us, he's never gone idle. I doubt he'll ever properly quit and exchange his existence for a lifetime of relaxing and lazing around. Since he quit the construction work with the company

I now oversee, he's taken up more handyman sort of tasks. He's also taken up a friendship with Marian that I suspect might be something more.

I'm glad if that's the case. Marian is a sweet woman, and I've always felt bad about her husband passing away when he did. She's been alone up on this mountain for so long. When Lauren showed up, then Caleb, they breathed new life into her world. Each time I see her, she's smiling like a doting mother on Lauren and Aubrey, and I'm relieved she won't be isolated and lonely for the rest of her days. She deserves love, and if she's got her eye on Jason, I'm damned happy for him, too. He's been a stubborn bachelor all his life, never wanting to settle down when he was committed to Dad's company. Now that I'm the man in charge of our "legacy," he seems much more open to Marian's company as more than her being a client of his work around the bed-and-breakfast.

*Meanwhile, Claire is kind of my client, a guest at a cabin I'm fixing up, but still...*I shake my head at my thoughts. Still, I never drive clients to Denver for the hell of it. Claire, whether I want her to be or not, is starting to sneak under my skin, which is decidedly inconvenient.

I park at the B&B and head inside to look for Jason. Lo and behold, there he is, on his hands and knees in the kitchen, three-fourths of the way done.

"You're not overdoing your back, are you?" I ask as I enter.

"I'm not even worth a hello or a greeting? Straight to the old-man jokes?" He peers up at me, grinning.

With a twenty-two-year age gap between us, this running inside joke never loses its fun.

"Nah. I'm serious."

Jason shakes his head, kneeling up as I lower to the floor to pick up where he needs the next slat of wood. "My back is fine."

But three years ago, about the time he considered leaving the company, he threw his back out, and it marked the change of his desire to keep up with the demands of manual labor outside with big equipment. It's a good fit for him, though, despite the ease with which we worked after Dad passed away. We are brothers from another mother, but Jason's two decades on me always made him more of a father figure than a sibling. Regardless, he is a solid coworker to rely on, a dependable brother, no matter what.

Unlike Kevin. I sigh, wishing I could move on past my issues with him. It wasn't all my fault. Kevin was never close with Dad, not like Jason and I were. He was into teaching, more studious and academic—less blue-collar and smarter, like Gina decided so long ago when she'd date me, then flirt with him. Date him, then still want to come back to me.

Kevin simply never fit in with the three of us, and when Dad passed and left Jason and me the company, a monetary grudge was combined with the differences between me and my youngest brother.

"Have you talked to Kevin lately?" Jason asks once we fall into a seamless rhythm of handing boards to one another.

I swear, it's like he can read my mind sometimes. I'm not sure how to reply, though. I never am. Maybe that's why Jason always brings him up whenever he can because he knows how both of us will resist reconciling. Kevin and I never got along that well as kids. Then Gina came between us, making me realize women would always want a stable man with a clean-cut job like Kevin's over my more rugged and unpredictable life in construction. And since then, we've festered in a limbo of awkwardness around each other. Kevin and I haven't behaved like close relatives for several years, but I can't see why Jason seems to think I'm the one to reach out to Kevin.

"Not really."

"Hmm." He carries on, slotting boards in and tapping them into place. Jason will never give up and mentioning Kevin in hopes that my answer will be different one day, but he's a good enough guy to know not to push.

Before he can follow up with something else, I speak up. It's more like blurting, a desperate spew of words that I've been thinking about constantly. Claire is always on my mind, so it shouldn't be a shock that she's the first thing out of my mouth. "I'm driving Claire, Dalton's cousin, to Denver when I go tomorrow."

Jason cringes slightly as he moves with the progress of the floor being put in. He can claim all he wants that his back is okay, but it looks like his knees are suffering more. "Short blonde? Yeah, I saw her when she stopped in here to pick up a delivery that Caleb had sent here instead of to the cabin she's staying in."

"The very crappy cabin." I shake my head, loathing how beat-up that building is. "Dalton hired me to do repairs there, and the list is long."

"And now you're driving her to Denver?" he asks. "Out of the goodness of your heart?"

I furrow my brow at his teasing. "Are you trying to imply I'm not good?"

"Depends on if you're taking her as a favor for Dalton, a paying client, or if you plan on taking her for something else."

I hate that he's reminding me that Claire should be hands-off. She's practically Dalton's little sister, and even though Dalton is paying me for my construction work, he's become a good friend, too. And dudes just don't go after a buddy's little sister.

I shrug, avoiding answering him altogether.

"Aha."

I shake my head. "No. I'm just a convenience for her."

"One and done?"

I shake my head again. "She just sees me as an easy-to-find supplier of manual labor. Just someone who can fix the issues with that cabin. Or drive her to Denver since I'm already going there to pick up my trailer."

"You're not convenient, Sawyer," he says tiredly, no doubt exhausted by the way I cling to that label.

One girl came between me and Kevin, and with the polar opposites between us, it's been impossible to get over that stigma that clings to me. Just a convenient laborer. Just another man. Dime a dozen and dirty. Someone Claire would never see herself with.

"When's the last time you dated anyone?"

I think back, trying to place the last time I went on a date or enjoyed a woman's company in bed. It's been a while, but I haven't been looking anyway, too busy with work. Jason can't accuse me of being celibate. I'm not. I've had girlfriends, but none of them were ever very serious. None of them ever made me feel like I couldn't get them out of my head, not like Claire.

I didn't mean to bring up Claire with Jason, but I realize that when I talk about her, I feel good. And when I think about her—which is nonstop—I can't get her out of my mind. The lines are blurring between viewing her as a client or as Dalton's guest and just a sexy woman I'd like to get to know better.

Maybe it's because she fights with me every chance she gets. That antagonism that is so natural between us makes her something like a forbidden enemy I'm lured to in the sense that we always want what we can't have.

Or maybe it's because deep down beneath the high-maintenance exterior, I can recognize and respect her drive and work ethic. A woman knowing what she wants and not giving up pursuing her dreams is such a turn-on.

Whatever it is about her, I'm starting to really look forward to bringing her to Denver with me. Even if I struggle with the knowledge that I've got no business wishing she could be a part of my life and belong in my world, she won't fail to amuse me or charm me.

So long as she isn't wearing another sexy robe in the truck...

I'm saved from having to answer Jason about my rusty love life when Marian pops her head around the corner. "Looking good! It's almost done!"

Jason grins up at her. "And soon you can resume sticking with your system in the kitchen, huh?" he teases.

"Speaking of…" she says with a wide, maternal smile for me. "Sawyer, are you staying for dinner tonight? Lauren and Caleb are coming over soon."

That's got to be really convenient. Caleb and Lauren had their big house built adjacent to the bed-and-breakfast, so they can wander over for this woman's delicious food whenever they want. I almost want to be jealous. Her chicken is to die for, but I know if I stay and enjoy the plate they might set out for me, I'll want to linger and talk far into the evening.

"Thanks, but not tonight." I want to go home and get to bed early. I intend to stave off this excitement about having Claire all to myself tomorrow, and being well-rested is the first step. "I've got to drive to Denver tomorrow morning."

And I can't wait to see how it goes.

I really am a glutton for punishment, craving the presence of one beautiful woman who will only see me as someone who does the grunt work no one else wants to put up with.

And I never learn, either.

CHAPTER 14

Claire

I pace past the front windows of the cabin, checking with each pass for Sawyer's truck. I've looked out for his arrival so many times over the last few days, but this time, a sense of expectation hangs in the air, too. I'm not just hoping he'll show up. He *will* be coming here, as planned. That excitement is enough to keep me on edge, but it's what follows that really riles me up. We'll be spending time together—alone—in his truck, then in Denver. And it seems like nothing more than a series of tests.

He is off-limits. Or he *should* be. I have too many reasons for avoiding a fling or hookup, but he's quickly appealing to me as just that. Sawyer represents a chance for me to feel something other than being trapped by my mother and the holds on my career. He's a new person, a new experience, and I can't deny my basic attraction to him. I have no way to talk myself out of being curious about him either. So putting myself in the position of being tempted by him sounds like a lousy idea.

If I want to stay sane.

Not only is this not the right time for me to try anything with anyone, he's also not the right person. Sawyer is not the kind of man my mother would ever approve of, and for so long, she's modified my thoughts. She's indoctrinated it into me that I shouldn't hope to meet someone I could one day love but someone she could parade as her influential son-in-law. She's trained me to think of marriage as a transaction, not a partnership, especially not with a common blue-collar worker like him.

And Colorado? This isn't where I belong. Even though every minute I spend here is a breather that I need after the hustle and bustle of studying in Paris, it's far from my ideal location for a dress shop.

Too many things stand against a future with Sawyer, but as I lean toward the window and smile at the approach of his truck as he pulls into the driveway, I can't deny the racing patter of my heart.

I open the door and wheel my suitcase out onto the porch, hoping he won't give me too much crap about my attire. Denver is a bigger city. It won't feel like such a backwoods place as this small town rural area of trees and quiet mountainsides. And being in a different environment, yeah, I plan to dress to impress. Sawyer's approval matters the most, if I'm being honest, but it seems like I already have that in spades.

He stalks up the drive and then climbs the steps, striding confidently in a way that reminds me how strong and masculine he is. His eyes stay locked on me, roving from my toes that show in my strappy sandals, up my bare legs, over my skirt and blouse, and all the way up to my short curls. At the sight of my smirking lips, he grins. It's a cocky smile that teases me, making me wonder what filthy thoughts he's got brewing in his mind with that smoldering look. The way he stares has me wishing he would act on that clear need to devour me, but he holds back.

Stopping at the other side of the porch, he gives me one last up-and-down look and grips the handle of my suitcase. He gives it a slight pull, and as the wheels roll across the wooden planks, his brows rise.

"We're staying for one night, right?" he asks with too much humor lacing his tone.

I roll my eyes as he pulls and pushes the suitcase back and forth, testing its density.

"One night," I agree. It sounds like so long, yet too short at the same time.

"*One* night?" He lowers the handle to pick up the luggage. "And you need *all* of this?" He pats the side of the suitcase.

"Yes." I tip my chin up. "Yes, I do." I don't. I doubt I'll even touch half the stuff in there, but because he's got me so worked up and nervous and excited, I feel vulnerable and unsure of what to do or wear. Hence, the obvious loophole of simply bringing too much and having more than enough options.

"You packing bricks in here?" he teases as he heads down the steps. "A dead body?"

"Oh, shut up."

He chuckles. "But what all is in here that you need for *one* night away?"

"Things." I shoot him a look, trying to take his teasing in stride. "You wouldn't understand."

"I'm not sure I wanna understand. I know you're high-maintenance and all..." He sets the suitcase in the back of the truck and then opens the passenger door for me. "But, damn, Claire. If you pack that much for one night away, I shudder to think of what you'd bring for a real vacation."

I enter his truck, pausing long enough to swat at his chest. It's a mistake I regret instantly. Brushing my hand against the rock-hard wall of muscles makes me want to rub up alongside him in a slower drag of torture.

As he steps back, I slam the door shut. I counted on his criticism and joking. Still, it annoys me. He isn't angering me, and as I sit there and watch him round the truck for the driver's door, I bite back a smile. If this isn't a case of a boy pulling a girl's pigtails for attention, I don't know what to make of his attraction.

"This *isn't* a vacation," I remind him as hotly as I can when he gets in and buckles up.

"Not for me, it isn't."

I frown as he reverses. Does he mean it's *work* to deal with me? Or does he mean he's seeing this trip as a business necessity for himself?

"I'm working," I tell him again. I don't care if he calls me high-maintenance. I am. It would be a lie to suggest otherwise. But it does matter to me that he understands I'm heading to Denver for a job.

"I need to find the fabrics for Lauren's dress."

"Hmm-mmm." He nods as he speeds up on the road. "Which is why you had to pack all your equipment in that case?"

I smirk, losing my fight with a smile. "No."

"Then what the hell did you put in that suitcase?"

"Options."

"For *you*? If this is a work trip, how many wardrobe changes do you need?"

I tilt my head, eyeing him closely as he drives. "Sawyer?"

He glances at me.

"Why are you obsessing about what I wear?"

The barest hint of a blush shows on his cheeks, and he shakes his head.

"It's more like I'm trying to stop thinking about what you're *not* wearing."

Oh, boy. I swallow, my mouth suddenly dry. I didn't think he'd take the bait like that and play right along with me. I can handle flirting as well as any other woman, but that comment has me feeling too warm. Too turned-on.

The most obvious reply is none. We sit there in silence for a few awkward moments until he clears his throat and asks about what Lauren's dress will look like. It's such a vague and open-ended question, and I have fun answering it the best I can. He might have overreached with that blunt flirtation, but as he sticks with small talk and asking about the dress design, we fall into a more comfortable companionship.

Despite our mutual urge to poke fun at each other, he is easy to get along with. We smile *and* bicker in equal measures, and as we enter Denver, I can't believe how fast the drive passed us. It's nice to be around people who don't have expectations of me for a change, and that's just how Sawyer treats me—like I'm just a woman in his truck along for a ride, with no expectations or obligations to meet.

He doesn't stop there. Once we're in the city, he's patient to type in each fabric shop's address and drive me to every single location. I thought he'd bring me here and ditch me while he went off to handle picking up the trailer, but it's clear that isn't his intention at all.

"Where to next?" he asks after the second stop.

I smile at him as we return to his truck. He's insisted on carrying the fabric samples from both of the places we stopped at so far, and it charms me. Maybe it's a simple gesture, him offering to carry my things and hold doors open for me, but I admire him all the more for it. He can be quick to tease me, but he *is* a gentleman, too. It's a nice balance I want to get used to.

"Are you sure? I know you've got your stuff to do."

He nods with a goofy grin. "Yeah. I'm sure. I'm...curious."

"About fabric?" I smile as we get into the truck together.

"About you and what you're doing."

I lean forward to tap in the next place on his navigation screen.

"But I don't get why you can't just buy the fabric now. Instead of collecting samples."

Once the address is in, I buckle up and face him. "Because this is very important to Lauren."

He laughs. "Well, I imagine every bride will think her dress is important."

More so for her. I can't tell him about her past. It's her story to tell him, not mine. "The details and approval of her dress matter, and I want to make sure every step of the way is meeting her needs. I want her full approval first. Then I can order it and have it delivered." I look out the window, watching the scenery. "I hope the shipping process is quick, though." Once I have Lauren's approval, I'll be more impatient to get going on it.

Sawyer shrugs. "I drive over here often enough for supplies. I can just pick it up for you."

I blink at him, stunned by his easy reply. "That's, um, that's really nice of you." Even as I say it and mean those words, I can't wrap my head around his genuine offer to be helpful. I'm not used to people doing things for me without expecting anything in return.

For the next couple of hours, we stop for a quick lunch and collect the samples and fabric I need to start framing the dress. I can at least get started on the actual creation of the gown, but I'll still wait for Lauren's approval to purchase anything more.

It has already been a long day, but I know it's far from over.

Sawyer still needs to get his trailer, and with my stops done, he heads toward the hotel we'll be staying at for the night instead of driving back so late.

"I appreciate your patience and offering to take me around," I tell him honestly. It may not seem like a lot to him, but it does to me.

"No problem."

"I took up your whole day," I protest. I feel like a problem.

"Then finish it off by sticking with me while I get the trailer." He winks. "Return the favor and keep me company at the store so I can grab my supplies, too."

I shrug and smile. "Okay, but *now* I'll feel overdressed."

He chuckles and changes directions to get the trailer.

Once there, I wait alongside the truck bed as he hooks up the trailer, and I struggle with the view. Seeing his arms flex reminds me of the muscles in his rugged physique. And later, when witnessing him in the hardware store as he grabs his supplies, I notice his confidence and knowledge of what to get and what to pass on.

It's a whole new world and a shopping experience that's far different from my line of work. But we're not so different. We're both in our own lines of services, and I take the moment to daydream further.

I run my hand down the smooth, polished surface of the long work-space of a counter as we wait to pay for Sawyer's things. This surface hosts the transactions for nuts and bolts, tools, and wood. If I had *my* shop, my counter space would let me measure and cut fabrics with multiple drawers and bins for fasteners and tools of my trade.

"What's that smile for?" he asks with a gentle nudge at my side.

I sigh. "Thinking about having a shop like this one day."

"To sell hardware?"

I giggle. "No. My own dress shop. It would be really neat to have someone build it just like this. Ample counter space, customized for my needs." I shrug, feeling silly to talk about my dreams that feel so far away.

"I know the feeling."

I tease him right back. "Of wanting to open a dress shop?"

"No. When my dad passed away and gave the company to me and Jason, I knew how I wanted to change it and make it better. Being the boss of your own company and having that executive decision-making never gets old." Before he steps forward to be cashed out, he smiles softly. "You'll find out what I mean."

Assuming I ever get there at all. It feels like I only grow further from making my shop happen but hearing him so freely support me like this makes me feel lighter. He'll never know how much his words matter, and they only endear him to me that much more.

I sigh and nod. *I hope so.*

CHAPTER 15

Claire

Even though I grew up in the States and I have my driver's license, I've spent so much time in Paris studying that I can't really imagine driving here again. It's a big part of the reason why I'm reluctant to deal with finding a rental. Why bother when so many others can drive me around, or I can have things delivered? I'm especially grateful for Sawyer's offer to chauffeur me around this city. I doubt I'd keep up with the traffic, and I bet it's worse than it usually is.

"Probably something going on at the convention center," Sawyer points out, aiming his finger at the flashing sign that we pass in the heart of the downtown area. Quite a few people have been standing at the entrances to public parking lots, asking for upwards of twenty bucks to park for an event.

"A concert, maybe," I guess after spotting more crowds of pedestrians wearing similarly styled merchandise and t-shirts with the image of the same band.

"Good thing we booked our rooms in advance," he adds.

I'm not sure I'd call that advance. We only just decided—or Dalton decided for me—that we'd be coming to Denver together for both of our business needs. A week isn't much of an advance notice, not if this concert was planned for months ahead of time.

I nod, though, not wanting to be pessimistic. Once we arrive at the hotel and head to the check-in counter, it's clear that we're out of luck.

"I don't understand," I protest again when we get the bad news. "How could you double book? We both made our reservations with plenty of time to spare." I hold up my phone toward the stressed woman. Sawyer's device is already on the counter with the screen showing his confirmation email.

"We've had a snafu with reservations from guests who've gone with a package offered by the concert host, and as such, communications were delayed. We did not have access to their systems, and once the information was processed on our end, it resulted, unfortunately, in double booking select rooms."

I scoff. "Yeah. Unfortunately." *For us. Not the people who took our rooms!* The clerk seems sympathetic, but it all sounds like mumbo-jumbo as far as excuses go.

"We do, however, have one suite available."

I roll my eyes. *One.* As in singular. Never mind my attraction and curiosity, Sawyer and I should *not* be sharing a room.

"Oh, yeah?" he asks.

I shoot him a look, which he ignores.

"Hey, our options are limited," he reminds me. "And I'm not crazy about driving through this downtown traffic again, not with the trailer." It's his turn to roll his eyes at the idea of it.

"It's a deluxe suite—"

"With two beds?" I interrupt.

"Well, no. Yes." The clerk nods. "It has a living area outside of the single bedroom, but the couch pulls out into a bed."

I guess that would imply two places to sleep. Sharing a combined room with him would likely mean sharing a bathroom. Both times Sawyer had seen me in a robe resulted in an awful lot of fluttering in my stomach, sensations I'd be better off avoiding with how much he tempted me the more I spent time with him. He simply draws me to him somehow, but so long as we have our own respective places to sleep...

"We'll take it," I reply hastily, intimidated by the prospect of having *no* room and of the pressure to avoid making Sawyer drive back tonight. He's done enough for today. While it's not my fault the hotel has screwed up and double-booked our rooms, I feel like I should be the one to reserve this new suite. Which means I need to say goodbye to more money. Dalton mistook my situation, assuming I have access to oodles of money, but my wallet is slim. My allowance deposits aren't much, and I fret that booking this bigger space will put a more significant dent in my spending. Still, there's nothing to do about it but—

"I'll get it." Sawyer steps closer to the counter, edging me aside.

"What?" I frown at him, elbowing him just as he did to me.

"*I* will get it." He repeats it with a firm tone but isn't mean about it. His offer to get the room is nice to begin with, but I have never cared for a man thinking he can push me around. It's bad enough my mother pushes me plenty.

"Sawyer, you—"

He thrusts his muscled arm forward, blocking me from handing my credit card to the clerk. His card is taken, and she swipes it quickly, perhaps wanting to end this bickering between us before it truly takes off.

Slanting me a sexy and serious look, he sighs. "Just because I work with these hands doesn't mean I can't afford a fancy room here." He holds them out to me, emphasizing that I should check out those roughened long fingers and calloused palms. Sawyer bears the evidence of hard, manual work. I'm used to delicate, moisturized hands, but in stark contrast, I can only think about *his* hands on me.

I'm stunned silent, staring and wondering just what else he could do with those hands. Namely on me. Parts of him *in* me. A furious warmth spreads across my cheeks, and I'm so stuck in the fantasy of Sawyer touching me that I can't care about how badly I'm blushing right now.

Stop. Not now! I shouldn't entertain these wicked thoughts about him ever, but shutting off those filthier ideas is easier said than done.

While the reservation is sorted out, and Sawyer gets the key cards, I stand there to the side. Flustered and irritated with myself, I wait for him to turn away from the counter. In silence, awkward on my part because I can't erase the idea of his hands on my naked flesh, we head toward the elevators and go up to find our room.

I can't tell if Sawyer recognizes that I need the quiet or what, but I appreciate that he doesn't tease or poke fun at me until after we're in the room. After we enter and he sets my suitcase with his one small bag near the door, he still doesn't speak.

We walk through the suite, and in unison, we glance through the doorway that leads to the one bedroom, then at the singular couch.

"You can take the bed."

I nod at him, smiling quickly. "Thanks." With another glance at the couch, I consider arguing, though. He's so tall that I have no clue how he could fit on the sofa. It seems like a safer idea to simply not talk about where we will be sleeping. I'm not confident I'll refrain from blurting out that I want to sleep *with* him, too weak to resist the visions in my mind after that blunt mention of his hands.

I remembered how hot his touch was at the cabin, and it's a memory that only eggs me on to want more.

I hug myself, folding my arms over my stomach. Flapping one hand to my elbow, I tip up on my toes, then sink my heels back to the carpet. I'm fidgeting, and I hate it. I was raised to always be poised and proper, not shifting and antsy. Standing around in this suite with Sawyer, I suffer intense uneasiness.

What are we supposed to do now?

Should I say something about him taking the bed instead, even though that will only end in arguing?

Are we just going to stand around and avoid making eye contact?

Why is he avoiding making eye contact?

Is he thinking the same thing as me?

What if he's envisioning us together on that one bed and—

"Kind of early, huh?" He mimics me, rocking back on his heels with his hands stuck in his pockets. His brows shoot up in question, and that cocky smirk is waiting on his lips.

"For what?" *Sleeping together?* I mentally groan at the thought, glad I have a censor not to speak it.

"Uh, anything." He clears his throat, and I want to grin at the possibility that he feels just as intimidated by me as I do of him.

"Want to get something to eat?" I ask. When in doubt, food is always a good option. A snack. A drink. A meal. It's too early for dinner, but for the lack of anything better to do, why not escape the stifling awkwardness of being alone with him in here and go out to eat?

"Sure!" He latches on to the suggestion so quickly that I'm more convinced he is equally off-kilter in here.

We head out to the nearest bar, located just across the street. The concert must be going on about now, though, because it's surprisingly not busy or packed. Everyone must be at the venue, and I'm glad we don't have to fight our way through a crowd.

Without throngs of people to get past, we get a table very easily, and once we settle into our seats, I take a good look around.

It's so...different. I don't feel like a true Parisian. I'm from New York. Still, I feel like a foreigner here because it's all just so new. The country music playing from the speakers is upbeat and not too twangy. It's not like anything I've listened to by choice, and I can't help but nod along to it. The TVs in the corners offer distractions to watch. Even the LED displays on the gambling machines at the ends of the bar top entertain me. The bar is dark with wood and neon signs, and as I marvel at it all, I realize I've never actually gone to a hole-in-the-wall kind of place like this.

"You're looking a little bewildered over there," Sawyer comments without lifting his gaze from the laminated single-sheet menu he peruses.

"Not bewildered, just..." I shrug. "Entertained." I'm used to fancy, boring restaurants where you don't go to simply eat but to be seen. The high-end clubs I've frequented are nothing like this loud, rowdy, and fun place.

I smile and fold my hands together on the wooden table. "You order for me, okay?"

He raises his brows. "You want me to name your poison?"

I nod. I doubt any cocktails they can make here would have any top-shelf liquor. My glance around the bar shows tall glasses of draft beer or bottles of it. I want to not only imagine fitting in here, but I also want to truly let loose and have fun.

Because why not?

I don't have classes to study for.

I have the samples and fabric to get me started as far as I can go with Lauren's dress.

And my mother and her acquaintances are nowhere to be seen to judge me.

I move to the music, enjoying the beat as he orders us two beers, chuckling at my enthusiasm.

"It's like you've never gone out before."

I haven't, with you. This isn't a date, but that doesn't matter.

If coming out to have an early dinner and drinks with Sawyer is the best way I can escape the awkward tension of being alone with him in that suite, then we may as well make the most of it while we can.

We clink our bottles together, and I grin before taking a long sip.

CHAPTER 16

Sawyer

The second we entered the bar, I could tell Claire was out of her comfort zone. She didn't sneer and look down at her surroundings. Instead, she gawked at it all as though she'd never set foot inside such a simple place. Maybe she hadn't.

Hours later, though, I realize she's not turned off by it. She has yet to stop moving her head to the music, sometimes tapping her fingers on the table and shimmying her shoulders. I highly doubt she'll claim to be a country fan anytime soon, but she sure as hell is going along with it tonight. The plates of greasy burgers and salty fries can't resemble any of the fancy-schmancy arty food she ate in Paris, but she ate every bite and seemed to want to lick her fingers, too.

Then the beer. Shots, too. I can't tell if she's on a mission to get wasted and pass out before we return to the suite as a way of avoiding sleeping with me or what, but she is not shy about drinking.

Maybe it's been a while for her. She did say she was busy in Paris, studying. She turned me down when I asked her if she'd like to come to the bar back home. Both of those clues have me suspicious that she's been too high-strung to have much of a social life. At the rate she's drinking, I have to wonder if she hasn't had a chance to just be and have fun like this. And on that matter, I'm more than happy to let her enjoy herself as much as she wants. Everyone needs a break, after all.

"What is this called?" she asks me with a glimmer of excitement burning in her eyes. She's tipsy, but cute and not sloppy about it. Like she's trying so hard to still be the proper and haughty woman she knows she should be. The alcohol is getting to her, though, making her more mellow.

"The shot?"

"Yeah!" She giggles, leaning into me as someone bumps into her at the bar. Half of the liquid sloshes out of the small glass, and she pouts.

"Hey, watch it," I tell the man who shoved into her. He ignores me, and with an even quicker exit from the crowded bar, he elbows her again, and she loses more of the scant liquid.

"Damn." She sets the glass on the counter, but as I lift my hand to hail the bartender again, she touches my forearm until she lowers it and holds my wrist. "Nah. Don't bother. I'm already buzzing, and I don't want to get *too* intoxicated."

I smile. *So much for the theory that she wants to get so drunk that she can avoid me later.*

"Okay. Your call."

It's been her call all night. From the first place where we ate to the next bar. And the next. And the next. I stopped checking the time around one, glad no one was shouting last call anywhere yet.

"Let's dance!" she insists instead of reordering a drink.

We're already sweaty from doing just that, but I'm in no mood to turn her down. I never expected to be tearing up the town with Claire, but it seems that beer is a quick way to get her to lower her guard and let loose because that's actually what we've been doing all night. Eating at one place turned into dancing at another. Ultimately, we shifted to bar-hopping, and I know this will be a night I'll never forget.

It *is* different for her. I can tell. She's not used to living it up and doing whatever the hell she wants, and with her enthusiasm, looking at this experience through her eyes, it's all the more fun and exciting. Hell, dancing with her is a torture I'll never turn down. While I've been careful with my drinks and mostly staying as sober as possible, I can't resist this opportunity.

She leads me to the dance floor again, and I don't hesitate or drag my feet. It was quickly clear her style of dancing doesn't match what everyone does here, but with my hands on her back and sides, my body pushing against hers as a guide, I show her how she can dance with me. As the drinks flowed, though, she didn't wait for or follow my lead. Instead, she took to gyrating against me and stroking her hands over me.

I'm not sure how much more I can take, and I expect my control to remain intact. She has no clue how much she's tormenting me.

Or maybe she does.

As the songs change and something slower comes on, she shifts toward me. She drapes one arm over my shoulder and presses her other hand to my chest. If she concentrates on the beat under her fingers, she'll know exactly how fast my heart is racing from being so close to her.

I keep my hands loose on her hips and rest my forehead against hers. We lock eyes, and I will my dick not to go hard right now. Just that stare. Her gorgeous eyes on mine, like I'm all she can see and feel...It's a heady feeling I never want to end.

"How about we get out of here?" she purrs. She licks her lips after she speaks, and I follow the path of her tongue.

"And go back to the room?" I feel dumb to ask, but with the way she's eyeing me like I'm the dessert she's been waiting for, and the way she sways her body with mine to the music, how could I not wonder about what she's asking. Her body signals something like surrender to this chemistry sparking between us, but I don't want to make the wrong assumption here.

She sinks her teeth into her lower lip. "No. Another bar!"

Giggling and full of energy, she grabs my hand and hurries me toward the door. I can't help but laugh. Her fun mood is infectious, but with this quick exit, I don't have the foresight or moment to reach back for her sandals she left on the stool.

And that's where we end up. At three in the morning, she's barefoot and finally ready after several bars to head back to the room I managed to snag at the hotel.

I hoist her higher on my back and she giggles so hard I think she'll start snorting. I laugh right along with her, clutching the underside of her thighs as I carry her.

"No!" she shrieks, laughing harder and wiggling on my back. "I told you."

"What?" I dig my fingers into her smooth skin again. "Ticklish?"

She roars with laughter, tightening her arms around my neck as I carry her. "Yes! Stop."

I cease walking, chuckling.

"Stop tickling me," she amends with fading laughter.

I do, focusing on carrying her back to the hotel in one piece. "I can't believe you lost your sandals."

"*You* did," she accuses playfully. She's quick to laugh as we head to the suite, but I hear the difference in it. She's not drunk or buzzing. We both drank so much water and sweated too much for the booze to be ruling us with all that dancing. Neither of us are in any shape to drive, but we're clearer now that we're in the open night air.

"You're the one who wanted to take them off in the first place," I remind her.

"Because they hurt."

I grunt. "Then why do you keep wearing them?" Here and back at the cabin. She's got such a fetish for wearing the wrong footgear.

"Because they look pretty."

"*You* look pretty. Not your shoes."

"We can agree to disagree," she says, instead of accepting the compliment.

We reach the hotel, and without letting her lower herself off me, I piggyback her right into the lobby and only put her down once we're at the elevator.

She sighs, glancing up at me as we ride up to our floor. "I've never done anything like that before."

"Piggyback?" I tease.

She rolls her eyes. "No. Just going out all night and having fun like that."

I blink in surprise. "Bullshit."

Her giggle is sweet and sincere. "No. Seriously. I haven't."

I step closer, wondering if she's going to put up those walls and be guarded with me again. "Never?"

She shakes her head, watching me with wide eyes as I move closer. "Never."

I reach up to tuck her springy blond curls back. "I find that hard to believe."

She grips my hand, holding it in place, not shoving it away. "Why?"

The elevator stops, and I twist my hand to take hers, guiding her out to the hallway and toward our room. "Come on. You? You're high-maintenance, yeah, but I thought someone like you would be a hit wherever you went. Life of the party."

"*Me*?" she retorts.

"Yeah, you. You're beautiful and funny. Young and adventurous." I pause in my praises and glance at her as I wait for the door to open from the key card activation.

Her cheeks are rosy again, and this time, without the exercise of dancing or laughing, I know that pretty hue is a blush of embarrassment, not an exertion of energy.

"Well, yeah, I'm young, but..." As she steps into the suite with me, she clams up further, frowning and stammering over what she struggles to say. "I'm not funny. Sarcastic, sure. But humorous? I doubt it."

I wheel around and close the door behind her, rolling my eyes at how quickly she resorts to self-deprecating thoughts.

"And I wouldn't say I'm adventurous at all. I prefer to hide, not face anything intimidating."

I turn toward her, sliding my arm around her back at the same time I use two fingers to take her chin and tip it up toward me. She's so short that I have to dip my head down to see her fully.

"Claire, that's bullshit, too."

She scoffs. "You can't tell me what I am. I know myself and—"

I sigh, brushing my thumb against her lower lip to silence her. "You're gorgeous. And hilarious when you want to be. And you damn well *are* adventurous. You showed me how all night."

"But I'm—"

I lift my thumb up to press against her lower lip again. "And you have faced plenty of intimidating things. Like this." I step closer, letting her see the desire on my face. "This chemistry between us. It's driving me crazy, but you're not running away from it either."

Yet. I don't want to think she will.

She swallows and draws a deep breath, lifting her soulful gaze of want to lock on me.

"I'll teach you how to accept a compliment, Claire. But right now, I'd rather show you how wrong you are about yourself."

Before I think twice, I lower my face to hers and cover her lips with mine, kissing her soundly.

CHAPTER 17

Claire

The moment Sawyer's mouth crashes over mine, I hold my breath and pray this isn't another dream. This whole night has felt like an other-worldly experience. I haven't been myself. The woman I normally am would not behave like this. She doesn't drink beer at common bars and dance barefoot with strangers on crowded, dirty floors. She doesn't let loose and enjoy the simplicity of music and a hot man's company.

The woman I'm expected to be is a refined, proper, and distinguished one, set apart from all the other women in the world, with manners and decorum.

It's certainly not this wanton example I'm showing Sawyer, clinging to him and kissing him back just as hard. This isn't who I'm supposed to be, but under his heated stare and exposed to his warm body, I can't help it. I can't even think about putting a stop to it or protesting his firm yet soft lips sealing over mine.

And I don't.

I'm not sure who I am in this moment, but I know that I want to follow his lead. I can only go with his direction and hope he—or this lapse in my judgment—doesn't hurt me in the end. The mere thought of saying *no thanks* or resisting this attraction that's been sizzling between us all night is abominable.

All I want to do, all I *can* do, is trust that he'll help me through this sexual panic. That he'll give me what I want without needing me to request anything. He can see it. He has to feel it in my touch and my kiss. If he's oblivious to how badly and desperately I need his mouth on mine and his hands gripping me tight, I'll go insane.

If he can't understand how much I need *him* but can't make myself vulnerable to ask or beg, I don't know what I'll do.

He breaks the kiss, parting from me with inches hanging between our parted lips.

"You're wrong," he repeats. "You are a beautiful, brave woman, Claire."

His words hit me hard, and I want to believe each one. I tip my face up to his, eager for more.

"Every." He pushes the strap of my shirt down over my shoulder and lowers to press an openmouthed kiss to my skin there.

"Single." As he trails his wet lips up along my neck, he shoves the other strap off my opposite shoulder. I shiver, both from his affectionate statements and his hot tongue dragging over my sensitive flesh.

"Inch." Tugging with both hands, he pushes my shirt down. He nuzzles his mouth up toward my ear, kissing, licking, and teasing me. My shirt is flimsy, and my bra is more for show than support. Exposed to the air with one layer removed, my nipples bead instantly.

"Do you understand me?" he whispers into my ear before he moves his mouth toward me and presses a tender kiss to the corner of mine. I close my eyes at the heat of him surrounding me. The hotness of his kiss. The warmth of his hand pressing at my back. Then, the searing intensity of his fingers as he reaches up to rub my nipple through my bra.

"Do you—"

"Sawyer, I don't know what the hell you're saying," I whine and wrench my eyes open to pout at him hopelessly. "I can't—I don't want to think right now. All I want is..." I swallow at the smoldering desire in his eyes. *I'm* doing this to him. Me. I'm the woman making him stare at me with that ravenous gaze.

"Tell me," he orders quietly as he tugs the cup of my lacy bra down. He doesn't wait for my instructions. Gripping my sides, he easily picks me up and closes his mouth over my breast. His teeth clamp down slightly as his tongue flicks at my nipple. The dual sensation of pain and pleasure rockets through me, building a naughty tension in my core.

"Yeah," I choke out the reply, dropping my head back as I wrap my legs around his waist. I thread my fingers through his hair and hold on tight, determined to keep his face at my breasts. "This."

"This?" he growls against my breast. He moves his mouth to the other one, still hidden by my transparent bra. His lips close over that nipple, too, and with a harder suction into his mouth, I swear I'm dripping wet.

"All of it. All of you." I won't beg, but it seems he hears the need beneath my shaky admission. He's already moving me to the bedroom. Sucking my nipples and laving my breasts, he unerringly navigates his way to the one bed. It's supposed to be mine tonight, but I'll be damned if he doesn't invite himself. Words are beyond me. I can hardly catch my breath with the rapid pace of my pulse. Between his teeth and tongue, I'm already delirious, and neither of us is naked.

He doesn't need to speak either, not with words. As he lowers me to the bed, his hands convey what he thinks of my needs. He's ready and willing to give me what I want, unable to cease kissing for more than a second to gasp for air, but not until he can see me.

When he struggles to remove my shirt, I distract him by unclasping my bra. With a dirty growl, he gazes at my tits and loses track again, kissing and groping with an increasingly faster and more frantic pace.

"Baby..." He cups them both, staring reverently as he swipes his thumbs over my hard nipples again. "I'll give you anything you want."

"Just this. You." I pull him back to me for a hard kiss, and he follows me down to the mattress, proving his words. In a fumble of too many hands and way too much clothing, the process of getting me bare seems to take too long. I can't manage the zipper of my skirt, but he can. He delays while dragging my panties down my legs, but I kick them off quickly. It's unfair how one-sided he keeps this, but each time

I reach for his buckle or zipper, and every chance I get to grip the hem of his shirt, he dodges my attempts.

"No. This time..." He presses his big hand over my stomach, keeping me flat on the bed as he crawls down. "This time is all about you."

I blink, staring up at the ceiling and trying to concentrate through the hazy fog of desire twisting my mind. All about me? I've never received such a dedication. Through all my twenty-three years on this planet, I haven't had such stark and utter consideration given to me, with nothing expected in return.

Then, once he fastens his mouth to my entrance, licking and sucking with vigor and without pause, I lose all trace of thought. I can only feel, and the wickedly good sensations he has coursing through my every fiber are out of this world.

A shivering streak of pleasure spirals through me, lighting my nerves on fire. The tension of a building orgasm coils tighter within me, and my muscles clench. He doesn't let up, not when I grip the sheets and cry out loudly. He doesn't retreat, not even when I clamp my thighs around his head and keep him there. And when I buck, arching my hips because I'm so sensitive to the sensual stroke of his tongue within my wet, throbbing entrance, he pushes his face onto me harder, doubling down on making me come.

I do, floating on a wave of pure ecstasy I haven't felt in a long, *long* while, so distant that I can't recall if Owen ever made me explode like this. I'm not sure *any* man I've been with has gotten me off as expertly as Sawyer just has, and I'm not inclined to consider anyone else attempting it.

Stop. Stop thinking like this. It's absurd, and after all, sex is just sex. This is physical. Sawyer is determined to prove his point and drill it into my mind—for the night—that I'm worthy of his praise and compliments.

"Like that?" he asks, crooning in that husky, deep voice.

I want him to climb up here and kiss me. For as quickly and powerfully as he got me to come, I need *some* kind of aftercare. But he doesn't move. Stroking my entrance with his fingers, he slows his ministrations and prolongs the climax. Smaller, lighter waves of my orgasm grip me, and all I can manage are gasps and moans.

"Or are you not done yet?"

He pairs that tease with another dip down of his mouth on me. My clit is too sensitive, and as he sucks on it, trying to make me come again, I cry out even louder.

"I—"

Crap. I don't even know what I'm trying to say. He's overwhelming me, but again, he somehow knows.

"What?" he asks, peering up at me as he kneels on the bed.

I lick my lips, panting as he peels his shirt off and tosses it to the side. It's my own private strip show, and just watching him reveal his hard body for me fuels my desire all over again, no matter how sensitive I feel from the lack of sex in my life.

"I want..." I pause and lick my dry lips again, eager for water. After all the alcohol, all the dancing, then this intense orgasm, I feel like I'll be dehydrated forever.

He stands, lowering his jeans and boxers together while keeping his eyes locked on mine. At the sight of his long, thick cock jutting into the air, I mewl and reach out for him.

"No. This time is for you."

Does that mean another time will follow? Soon? Because I adore the way he wants to worship and prioritize me, but I feel deprived of tending to him and his needs, too.

He rolls a condom on, still gazing at me with that deep stare of hunger. Before I can think to reply or argue, or even string along a coherent sentence, he climbs back over me. Hovering and flexing all those rock-hard muscles as he braces himself, he reaches for me again.

In a flash, he hooks his hand beneath my thigh and pushes my leg up, giving himself a better angle to enter me. The stretch of his cockhead is a delicious burn. When he slides into me hard and steady, driving his erection all the way in, I growl and clutch at his back, uncaring if my nails score and mark his skin.

It feels that good. Too good. And if he doesn't move soon, I'll go crazy. I've never felt so full, so stretched, and eager for that dragging slide of his veiny dick against my inner muscles.

"Please." I kiss his neck, and he grunts. Leaning closer, he wipes my juices off his face, rubbing them onto the pillow. Then, as he turns his face to me, he kisses me deeply and pulls out. The second full pump into me is more forceful, and I can't get enough of it.

Over and over, he thrusts into me and devours my mouth with sucking, demanding kisses that could almost make me come alone.

This is no delicate time ruffling the sheets and chasing a quick orgasm. He's pounding into me with full-body friction, shoving the linens and pillows into disarray.

This isn't a simple act of slotting his cock into me with just enough thrusts to get himself off and hurry to the shower, kissing me here or there to remind me I'm not alone. This rugged man is owning me, taking command of my body, and bringing it alive in a dirty, wonderful way.

I've never had a lover like this. I've never been so entirely consumed by a man. Because he is already my master, pulling a second, and even more forceful, orgasm out of me. I shatter and cry at the blissful release, and as I milk him, he stills deep inside me, groaning as he reaches his pleasure, too.

I don't know how long I lay there. We both doze off, but over the course of the night, we do manage to find the covers and snuggle under them together.

After that restful, deep slumber, though, I wake alone.

No. It couldn't have been a sex dream. As I sit up, feeling the aches and sweet soreness between my legs, I sigh. It was real. Silky smooth sheets caress my bare skin as I sit up fully. I *so* had sex with Sawyer last night, but he's no longer here.

My heart races, because instead of waking in his arms and easing into a greeting after that momentous night we shared, I now face his return with anticipation.

I don't have long for nerves to build up. Not wanting to be caught in bed when he's already up and about, I slide out of bed and rub my eyes. I don't have any excuses to hide behind now. There is no freaking way I can ignore or avoid what we did last night, and I panic, wanting to know what my story should be so I can stick to it.

As I slide my arms into a robe and tie it, he strides in. He's already dressed, carrying two to-go cups of coffee. "Hey, you're up." He smiles, but there's nothing special or secretive about it. He's not giving me that knowing, cocky grin that suggests he's thinking of something naughty. He's not even speaking in a tender tone. Just casual. Whatever, like this is any old day, and I'm just another random person who shared a bed with him.

And it hurts.

It burns. This...coldness pierces me, but as soon as I recognize that I feel so wounded, I slap on a mask. We just had sex. Nothing more. But still...

I smile. "Yep. Sorry to keep you waiting." It kills me to be so cavalier like this, to play along with his attitude. It's crystal clear that he has no intention to treat me as a lover, as a woman he wants to worship. I'm just...Claire. I take the coffee, eager for a prop, for anything to focus on instead of trying to figure out why he's acting like this.

As I take the cup, though, I almost drop it. Then, so off-kilter and riled up while trying to hide it, I overcompensate and almost trip over my own feet. This clumsiness isn't like me. His stare is too potent on me, and I know my cheeks are burning up as I fidget under his gaze.

"You okay?"

I nod too quickly and gulp my coffee, effectively scalding my tongue.

"You seem jittery."

"Nope." I press my tongue to the top of my mouth, wishing I could cry; it hurts so bad. *Damn coffee!*

"Oh. I get it. You..." He rubs the back of his neck, arching one brow at me. "You wanna talk about last night."

"No!" I hold up my hand and force a fast smile. He sure as hell doesn't want to, and I'm not strong enough to explain why this sudden distance hurts. I knew nothing could happen between us, but apparently, I can only believe it after proving it with a huge mistake.

"Cool. Me neither."

That's freaking obvious.

"So, we'll just, uh, hit the road then." He smiles, but it lacks that warmth I've grown accustomed to. And right now, hating how quickly he's dismissing me, I feel cold and alone, wishing I'd never come here with him at all.

CHAPTER 18

Claire

The drive to Denver was awkward at first, but as we pass landmarks on the return trip, I think back to all those moments when the alone time with him on the ride here was fun. We talked. We got to know each other. We shared details about our work. I told him about wanting to open my shop. He explained more details about his brothers, how he's close with Jason but has never been able to connect with Kevin.

When we were heading to Denver, we experienced a sense of companionship that resembled a budding friendship. But after we slept together and tried to morph that into a sexual connection, we screwed it all up.

This ride back to Breckenridge is fraught with tense silence. I break up the unbearable quiet with squeaks on the cushion of the bench seat, courtesy of how often I fidget. I'm so antsy I can't sit still. It's a weird lull of no communication at all, but I can't bring myself to break it. I don't know how to end this funky tension of no words between us. And I'm not sure that I need to be the one to try to salvage anything between us.

"Too cold?" he asks, jarring me from the overwhelming silence.

I flinch at his voice, and he clears his throat after the words come out croaky. Neither of us has spoken in almost an hour, so yeah, of course, his throat is dry. Mine is, too, dry and tight with emotions, but I rely on a shake of my head instead of telling him *no*.

"Okay. Just checking." He lowers his hand from the control for the AC and resumes driving, as though he doesn't have a care in the world. It baffles me just how oblivious he is. I'm not cold and shivering from the AC blasting at us. I'm on edge and wanting to hug myself because his distance is icy and harsh.

I can't make sense of the one-eighty. Last night, he proved how thorough of a judge he was of me. He could read me like an expert and show his mastery in knowing my body, how to please me and push the right buttons. Yet, today, he is clueless and ignorant of this gap widening between us.

Do I truly mean that little to him?

Sawyer is the hottest man I've ever seen. He, without a doubt, can't struggle to find interested women. He's built like a hulk, all chiseled muscles, and oozing testosterone. Sure, he's had lovers before. I know that without having to ask for details that aren't mine to learn. I can't be the only woman he's slept with before, and I wonder if this is simply how he does it and if women are all random conquests to enjoy, then discard the day after. This might just be his style and how he behaves.

Or did I do something wrong? That was the worst fear, that I'd erred somehow. He made it all for me, about me, but maybe that was a turn-off in the end. He already called me high-maintenance. Maybe he's decided I'm *too* high-maintenance.

It wouldn't be so hard to ask and be direct. I'd rather know what mistake I made to have him wanting to treat me so coolly, but I can't find the courage to ask. We reach my cabin before I can think of how to ask if I've turned him off.

Still without a word but offering me a slight, casual smile, he pulls in and parks.

I have to have done something wrong! It's going to pick at me, wondering and worrying, but I exit the truck, sighing as I watch him get my suitcase and gather my samples.

Dejected and hating this awkwardness, I offer him a weak smile and show him where to set the things I've picked up.

He lingers at the doorway, and while I get my hopes up high that he'll explain himself, he turns to me. "I had a really nice time with you."

Nice? That's all he can say about it? It was *nice*? I give him a weak smile, clinging to this stubbornness to hide my dejection. "Yeah. Me too." *Nice, my ass.* The sex was amazing. His compliments, even more so. When he leaves, though, a weird feeling settles in my stomach. It seems a lot like disappointment and a strange sense of missing him already.

It's not just about the sex. I *like* him. A lot. But it's soured by the realization that he has regrets about what we did.

Instead of picking at it and overanalyzing, I dupe myself into thinking it will be a case of *what happens in Denver stays in Denver*. Setting up my fabric samples and arranging my equipment is a solid distraction that carries me into the evening. I'm only pulled from it all when my phone rings. I stupidly hope it's Sawyer, while a bigger part of me knows it won't be.

But I'm not expecting the name that shows on the screen.

I answer, uncaring how bad of a mood I'm in.

"Mother." I'm curt and if she doesn't like it, tough.

"Claire. Where in the world have you been hiding?" she demands without raising her voice, so used to getting her way. "You couldn't tell me that you wanted to leave Paris for a while?"

That was the whole point. Not *to tell you.*

"What are you even doing out there? Not even in a city."

I lick my lips, using my confusion about Sawyer's coolness toward me to fuel my anger. Boldly, I tell her the truth. "I've come out here to design a bride's dress. It will be my first job to kick off my career."

"*Career*?" She huffs. "You're talking nonsense."

"No, I'm talking about my dream."

"You don't *need* a dream."

I shake my head, unsure how to make her understand. How does one argue with a heartless, soulless person who's never had a goal other than to be rich and spoiled?

"It's my passion. This is all I've ever wanted to do and—"

"No, Claire. This is just nonsense." She sighs dramatically, like she's exasperated after dealing with a child. "What you need to do is come home. I expect you in New York next week because I've secured you a date with a Rothschild."

My chest convulses. A bitter rage brews within me, but I don't let it out in the scream that teases in my throat. I can't run from my mother forever. She's already found me here. She foiled my hopes to elope into a loveless marriage once. Why did I ever think I could escape?

"Shall I remind you that *I* paid for you to go to school in Paris? Hmm? I pandered to your whims and so-called dreams. I gave you a chance to get that silliness out of your mind."

"No! That money is mine. It is rightfully mine, Mother. It was left to *me* when my father died."

She draws in a short sharp breath, cut off with that line of reasoning. She never liked it when I reminded her of the details of *my* wealth. My father wanted to see to my future up until his death.

"I'll find a lawyer. Here or in New York." I bet Dalton and Caleb can still help. I hope they can. "If you don't leave me alone, if you don't stop with your matchmaking crap, I'll find a lawyer and have them deal with you."

She chortles, a nasty, wicked sound. "I'd like to see you try."

"You think I'm bluffing?" I stand and pace. "I'm sick of you meddling in my life and trying to dictate what I should do and who I should be with!"

"No lawyer you find will ever get around *mine*."

Oh! I grit my teeth, slitting my eyes.

She laughs again, louder, like she's tolerating a toddler's tantrum. "The ticket home will be in your emails."

"I don't care."

Her sigh is heavy and dramatic. "Your trust fund had stipulations, dear. You can access it when you marry, and only someone of my choosing. That's what your father wanted."

No! My father loved me. I was his only child, the apple of his eye. He cared for me and doted on me the best he could, with my mother trying to rule his personal life. I cannot fathom how he ever would have added such a detail to the will. He set that trust fund up to provide for me, not hinder me and trap me into a situation lacking true love. My mother always put me off when I wanted to see a copy of the will, but hopefully, with Dalton's help, I can get access to what my father left for me.

I don't have a chance to argue.

She hangs up, and the click of the disconnected call burns another hole in my battered soul. I refuse to admit defeat. I will not agree with what she claims, but the world presses in on me, rendering me numb and empty. Shell-shocked once again.

I sink to the floor and hug my knees to my chest. With my face smashed against my knees, I steady my breaths and will this hopelessness to fade away.

She can't win.

It's a horrible thought I don't want to allow myself to believe.

But it seems like no matter what I do, with my head or heart ruling me, I can't win either.

CHAPTER 19

Sawyer

I do my best to keep busy after I drop Claire off at that luxury cabin. If I'm too idle, if I have too much time to think and second-guess myself, I'll overwhelm myself with doubt. I leave the trailer where it should be ready for the upcoming workdays, and after that, I head to the construction company's warehouse to set the supplies out for my crews. Every time I think back to the exact moments when I picked up all the items, though, I'm bombarded with memories of Claire. Of how she smiled at me or how we'd joked about something trivial. She was so animated, talking about her dreams for a custom shop for her bridal gowns, and I fell right back into the rabbit hole of obsessing about her all over again.

Wasting time at the warehouse doesn't help to distract me, so I head home to shower and prepare for the next day. Nothing's set on the schedule, just odds and ends of errands and tasks I need to see to at home, and with this morning gone and the afternoon stretching out with too much free time, I struggle to get over her.

Claire is on my mind. She has burrowed her way under my skin, and I can't dislodge her. If I zone out, I'll recall the image of her naked on that bed, open and willing and trusting me. If I turn up the radio as I tidy up my condo, I'll think back to how each time she moaned or growled my name made me that much harder.

"Dammit." I toss my phone to the couch and drop my head back against the headrest.

Nothing I can do will pull me from thinking about her, and I know that's clearly a bad sign.

I open my eyes and scowl at my living room; all the details of the modern and minimalistic layout a blur I don't notice. Jason never fails to tease me about my residence. It's all modern, with sleek angles and gray tones. Nothing rustic or earthy, which, according to him, is expected from an outdoorsman like me.

It's not just the mere thought of her that is irritating me. If I'm being honest, she's been on my mind since the day I met her. It's the way I left her. The way I went overboard in setting up boundaries between us the morning after I ravished her.

I feel awful about being so weird around her. She doesn't deserve it, but I couldn't help it. I felt awkward and lost, and my first reaction, my initial and instinctive idea was to push her away, to erect some distance. In my mind, I was only seeking a buffer for a temporary need to figure myself out.

When I woke up and watched her sleep, so sexy and serene in that bed with me, I realized how damn much she was getting to me. She was out of my league, just like Gina, who got between me and Kevin. Claire is not my type. She's not the kind of woman who would make sense in my life or fit in it at all, but there's not a chance in hell that I can deny the strength of what I feel for her. After she gave me permission to love on her, I felt such a deep connection, something so profound I've never felt for anyone else in my life.

The severity of how much she matters scares me. She has so much power, this undeniable sway on me that pulls me to please her, that encourages me to impress her. And all for what? To have my heart broken again? I can't help but be drawn to her, but I can't shake the common sense in my brain that warns me not to. I've gone through this before. I've gotten close to a girl too fancy and pretty and high-maintenance for me, a woman from a whole different world than what I'm used to as a blue-collar construction guy.

And it burned. It stung when Gina left me. Just like Kevin predicted she would. That women will only ever see me as the rugged lover, good for a quickie, nothing lasting and deep. That I'm nothing but convenient eye candy, not a representation of a man to keep for good.

With those reminders of a similar heartache and loss, I didn't have a clue about how to act around Claire after experiencing such strong feelings after having her.

There is no simple way to view Claire being in my life, even as a fling. Yes, she's out of my league, and she's used to such a different life than I am, but that's not it. She's also Dalton's baby sister. Technically, she's not. They're cousins, but I noticed how he looks after her. He's allowing her this stay at his cabin so she can work. He's focused on helping her out however he can, so much so that I worry about what he might think of me afterward. If she were to cry to him about a broken heart or any other jaded feelings, he might alter his ties with me. I can afford to lose his business, but I've become friends with the man. I'd hate to ruin my friendships with Dalton and Caleb because of things turning sour between Claire and me.

"What's the point anyway?" I mumble out loud.

Claire will never be anything more than a fling, a short-term lay. She spoke of her dream shop, but I know where she saw it happening. Not here. In Paris. Or some other big, glamorous city. The woman who's hogging all of my thoughts doesn't want to stick around here, and it's a painful pill to swallow.

I don't need to be reminded of why I shouldn't let myself get any more connected. I shouldn't let these feelings grow and linger because she's not only a forbidden girl out of my league, but she will also soon be gone from this area completely.

I rub my face and sigh. "Enough." I stand, shaking my head and wishing it was closer to the time I told my crew I'd meet them for today's work. I'll be early. It doesn't matter. Whiling away my time here at home and trying to find something to occupy myself with isn't doing me any good at all.

I head out to my truck, shelving all my thoughts about Claire. I put a lid on the emotional turmoil and check through my tools one more time before heading out to meet the crew. It should be a short and simple check, going through and making sure everything is in my bag and in the lock box on the bed, but I'm missing something. My tape measure isn't anything fancy, but that's the tricky thing about them. You think you've got one handy for when you need it, but if it's missing, you can never locate another.

"Dammit."

I remember using it at Claire's cabin. I can't tell if details are sharper when they have to do with her or if I'm borderline obsessing about her now. But I do know that stupid tape measure is at her place.

I get in my truck, mind made up and decision chosen. I'll swing by her place on the way. It's *almost* on the way. I'm due to meet my crews to start demoing the older cabins on the other end of Dalton's property, so I'll stop at Claire's to grab my tape measure and leave.

It won't hurt either of us if I see her. It's no harm to merely glance at her and see if she's okay. She held up all right for the ride home, didn't she? It seemed like she was managing, but deep down, I feel like crap for even putting doubt in her mind.

I'd never felt that close to a woman before. And while I am confused about how to navigate things post-sex, I refuse to outright hurt her intentionally.

I arrive at her cabin and try my best to calm my racing heart. She always riles me up. Just thinking about her can make me feel more flustered than I should, and after the shitty way I blew her off and reduced our hot night of sex in Denver to a one-time thing, I'm more on edge than usual. It's *my* fault if she is bitchy with me now. It'll be on *me*, not her, if things are awkward and tense between us, and it's a damn shame because on the way there, then all night long bar-hopping and dancing with her, we'd truly gotten close.

I hold my breath and knock on the door, but I don't receive an answer. I try again, watching from the corner of my eye to see if she's peeking through the curtains and seeing me here. I wouldn't put it past her to avoid me and not open the door out of spite. She's got to be confused, too.

I try the doorknob, wondering for a fleeting, panicking second if something could have happened to her. I've been trying to weed through the laundry list of jobs this cabin needs for updating, and I started with the most potentially dangerous things first. I wouldn't be okay with her staying here if I thought it was unsafe. Nor would Dalton. The door opens easily, though, and I see her in the front room, a gorgeous proof of life.

With her music blaring, she can't hear me enter. And with her position of sitting facing the opposite direction, granting me a view of her profile, I can tell she won't see me, either.

Dangerous. If someone else would happen by and want to walk in...

I stride toward the kitchen. From the distance across the cabin, I can clearly make out the bright orange of my tape measure I've used for years. It's sitting right there on the counter, and I see no reason why I can't grab it from where I left it. I consider shouting hello so as not to startle her if she catches a glimpse of me or my reflection in the window, but the music is blasting so loud—some old-school classic rock I wouldn't think she'd care for—I doubt my shout would be noticeable over Brian Johnson's lyrics.

As I return, aiming for the door, I clip my tape measure onto my pocket. I glance at her as I pass by, finding her in an explosion of fabric. She sits in the middle of the pile. A few pins stick out of her mouth as she concentrates on the dress form. It seems my closer look on her is what it takes to pull her from her work. She jumps a bit, noticing me in surprise.

"Sawyer?" Her cheeks turn pink as her eyes widen.

I unclip the tape measure and hold it up. "Sorry for barging in. The door was unlocked."

She taps her phone, still blushing, and the music goes down a few notches on the speakers.

Having her undivided attention, I clear my throat. "Sorry to barge in like this," I repeat. "I forgot this and wanted to grab it before heading to the job site."

Her lips clamp together in a tight line as she nods. I can't look away. If that little tip of her chin was a dismissal, I'll disobey it. I'm not done looking my fill. I've never seen her so dressed down and casual like this. Her hair is clipped back in a messy bun, no makeup covers her beautiful face, and in a tank top and terry shorts, she's simply gorgeous.

"Sorry," I say again, unable to stop apologizing.

She shrugs, glancing at the tool in my hand. "It's fine."

I nod, stupefied into staring at her.

She arches her brows. She's not inviting me to talk much or acting welcoming. Still seated, she makes no move to greet me like she used to.

Which is no one's fault but mine...

"How are you doing?" she asks neutrally.

"I'm fine." *Not fine. I can't get you out of my mind.* "I'm all right. You?"

I hate this stilted talk.

She shrugs again.

"What are you doing?" The question doesn't satisfy my need to get close, but I blurt it out, interested in this mess and her creation.

"Framing the dress." She states it simply, like it should be obvious.

It's not obvious at all, not to me, but it's incredible to witness her in her element, working so passionately. She's open and comfortable, laid-back even. I want to ask more about her creative process, but I can tell how I threw her off, arriving unexpectedly like this.

"Well..." I lamely hold up the tape measure and sigh as I turn. "I'll head out." I do. I hurry to the door before she can say anything that would make this more awkward. It's cowardly, running from her after giving in to the urge to see her, but I no longer have the time to dawdle and not make up my mind about her. I still can't figure out what getting a glance of her could do other than ignite my need to see her more and more, but I shelve it. I set aside all thoughts of her and try my best to focus on the jobs today.

I find Dalton and Caleb inside the first cabin to be demoed, and I'm surprised. Dalt's not a micromanager, and Caleb is usually busy on his property closer to the bed-and-breakfast. They're not unwelcomed, though.

"You don't mind if we stick around?" Dalton asks after I greet them.

I shake my head. "No." It's his place. His call, anyway.

"We're in the mood to destroy some stuff." He pulls his work gloves up his fingers and glowers at the old, wallpapered wall.

"Bad day?"

He rolls his eyes at me, nodding. "My aunt has been hounding me the last few days."

I raise my brows. "Your aunt? As in...Claire's mom?"

He nods again. "I, uh, I might have to go to New York with Claire next week."

"So soon?" I ask, instantly hating the whininess in my voice. "Why does she need to go to New York? She said with all the samples she got in Denver, she'll be super busy on Lauren's dress. Is something wrong with her mom?" That would stink. I'd hate for Claire to be distracted from her first big job of her dream career with a family emergency.

"Plenty is wrong with that woman," he mutters darkly. "My aunt is essentially trying to sell Claire off to a Rothschild. Some antiquated crap about the 'old money' marriages and needing to keep with the lines and all that."

Sell Claire off? Like fricking chattel? I see red. Anger immediately sweeps through me. My muscles tense, and I grind my teeth together to ensure my mouth stays shut long enough for me to keep my cool.

Claire is going to New York to be sold to some rich punk over my dead body.

CHAPTER 20

Claire

I don't have a lot of time to perfect Lauren's dress. Since it's my first "real" design, making it as close to what she envisions is critical. The pressure of the deadline looming closer and closer adds another layer of stress as well, but I'm glad for it.

Waking up every day with something to work toward is the drive I need to get through the first several days after the trip to Denver with Sawyer. It's also the project I devote my brainpower to so I don't dwell on how things went rotten with the man I can't keep out of my thoughts. More than that, though, having Lauren's dress to design grounds me from getting carried away with worry and anger about my mother.

Demanding me to come to New York. Like I'm a dog trained to heel and stay! I already vowed not to forgive her for contacting Owen and turning him against the idea of eloping with me. In hindsight, I realize that was a blessing in disguise. Having moved on to meet Sawyer and see how a real man makes love, I'm glad I evaded that marriage. I won't hold a grudge against Owen. I wish him well. But I am happy I avoided a loveless and subpar marriage with a man who doesn't challenge me at every turn and excite me during every minute of the day.

I deleted my mother's email with the flight information, and if she dares to send it again, I won't see it. I'm so fed up with her that I finally took the ultimate step of canceling her right out of my life. Her emails are on my spam list. Her calls are blocked from my cell. This complete and total act of ignoring her summons is the lifeline I've needed. Not dreading her calls or texts is a beautiful and freeing experience. Never seeing her email address in my inbox has me breathing easier.

Between the closure of communications with her and Lauren's design, I'm seeing to my own happiness as well as I can. Sawyer is a whole other matter, but I refuse to let him dominate my mind now.

Lauren and Aubrey show up right on time. I asked Lauren to come by and finalize her fabric choices, but once they enter my makeshift workshop in the cabin's living room, we don't talk much about the dresses, not for the lack of my attempts.

"But what else is new?" Aubrey asks after I point out how I've added equipment and necessities to the cabin. Both of the women are excited about how I've transformed this room. The last time they were here, I didn't have all the samples, equipment, and forms arranged. With an almost childlike curiosity of seeing something so new and different for the first time, they ask me question after question about what does what and what step happens where. I entertain them, glad for the chance to talk about something I love. The process of designing a gown *is* a complex concept, though, and I do my best to steer them back to the samples I picked up in Denver.

"I got these from two shops in Denver," I say as I hold out the two booklets to lay them on the coffee table. Lauren and Aubrey face me, seated together on the couch, while I wait in a chair, eager to stand and get moving the moment Lauren makes her choice. It's so important for her to have this say in her dress. I feel confident in my hunch of what she'll pick, but until I have her approval, I'm at a standstill.

"Denver, huh?" Aubrey's tone is teasing once Lauren confirms her final picks.

Yes! Now I can go, go, go. Lauren nods, smiling wide with her decisions, and I sigh in relief that I've guided her well, so well that she feels good about the design. I no longer have to wonder, worry, and wait on her choices.

"Yeah, about Denver," Lauren says coyly.

In our group texts thread, they've been hounding me for details, but it seems I'll no longer have the ease of evasion here while they hang out.

"I..." I set aside my notebook and slump back in my chair. "Well, I slept with Sawyer in Denver." I throw my hands up in a huge shrug. "There. The truth is out."

Aubrey rubs her hands together. "*Ooooh.* I knew it!"

"Really?" Lauren laughs.

I nod. "Apparently, nowhere in Denver had more than one room available and—"

They break out into giggles, snorting over each other as they try to calm down enough to speak.

"Same thing happened to me...with Caleb," Lauren says.

Aubrey points at herself. "Yep. Me and Dalton, too."

I shake my head and laugh. I can't stop smiling, even though this girl-talk thing is weird. It's strange because I've never actually done it. I've been expecting them to turn their noses up at me for sleeping with Sawyer, maybe ready to slut shame me or something, but instead, they seem happy and extremely curious about him. If this is what *kiss and tell* is all about, it's not so bad. Lauren and Aubrey are real friends—another first—and it's too easy to giggle and chat right along with them.

Once they leave, though, after an hour of joking and sharing the minimal details about my hookup, the cabin seems overwhelmingly empty.

I close the door after them and lean on it as reality kicks in. It's all well and good to do this girl talk with those two, but Sawyer is avoiding me. How can I sit here and giggle and smile about how great he made me feel when now, he's doing the opposite? The lack of communication with him still hurts, and with every day that passes without him reaching out to me, another chunk of my heart cracks off and shrinks.

Or...I could reach out to him. I've never considered myself the kind of woman who chases after a man. It's not my style, or at least it never has been. Now, as I think hard about why I'm still so eager and hopeful to reconnect with Sawyer, I wonder if I've never chased after a man because none of them have ever mattered as much as Sawyer does. I've never yearned for another guy. I've never woken up wondering about a man and or gone to bed missing one like I do with the rugged smartass who drove me to Denver.

Maybe I—

Knocks sound on the door. I'm still leaning my back against it, so the vibration against me, coupled with the closeness to the noise, has me jumping away in shock.

I peek out the window, seeing Aubrey driving away with Lauren. It's not them, but my cousin. Dalton's truck is parked in the gravel drive.

After I open the door, he enters and sighs at the mess I've made. No, not the *mess*. The excess of my creativity. Calling my workspace a mess feels too derogatory.

"Hi, Dalt."

"Hey, Claire." He walks closer to the dress forms, eyeing my preliminary progress.

"Lauren *just* chose her fabrics. So it'll come together quickly now."

"That's great. And I love to hear you commit like that."

I furrow my brow. *Because I'm just out of school? Because I'm too young to know how to commit yet. Pu-leeze.*

"I came by to talk about your return to New York." He arches a brow at me expectantly before approaching the other dress form.

I shake my head and cross my arms.

"I'm against it, Claire. All of it. My lawyers are looking into what they can do on your behalf."

"She more or less laughed at that idea. I think she's convinced her legal team will overrule any other."

He rolls his eyes. "Not true. Some of these things take time. Like that mess with Jeremy. It's still a work in progress."

I shrug.

"Even though I'm against you going, I will come along to support you."

"Not necessary."

He grunts in frustration. "I know you prefer to handle your problems on your own, but—"

"No. I'm not going."

"Really?"

I nod, trying my best not to smile. "I'm not going to New York. Period."

He comes close and pulls me into a hug. "Thank fuck."

I giggle, hugging him back.

"This calls for a celebration. The day you stood against Adelaide."

Little does he know, I decided this the day after she called me about coming to meet some doofus who exceeded her expectations.

"Come out with us. This calls for a drink."

I step back, brushing my hair from my face. "Where?" I'm not aware of all the nightlife this small town has to offer. In the heart of Breckenridge, sure, but here, further out?

"Caleb and Lauren want to go out for drinks with me and Aubrey at the hotel they renovated last summer."

"The one in Frisco?" I ask.

He nods. "Yeah. That's the one. Come join us, and we can have a celebratory drink."

His invite is tempting. Because if I turn him down—which is my lingering instinct I am trying to grow past in an effort to be more social—I'll be here in this cabin, alone and creeping closer to misery.

"I'm not sure I'm in the mood to drink tonight…"

I doubt it matters if I'm here alone and sad or if I'm with them and drinking and still feeling so stressed. Dalton has no way of understanding how heavy my head and heart are right now. I'm torn and stuck, and it's an ugly position to remain in limbo for too long.

"Okay, no drinks. Just to celebrate?"

I sigh, knowing he won't give up easily. I nod, reluctantly agreeing to head out even though not even a teeny bit of my soul wants this.

Too many things are getting twisted in my life, and worst of all is the niggling reminder that the last time I headed out for a drink or two, it was with Sawyer.

And look how that *ended up.*

I roll my eyes and shrug. "Okay. I'll go out with you for *one* drink to toast my independence from my mother."

He grins and hugs me again, clueless as to how much I wish Sawyer might be there as well.

Nope. I know he won't be. For whatever reason he's sticking with, avoiding me is the best path forward.

And damn, does that hurt.

CHAPTER 21

Claire

Once we arrive at the bar in Frisco, I begin to feel glad that I gave in and came. These four are so welcoming and inclusive that I should always know that they'll have my best interests at heart. I grew up with Dalton as my only likable relative, and Caleb has been the second brother I never had. Both of those men are protective and caring, and the women they've decided to make theirs are just as good of company, if not more. In Lauren and Aubrey, I have real, honest-to-goodness, actual friends for the first time.

Still, being here with two couples reiterates the fact I'm a fifth wheel. I'm a single with their pairs. I don't fit in. Watching them together makes my heart sink just that little bit more. I fall back into the pit of missing Sawyer and wishing for something more with him. I envision him here, smiling and holding my hand as we complete the night as a third couple.

But he's not here. Other than stopping in my cabin to scare the crap out of me, just walking inside to pick something up, I haven't seen him or heard a peep from him. No calls or texts. No plans to work on the cabin. It was so weird, knowing he saw me like a mess as I worked on framing the dress, but he hadn't shown any sign of being bothered by my appearance.

Sawyer has fallen off the face of the Earth as far as I'm concerned, so when Aubrey introduces me to a man who resembles the cocky contractor I can't stop thinking about, I'm intrigued.

"Claire, this is Kevin, Sawyer's brother." Aubrey beams at the man as he approaches. He seems to have had the same idea as us, to grab a drink at this bar connected to the hotel Lauren and Caleb flipped last summer.

"We both teach at the same school," she says. "Kevin, this is Claire, Dalton's cousin."

"Nice to meet you," I tell him after he says the same and takes the seat next to me. "Younger brother?" I guess.

He nods. "Yeah. Jason's the oldest." A wry smile hits his lips. "Obviously. Then Sawyer and me."

"I've met Jason at the Goldfinch." And I've heard about Kevin. Sawyer mentioned him previously, but he never put many details into their relationship. Honestly, I forgot about him, and I can't help but wonder if Sawyer intended that. If this relationship isn't a fond one.

"Jason's been up that mountainside more than ever," Kevin says as his drink is delivered.

I nurse my cocktail, not very interested in seeing it disappear too soon. "Because of Marian?"

He chuckles, and I notice how different it is from Sawyer's. Sawyer's voice is deeper, sexier, no matter if he's joking, whispering, or laughing. Kevin is much more proper, more like a man my mother might approve of. Not crude and laid-back enough to let loose like Sawyer.

"Jason and Marian are a good fit. I wonder when they'll both give in and just admit he's going to move in there to be with her. He's got to be getting tired of pretending to be needed or wanted there for projects that need to be done."

"Maybe it's like a slow build-up."

"Maybe," he agrees. "And with how long Marian's been alone after her husband passed away, it makes sense that she would be slow and cautious to officially announce anything with anyone."

I smile, loving how everyone not only knows the older, smart woman running the B&B but also how they admire and look up to her. It's something I sure lack practice with. The only maternal figure in my life, my mother, has never encouraged admiration from me.

"It would be good for Jason to settle down. He's always been a bachelor, and now that he's retired and has given Sawyer his half of Dad's company, he'll have plenty of time to finally spend it with someone."

His comment seems multilayered, and I'm not sure what to pick at first. "Jason and Sawyer run your dad's company?"

"Sawyer does. When Dad passed away, he gave it to both of them."

I raise my brows. "Nothing to you?" That sounds like fodder for resentment.

"No. I got some money. I've never been interested in construction, not like those two are. Jason grew up with it, so it's natural that he would follow in Dad's footsteps. After Jason's mom passed and Dad remarried, Sawyer came along and fell right in with the business."

"You didn't?"

He shrugs. "Like I said, I was never interested. I was already halfway through getting my education degree when he passed away. My calling has been to teach, not bang a hammer around outside all day."

I frown at my drink. There's resentment, all right. Sawyer is a hard-working man in a manual-labor field of careers, but even I know he doesn't just 'bang a hammer around all day.' He's smart, analytical, and probably one of those super wise math geeks who can master chess and just *see* how dimensions line up. I've never been good at math, much stronger in the creative department, but it saddens me that his own brother would be so quick to belittle him.

More so, it's depressing to realize even closer-knit families with siblings can still be as dysfunctional as the relationship between me and my mother.

Kevin shrugs again, almost as though he wishes he could get the topic of his brother off his shoulders and out of his mind. "Sawyer and I have never been close."

"That's understandable. You have different interests. Dalton and Caleb are the closest things I've had to a brother, and I know they will never relate to my career or even understand it."

"What do you do?" he asks, looking me up and down.

I almost want to bristle at his tone. Was he implying he's surprised that I do anything? That I look like a spoiled woman who never works? I feel like he's judging me just like that.

"I'm a fashion designer. Bridal gowns, specifically." It feels stupid to claim that. I haven't actually *done* that yet to declare it as my job, but once Lauren's dress is finished, it will be true—with or without my dream shop.

"Ah."

"So, I get it. If I had a sister or a real brother, I bet they'd have their interests while I have mine." He doesn't reply, staring at his drink. I'm waiting for a deeper explanation about why he and Sawyer aren't close because I'm that thirsty for more clues about the man I can't get out of my head.

"Are you not close with Jason either?" I ask. If the difference of interests is what split the brothers, it seems Kevin wouldn't be close with Jason either.

"He's all right. We get along. But Sawyer..." He sighs and faces me, studying me directly. "You're really curious, aren't you?"

I smile, not sheepish to show that he's caught me there. I *am* curious about everything about Sawyer, including details about his family members and why his brother might not be close to him. I'm deluded, thinking the more I know about that sexy man, the better I can be rational with my decisions about him.

Yeah, right. I'll only want more and more. It's a scary notion, this need to get *more* involved with Sawyer when I know nothing will ever last. I meant it when I told Dalton I'm not going to my mother in New York, but that doesn't mean staying *here*. The urge to rub my face hits me, but I refrain from showing my frustrations like that in public. Simply put, I have no clue what to do or where to go. I see no answers anywhere.

"Sawyer is a..." I can't even figure out what to call him. He's more than a friend now, one who wants to pretend I don't exist.

"Ah." Kevin nods. "*That* kind of a friend."

I purse my lips, hating how he might be judging or viewing me now.

"I'm surprised."

Okay, red flags galore here. "Why?"

"You're not his type."

I giggle. Well, everyone would think that. I'm confident that Sawyer's far from what should be my type, too. "We do seem like a case of opposites attract." I smile, twirling my straw in my drink. "He calls me high-maintenance."

Kevin smiles, not making eye contact. "I would think he'd know better then."

I frown. "Because...a 'high-maintenance' woman isn't worthy of his time?"

"No. It's just what you've said. He's your opposite. Sawyer is, uh, not high-maintenance. He's a simple working man."

I furrow my brow as I focus on my drink. I don't want to dignify that comment with looking at him. That's a cruel comment. Sawyer isn't *simple*, and to know his brother views him so poorly hurts.

"I'm not one to claim to know Sawyer, all right? We're not close, so please, whatever you've got going on with him, don't take my words to heart."

Ha. Too late for that.

"Well, we're in the same boat there. I feel like I don't know him that well either." *Except, um, in the naked sense.* "And I have a hunch Sawyer doesn't really know what he wants anyway."

Kevin nods. "Yeah, that sounds about right."

Maybe he thinks I've said something accurate, but it feels wrong to speak it.

This funkiness remains with me for the rest of the night. Even though Kevin moves aside to chat with Aubrey and another colleague from the school they work at, I can't shake Sawyer from my mind.

I miss him. I wonder what I've done wrong to make him want to avoid me. I hate that he can't have a good relationship with both of his brothers. And more than anything, I wish that whatever changed his mind about me could no longer stand between us.

I don't know what to do next or where I'll go in the next phase of resisting my mother's efforts to marry me off, but I wish that while I am here in Colorado, I could spend every possible minute with Sawyer.

***

Dalton and Aubrey drop me off at the cabin, and I jump right into working on Lauren's dress. It's all I have to distract myself. My hope is that I will tire out my eyes and force a decent night of sleep on myself.

Headlights flash through the windows, though, capturing my attention. No one ever drives out this way, and since it's Dalton's private property, no one should be out here.

Except...

Sawyer headed to those older cabins.

I cling to the idea that it could be him driving so late, and I hurry to the porch.

Too many questions sit in my mind about him. While I'm stubborn enough to avoid the vulnerability of reaching out to him, I wish he would come to me.

Stop getting your hopes up. Clearly, it was a mistake. As I prop my forearms on the porch railing to watch him inevitably drive past, I sigh and think back to how Kevin judged me earlier. He was so quick to think Sawyer wouldn't ever be with a woman like me. He pointed out that I was the opposite of his laid-back brother, and it hit me like a lightbulb going off.

Was I too needy that night? Doubting myself and rejecting his compliment? Did I make myself too vulnerable that Sawyer felt like he had to take care of me, getting nothing in return? Maybe that's why he's done and moving on.

To my surprise, his truck slows, then stops in the drive.

I hold my breath as the driver's door opens. It's like I've summoned him here, and I don't know what to think or how to act.

He steps out of the truck, his intense gaze on me. The lights on the porch show me plenty of details on his rugged face, and I swallow at the instant hit of desire that cloaks me.

I want him. Damn, do I want him as he stalks toward me, climbing the steps to reach me up here. Without a word, he stares at me so intensely, and I fall under the spell of wishing he could just be mine.

"Did I do something wrong?" I regret that it's the first thing I blurt out. Not a hello. No question as to what he's doing here. Just an automatic worry and assumption that Sawyer and I can't work. That Kevin is right to scoff at the idea of his brother wanting me.

Sawyer shakes his head, sighing as he sets foot on the porch. He pauses for so long that I get impatient, too curious for any mind games.

"No. You didn't do anything wrong," he says carefully.

A tense moment spans between us, but beneath the silence of our stare-down, I want to crumble under the suspense. This electricity still sizzles between us, and more than ever, I'm drawn to him.

"I—"

I lose track of whatever I was going to blurt out, cut off by his quick steps over the wooden planks. He approaches me swiftly, sauntering toward me with an unreadable expression that looks a lot like desire.

He reaches out to grab my sides, and I give in. I cave. Leaning close, I fall against his hard chest as he hugs me tightly and slams his lips to mine.

CHAPTER 22

Sawyer

Hearing the worry in Claire's voice cuts at me, but feeling her soft lips pressing against mine soothes that ache. I have her in my hands, and as I clutch her sides, I feel better just knowing she's here, with me, and still holding this passion that I can't shake off.

The very idea of her doing something to turn me away is ridiculous, but I'm not shocked that she's taken that route of wondering and fretting about where things stand between us. Avoiding her like I have been, I've given her nothing but every reason to assume the worst of this situation.

But it's not her fault. None of this is her fault. Shying away from the depth of my feelings for her is all on me, and I hate that I went so far to push her away.

"No," I tell her again as I walk her back to her still-open front door. "You didn't do anything wrong."

She peers up at me with wide, trusting eyes. I see the vulnerability there. She has a shaky, iffy trust in me now, but she's giving me hope at the same time. I'm glad she doesn't protest and demand that we stand out here and talk. Instead, she's open and willing, maybe just as desperate as I am, to be led inside her cabin.

I kick the door shut after we enter, and I waste not a second to cup her face and kiss her soundly. Her moans make my dick hard. Every time she pushes up to secure our mouths in this sloppy, messy kiss, I want to growl. And when she slips her tongue out to find mine and duel, I stumble through her living room.

I kick my boots off and leave them by the door; I don't want to dirty up her personal space by bringing the outside in here.

"Then why—" She pants hard, catching her breath as we cling to each other and weave our way toward her room. "Why—" She's not stammering or stuttering, but confused and torn. I wouldn't expect any less of her. While she wants me, she's not a pushover to forget about the way I've shunned her after Denver.

At the door to her bedroom, she fists my shirt and sharpens her gaze on me. "Why did you dismiss me? Was I too needy?"

I choke on a laugh, incredulous that she'd ever go there. Too needy? "When the hell did I ever suggest that?"

"When..." She licks her lips, reaching for my jeans and sliding my belt through the buckle. "When you took care of me. When you treated me so affectionately. Like I was fragile and delicate—"

I pick her up and carry her to the bed, where I drop her onto the mattress. She bounces and looks up at me, grinning as I stare down at her. I've never wanted a woman more, and I hope I'm not making a bigger mistake by going weak with her.

Claire just gets to me, and I drag in a deep breath before I rush it all.

"I don't want you to view me as needy. As high-maintenance." She crawls onto her knees and comes to the edge of the bed. Pulling up at my hem, she removes my shirt. "I want to please you, too," she promises.

I grin and watch her drag her hands down my chest. She traces her fingers along my waist, going back for my buckle. I haven't ever doubted what she can do. She does please me, a lot, but I'll let her continue to show it. If she was worrying that she was demanding too much of me, a silly thought that doesn't make sense, I'll let her appease herself by showing me otherwise.

"You please me, baby." I brush her hair back from her face as she unbuttons and unzips my jeans. "Never doubt that."

"Hmmm." She pushes my jeans down, rubbing her knuckles along my erection confined under my boxers. "I want you to know I'll take care of you, too..."

I hold my breath as she crawls off the bed. She keeps her hands on my jeans, turning me to give her room to reach the floor. Once she's on her knees again, she pushes me toward the bed. Then she takes hold of my boxers and pulls them down.

I'm unable to look away. My dick springs free. The tip is shiny with pre-cum, jutting out inches from her face. Her eyes lock onto the sight of me hard and ready for her, and with a slow, sexy lick of her lips, she hints at what she plans on.

"If you'll let me." She pushes, urging me to sit, and she follows me to the bed.

I'm glad I took my boots off after entering the cabin because as she presses her fingers at my knees, I part my legs and let my jeans and boxers fall to the floor. They hang off one ankle, but she merely nudges the mess aside to kneel closer. And closer.

The second she touches the tip of her tongue to my dick, I tense. My abs contract, and I brace myself for the many hits of need that strike through me.

Dammit, she's hot. She's a wet dream come to life—no, she's *my* dream. A bold woman who knows what she wants. A sensual lover who's not afraid to go for it, either.

As she closes her lips around my dick, I groan and watch her suck the head in. Her cheeks hollow, and keeping her eyes on mine, she hums in appreciation.

"Baby," I croon, sliding my hands through her hair to hold her head. "Damn, baby. Feels so good."

She smiles around me, and as I stretch her lips, she sucks me further down her warm, wet mouth. Even though she's tormenting me, taking this so slow, I can't bring myself to push into her. I want her to take the lead. It's ridiculous for her to think I was turned off by her behavior in Denver. She wasn't needy. I just wanted the freedom to worship and memorize her so I could hang on to the memories after she's gone. But I understand why she might need to do this for me—for herself. For her own sense of pride and power over me.

I don't care. As she sucks me off, using a damning pressure with her lips and throat, I get closer and closer to shooting my load into her mouth. I realize I have no power to say no to this woman, and if that makes me the idiot, so be it.

I breathe faster and harder, feeling my balls tighten with the threat of an orgasm ending the fun. I flex my fingers, losing hold of her head, and as I firm the muscles in my legs, she strokes her nails over my thighs. She slows her up-and-down bobs on my cock, and as she pauses, catching her breath, she licks my tip like she'll never get enough of my taste.

"Can..." I swallow hard. "Can you ride me?" I scoot back on the bed, not waiting for her answer. "If you're determined to rock my world, I wanna feel you around me. I want to feel you milking me." As I lie back, she stands and strips quickly. Then she dips down, sucking me into her mouth again before she releases me and reaches toward the nightstand.

She returns with a condom, which she rolls over me. Before I can speak or move, she straddles me and sinks down in a brutally tight grip.

"Oh, yeah." I grunt at the feel of her sheathing me, and I let my head roll back onto the bed as she lifts up to grind back down. "Just like that, baby."

She sits up more, giving herself a deeper angle. I clamp my hands on her hips to guide her, but I'm lost in the sight of her ravenous, lusty expression and her gorgeous breasts bouncing and jiggling as she picks up her pace.

"Like...that..." I growl, lost for words. I can't even think, and I'm not sure I want to try. All I can concentrate on is the sexy woman getting herself off as she tempts me to let go.

Come on. You've got to get there first. I can't without it. I grit my teeth, willing her to come with me, but she grimaces and falters.

"Please, Sawyer."

"Come with me," I argue, always ready to quarrel with her.

"No, I won't."

"Come with me, Claire!" I dig my fingers into her hips, falling just that much more in love with her because she's so driven to please me. As if watching her ride me like a wanton, wild woman isn't the epitome of all I want.

She tightens around me, then cries out. Her head drops back, showing me the art that her body is. The slender length of her neck, the generous swells of her breasts, and her flat stomach, all the way down to here, where we're connected. She's magnificent and raw, so full of passion.

All for me.

I know this now.

I should have accepted it earlier instead of being a coward and worrying about how to treat her. It's clear. This woman just very well could be it for me, and I'll be damned if I ever give her another reason to doubt my feelings for her, as complicated and undefined though they may be.

I lose control, giving in to the demand to come, and with a deep groan, I push up into her. Every fluttering clench of her muscles sucks me in more, and as I release into her, shaking from the intensity of my orgasm, I catch her.

She falls atop me, shivering and trembling, and I hold her tight as I close my eyes.

What have I done?

Coming here because I missed her felt like an impulsive decision, but sleeping with her again is anything but. A harder question follows up the first.

What happens now?

***

Hours later, once we've showered without a word, we sluggishly end up back on her bed. This time, we're under the covers. I just woke up, shifting to get more comfortable, but for some reason, I remain awake.

In Denver, I had nowhere to run but to get coffee in the morning. Stranding her there was never an option. Here, though, I feel caught by the indecision of staying or leaving. I don't want to be a coward. I don't want to struggle with how hard and fast I'm falling for her when we both know the odds are slim that we can last.

I'll hate myself if I go, but I need space. I need time. I need a slight separation from her to begin to come to terms with this. So, I ease out of bed and slip my jeans on. I don't want to alarm her or wake her, and heading out to the living room seems like the only alternative.

As I sit on the couch and try to compartmentalize what I'm doing by letting Claire into my life, I zone out and eye all her things. I guess it's less of a living room now, taken over by the evidence of her work. She's transformed this cabin into a dress shop, and I smile at the faint and faraway fantasy of giving her the real thing. Her own dress shop, here, not in Paris. It sounds stupid and corny, like I'm grasping at farfetched wishes, but the more I really think about it, it doesn't sound that bizarre. Why *couldn't* she have a dress shop here? I bet she would worry about not having the same types of clients as she might easily find in Paris or a bigger city, but since when does a thing like distance matter in the age of technology and the internet? She could have her dream shop here, with me, and still reach out to clients from any niche of the world.

I gaze at her sewing stuff, knowing she's not that different from me. She's meticulous and incredibly talented, and most of all, passionate about what she makes. Just like me. My "creations" are locked in place here as buildings, but I know I could help make her dreams come true here, too.

But would she even want that? I can't tell, and it frightens me how quickly my heart is following this pull to her without letting my logical brain catch up. I still have so much more to learn about her, but the infectious hope of her staying here while seeing her dreams come true is too tempting. It's all I can think about, and as I head back to the bed and crawl in beside her, I want to hold on to the chance of us working out. She sighs as I pull her against me, and even though she's asleep, I treasure the way she automatically leans into me and seeks me out.

I've always been guarded. Ever since a big-city woman wounded me, I've been cautious not to let another girl get close enough to destroy what's left of my heart. Claire is breaking me out of that guardedness, though, and I hope I can have faith in not only her but the depth of her feelings for me.

CHAPTER 23

Claire

I wake to the glorious smell of coffee brewing in the cabin. The fragrance carries to me in bed, and as I smile at what this means, I stretch under the covers and luxuriate in the tenderness in my thighs from the "exercise" I gave myself on top of Sawyer last night.

If I'm sleeping in here, and *someone* is making coffee in the kitchen, it means he's got to be here.

He didn't run!

I sit up, waking up faster, and grin.

So maybe he won't be weird and hide from me again!

I suspect the "adult" thing to do would be to approach him calmly and patiently. I should ask him what the heck was with his attitude after the first time we had sex. At the bare minimum, I deserve an explanation.

No one should get the cold shoulder and indifference like that after such intimacy.

And the first step to seeing if Sawyer will react differently to this episode of hot sex requires me to get out of bed and go find him in the kitchen, presumably making coffee.

I slide out of bed and grab my robe before heading out there. When I pad into the kitchen, I slow down and take a seat at the bar. He's still here, much to my delight. I was so convinced he would bolt again, but still, the chance of that happening hadn't dissuaded me from sleeping with him last night.

While I'm glad he's here, I didn't count on him *working*. Coffee has been made, yes, but it seems his use of my coffeemaker has warranted a repair of said machine. Parts lie all over the counter. A bowl of brownish water suggests he's drained and cleaned it. But as I sit, he's so into his project that he doesn't look up at first.

"Problem?" I guess.

He sighs, setting down the screwdriver. Then he looks at me and smiles, making my heart sing. It's not an expression of indifference. I can tell he's not plastering on a grin for the hell of it, either. He's...happy. With me. With us.

Before I let my hopes get too high and become giddy, I remind myself to tread carefully. He's proven a flight risk before, and until we talk about why that is, I need to be easy.

"Morning, baby."

Ooooh. That endearment gives me hope, too. He really *is* in a good mood.

"Why didn't you mention this thing leaks?"

I mock a wince. "Whoops." I can't say that I didn't warn him because I hadn't counted on him staying the night and then taking the initiative to make coffee for us.

"You didn't put it on the list," he adds. "Of things for me to fix or update."

Oh. That's what he meant. "Well, it does make coffee." I frown at the mess of parts. "Or it did. And I wasn't aware you could update a coffeemaker. I planned to get a new one and just replace it."

He nods, chuckling as he leaves the clutter of his disassembled parts on the counter to face me across it. Pushing a mug of steaming liquid toward me, he winks. "Yeah, replacing it might be smarter than trying to fix it."

When he slides my almond milk over, he smiles. "Don't forget your fancy creamer."

If he's not trying to get me to fall in love with him, I'm not sure how to interpret his consideration. He gets me. He knows that I have particular tastes, but he's not judging me for it.

But I can't go down that path. I'm too scared to jump into the lovely hope that we could make "it" and that he's genuine about wanting me in his life.

I'm still confused about why he put distance between us the first time. I need an answer for it, but not right now. We're in a good spot, and I don't want to ruin it or complicate it. It's on the tip of my tongue to tell him I'm thinking about staying here. It's not a matter of simply wanting to see where things can go with him, but I also don't want to give up the chance to fit in with the two couples who have made me so happy here.

When I came here, with the prospect of making Lauren's dress, I was mostly convinced I wouldn't need that apprenticeship in Paris. I have my work experience with Lauren's gown now. I'm not at all sure how I can ever make my dress shop happen, but with Dalton's support and maybe a huge adjustment to living in this cabin until I can sell enough dresses, I'll take the painstakingly slow approach to reaching my dream.

The only thing that's clear is that I cannot go to New York and deal with my mother. I mean it. I'm done with her, and I can't retreat.

Dumping all these thoughts and worries on Sawyer would be a mistake, though, and for the sake of not putting too many expectations on him this morning, I decide to avoid wading into the "what is this" topic between us.

At the same time, I feel the need to clarify *something*. "We're um...What we did last night..."

"Yeah?" He grins that sexy, smug smile that somehow never fails to annoy and excite me at the same time. "It was fun."

There we go. *Fun*, I can work with. Last time, he said it was *nice*, but *fun* is an ice-breaker.

"Yeah. I had fun, too. Because"—I clear my throat and look away, hoping he can't read me so well he believes that I mean this—"that's what we're doing, right? This is a hookup?" I widen my eyes at the cheapness of my words. "Um. Exclusive hookups?"

He smiles, seeming to hold back a laugh. "Yeah."

I don't want him to think I'm merely hooking up, but until I sever all ties with my mother and solidify my plans to stay here, I can't let him think what we're doing is over.

He nods and sips his coffee. "That's fine. Just make sure you let me know when my next appointment is."

His tone is casual, but it lacks the awkward coldness I heard and felt in Denver. Maybe I'm not convincing him. I can't tell what he's thinking, but I feel good about this. It's the best I can manage until my life isn't as messy, and I'm elated he's still here.

I smirk, though. "Appointment? You're making me sound like a sex worker."

He roars with laughter, shaking his head. "Hell no."

As I sip my coffee, he heads into my room and gets dressed. After he comes back out and kisses me quickly, he says, "One of my guys has to go pick up some equipment in Denver tomorrow, so I can pick up anything you need."

"Perfect!" I perk up at this offer, excited as I follow him to the front door. "Thank you. I'm so grateful for your help."

"Hmmm." He lingers at the door, sliding his boots on. When he reaches for me, I'm careful not to spill my coffee. "Sorry about the mess on the counter. I'll order you a replacement. Since I do like my coffee after 'hooking up.'"

I accept his kiss and smile back at him. At this rate, it's almost like he's mocking me, seeing right through me and getting used to the possibility that we've got something much more significant and meaningful than a mere hookup.

I wave goodbye to him, wishing him a good day at work. As I turn to the cabin and eye my workspace, I feel light and happy. Sawyer isn't avoiding me after intimacy. We have to talk, but that will come. I'm considering *how* I can make my life here without much money, and I've got a project of a lifetime to concentrate on.

What more could a girl want?

I need nothing but some music, and once I get positioned, I lose myself in my work. Before I move forward with the design, I check over the progress so far. I've framed Lauren's dress, and I'm ready for the step that involves the more expensive fabric. I never want to make any mistakes with someone else's gown, but it's getting crucial that I am extra careful with the costlier resources now, too.

As soon as I reach for my scissors, the reflection of sunlight glints off a windshield. I frown, peering through the windows as an expensive-looking car rolls up the drive and stops. It's not Dalton or Caleb. Remaining still, annoyed at the interruption, I watch as the door opens and my mother steps out.

Oh, shit.

My heart races, and I press my lips together tightly so as not to scream in frustration. "What the hell are *you* doing here?" I seethe out loud.

My mother stands tall in her Versace dress and Louboutin heels as she looks around at the scenery. Her lips twist in a grimace and the smirk on her face that follows suggests she's disgusted to even be here. Without a hint of approval, she walks up the drive and begins to climb the stairs.

Shit! I consider hiding, but I know it won't do me any good. Clearly, she's found me. She wouldn't have randomly shown up right here without having it on good authority that she'd locate me here. I know Dalton wouldn't have sold me out like this, nor Caleb, but my mother is nothing if not resourceful and determined to get her way.

She doesn't give me a chance to hide either, opening the door and striding right up the porch. I cringe, regretting that I didn't lock it after Sawyer left.

Without knocking, she enters like she owns the place and sneers at me. "You were supposed to be in New York yesterday. I figured I would come fetch you myself."

"I'm not a thing to collect!" I stand and cross my arms.

She smirks, turning her attention from me to the dress form. As she approaches it, she rolls her eyes. "No, you're a wayward daughter, delusional in thinking *this* is fashion." She flicks her hand at it like it's garbage.

Her words are intended to hurt. I know that, and I try to ignore her, but it still stings.

"This is tacky, Claire. Just trash. I want you to give up this nonsense and come home to get married already." She sighs, like I'm being a stubborn child. "I've let you play out your fantasies. I've catered to letting you think you're a 'designer', but this is nothing but an embarrassment to the Rennard line."

I fume, so furious that I lack the ability to speak. The bottled-up scream will slip out before a single word.

"I've given you plenty of time to sow your wild oats and get your useless, fancy degree, but it's time to come home."

"No." I exhale it with all the heat of my anger.

She smirks. "Listen. Any money you have access to belongs to the Rennard estate. I can easily take it all away."

When the door opens behind her, she pauses to turn and watch Dalton rush in. "Oh. It's *you*. Come to meddle with more gibberish about what your lawyers want to tell me now?"

"Claire, don't agree to anything she says," he warns me, backing me up.

I shake my head. "Never." It's taken me too long to stand up to her like this, but I can't imagine caving anymore.

"You're better off staying quiet like usual, Dalton." She turns her sneer to him. "This doesn't involve you. This conversation is between me and my embarrassing, pathetic daughter who thinks she can enjoy fulfilling her big, stupid dreams instead of doing what the women in our family are expected to do."

"I won't marry someone I don't love!" I shout.

Dalton stands next to me, putting his hand on the small of my back.

"Who said anything about *love*?" she sasses back. "You will marry the man I arrange for you, and that is final."

She turns again, as Dalton and I do. The front door remains open, leaving Sawyer a clear path inside. He enters confidently, his narrowed gaze on my mother as he walks right in and slams his toolbox onto the counter so hard it cracks the smooth surface.

CHAPTER 24

Claire

I blink, tense and anxious, as Sawyer glowers at my mother.

"Get out." He orders it firmly, looking directly at her and not backing down.

I'm not sure how much he's heard, but he's livid. I've never seen him this mad. I've never seen *any* man this furious before. All the muscles in his arms are locked tight. His hands remain in fists atop the counter he's just cracked. He stands there taut with anger, and as he slides his jaw, clenching his teeth at the sight of my mother smirking right back at him, I almost give in to a helpless whine.

As I snap out of the shock, flinching and hurrying to intervene and stand between them to mediate this mess somehow, Dalton takes hold of my wrist and prevents me from getting in the middle.

I already am in the middle. I'm in the thick of it, with my controlling mother on one side of the room opposite the man I think I could love with all my heart if I let myself lower my guard that far.

"Mother—"

"I said *get out*," Sawyer tells her as he stalks around the counter to face her. He doesn't stop, walking all the way over to me. Passing Dalton, Sawyer continues until he stands at my left and takes my hand.

I tremble with nerves, so fraught with tension and anxiety that I can barely register his gesture of support. He squeezes my fingers, and I draw in a deeper breath, but I can't bear to look at him. All I can do is watch as my mother snaps her stare from me to him. Then she curls her lip at our joined hands.

"Who the hell are you?" she retorts haughtily.

"Get. Out." Sawyer is bold and unwavering with each repeat of his demand.

She laughs, scowling as she loses it to some twisted sense of humor. "You think *you* can tell me what to do?"

"Adelaide," Dalton says in warning.

She pays my cousin no mind, laughing and pointing at Sawyer. "You think you can tell me what to do? When I'm having a private discussion with my daughter?"

She wants him to feel insignificant, but Sawyer is impervious to her tone. Again, she glances at our hands together. "I always knew you were trash, Claire." Her lip curls in disgust as she rolls her eyes. "Sleeping with a man who carries around a filthy toolbox. I think *not*." She screeches the last part.

When she turns her sneer to me, I want to hide behind Sawyer's tall frame. I don't. I swallow and stand firm, lifting my chin up at her in defiance.

"You can try to embarrass me by being difficult. You can try to humiliate me with your stupid dreams about fashion." She picks up my coffee cup from the counter and rushes over to the dress mannequin before she throws the dregs of my coffee over the beautiful white fabric. She then shoves both hands against the dress form and pushes hard.

I gasp, covering my mouth as the entire thing falls over. In a blur of white and brown, the fabric and mannequin topple to the floor with a resounding thud that hits me deep in the heart.

"But I'll be damned if you think about dragging the Rennard name through the mud by sleeping with the likes of someone like *him*!"

I stare at the mess on the floor. Tears sting my eyes, and I can't bear to face my mother as she storms out of the cabin. I heave in hot breaths, shocked and wounded at her cruelty and the destruction of my hard work. I wheeze in air, trying to accept the instant and total disregard she left in her wake. Sawyer lets go of my hand as I run to the dress form and the scattered fabric that has flown all over the floor with her vicious push.

"Claire." Dalton rushes toward the door, following my mother out. He pauses and nods at Sawyer, who comes closer to me as I drop to my knees. Then my cousin is gone, chasing after the cruel person who disrespected my efforts.

I sob, frantically trying to set the bulky dress form upright again. Fabric is torn and smeared with the coffee. It doesn't matter, and the darkness shows on the pure-white fabrics I've just purchased for Lauren.

Sawyer reaches out, grabbing the form when it again falls to the side. I can barely see through the tears in my eyes as my life crumbles apart. I cry and blink, straining to see why the form won't stay upright. With the fall, one part of the legs at the bottom busted. Even if I could get the form to stand, it wouldn't matter.

My creation, the start of it, is ruined. I sniffle and grasp the soft material I've labored over. Sawyer sets the form up, canting to the side and resting against the armchair. It doesn't tip again, but it's pointless. The fabric is dirtied and has snags. The coffee stains the delicate embroidery it took me painstaking hours to complete.

"I...I've..." My tears splatter on the lace in my hands. "I've spent so long making this by hand. I don't—I don't even have a machine to make this properly, and I've put hours into embroidering this..."

"Claire." Sawyer's voice is soft and gentle as he lowers to his knees to help me gather it all. But it's no use. It's all ruined.

"All that time. All those painstaking moments of trying to get this perfect..." I sniffle and cry harder, broken inside by the loss.

"Come here," he tells me carefully. He holds his arms out to me, but I can't cave. I want his comfort and sturdy support more than ever, but I simply can't turn toward him and let him console me. Not now. This utter act of ruin is too large to fathom, too heavy to accept.

All my work, gone. That's not even touching the pain of my own parent, my mother, wishing to cause this ruin. The one person who should love and respect me out of an unconditional bond as mother-to-daughter has destroyed my first real project.

She's never cared about my passions. She's never stood by my dreams and how hard I toiled and studied for them. She's only ever wanted to ridicule and squash my goals.

But knowing she thinks so little of me didn't prepare me for her acting on her hatred like *this*.

"Here," he says when I don't turn to him.

I scramble to pick it all up. It's a stained mess, and there is no way that I can salvage it, but I can't bear to see it lying on the floor, wasted and rejected.

He reaches out, scooping up what he can. I can't see through the shock to appreciate how he's helping. Nothing can register. I can only wallow in the scream locked in my mind as I grapple with my work being reduced to this mess.

"Claire, come here," he says again, gesturing for me to fall into his arms that he holds out for me.

I can't, though. The second I lean on him, I fear I'll never get out of this rut.

"Just go. Leave, Sawyer." *Leave and let me suffer in the peace of my privacy.*

He doesn't listen. Nope. He grabs my shoulders and jerks me as he roughly pulls me into his embrace. I'm on my knees, slanting into him until he stands with me in his arms. I hug him close, jarred from the pain of the dress being ruined to gasping in tears and desperate for his strong arms to hold me up.

I break down, crying on his shoulder. He keeps me close, stroking my hair away from my tear-streaked face and rubbing his hands over my back. I hear him speaking soft, soothing affirmations, but I don't understand a word he says. It's all white noise, in and out of my ears, as I cling to him and cry.

"All I've ever wanted was to be a fashion designer. I know..." I sniffle, losing my strength to carry on. "I know some people might think it's silly, but it's all I've wanted. All I wanted was the chance to design something that would make a woman feel beautiful and complete."

"You can still have that."

I shake my head and pull back to face him, tears and all. "No. Not...no. You don't understand. My mother is holding my trust fund over my head. I have no money. I have nothing to start a business with." I sniffle again, growing bolder to at least just get all of this off my shoulders once and for all. "I can't open a bridal shop with no money, and she's holding it out of reach. I almost eloped with a man I didn't love just to access my trust fund to start my shop. I, I just—"

Tears overwhelm me again, and he holds me, stroking my hair and my back.

"It will be all right." He presses a kiss to the top of my head. "It will be all right, Claire. I promise. One way or another, it will be all right."

I let his words be a mantra through my mind. I can't believe him. I want to, but it all seems so impossible. Still, as my tears slow and I steady my breathing, I let his words play on repeat in my mind.

I want to agree. For once, I don't want to argue with him on this point. I so desperately want everything to be all right, but after being trapped and hopeless for so long, I struggle to see *how* anything will ever be right again.

"Are you calmer now?" he asks once I stop crying.

He cups my face, peering at me, and I nod as I draw a deep, fortifying breath. "Mostly."

I'd be lying if I told him I'm fine.

Lifting a handful of fabric I'm clutching in my hand, I sigh and shake my head. "I'm calm enough to try to clean up more." I scoff, dejected, as I look at the destruction.

"I'm going to head out for a minute. Okay?"

I blink and nod. "Well, sure. I don't...I don't expect you to be here and—"

He kisses me, silencing me with his lips, but it is a tender and firm press, not a sexual one.

"I'll be back. Okay?"

I nod again before he leaves.

He can promise to come back, but I'm not sure what to tell him if he hopes to see the woman I was hours ago.

My soul is crushed. My spirit is broken. And I have nothing to offer him right now.

This, this is rock bottom.

CHAPTER 25

Sawyer

I hate to leave Claire, but I'm eager to get to Dalton's house and speak with him. Besides, Claire doesn't need me. That's a lie. She does. And I want more than anything to be the shoulder she can cry on, but that phase is over.

It is just a dress, not a finished garment, but the start of a beautiful gown if Claire's sketches are accurate. It's not *just* anything like a sewn-together mixture of fabrics. I realize it. This is a loss she needs to grieve. It doesn't matter if it's an inanimate object or not, Lauren's design symbolizes a lot to Claire. It's the start of her career, and Adelaide has stomped all over it.

As I hurry out to my truck, my heart feels so heavy and chipped. I hurt because Claire is hurting, but still, I know I'm not making a mistake in leaving her right now. I will be back. And I hope that I can further help her if I step aside for a few minutes to speak with Dalton.

Besides, tears are only one step of the grieving process. When I lost my father, I cried myself out. Afterward, I needed the space and time to *think* it all out, too. I recognized that shift in Claire. She cried on my shoulder, but as she calmed down, I saw that she likely would appreciate a chance to think and accept what has happened.

"It will be all right," I whisper to myself as I get into my truck. I glance back up at the cabin, worrying about her even though I understand she needs to grasp this loss herself. I can't force her to feel better. I won't lie and trick her into thinking it's not so bad. She deserves a chance to fully recognize and come to terms with her emotions about this.

But I refuse to lose faith. I've stumbled and erred my entire way to get here, but now the truth is a brutal force that opens my eyes wide. It *will* be all right. Claire will not go with her mother, and she won't be bartered or manipulated for the sake of marriage or prestige. I will fight for her because she matters that much. I've known it since I met her. From the second I first saw her, I just knew she would turn my world and my life upside down if I let her.

I didn't only let her, I welcomed her into my existence. I chased her. I encouraged her to pursue me, too. Claire matters to me and always will in an undeniable way. My feelings were so strong for her after we slept together in Denver because I could tell that she was the part of my heart that was missing. That she was the light I needed to be a better man. I began to accept how much I cared for Claire last night, but after seeing her mother try to abuse her like this, it was strikingly clear that I would never look for a stupid excuse and try to guard myself against her ever again.

She needs me.

And I think I need her even more. The thought of her leaving is too horrible to consider. I wouldn't be the same man if she were to surrender and let herself be pushed around in such a fatalistic way.

I speed over to Dalton's house, which isn't a long trip anyway since I'm on his property. The cabin Claire is staying in isn't within sight, but I'm grateful I don't need to be any further apart from Claire.

Dalton must have seen me pulling in because he's there at the door when I reach it. He opens it wider, and I don't have to ask him how he's taking this blown-up mess of an afternoon.

His lips are pressed in a furious tight line, and he stands so stiffly, I wonder if he's bottling in a shout like I was.

I know this man well enough to be aware of how livid he is right now, but I also understand he's a man of few words. Words I need from him about what the hell went down.

"She just left." He scowls over my shoulder as though darkening the whole drive with his glare. "I just kicked my aunt out. She thought she could argue with me, but I refuse to put up with that."

I nod, glad he removed the pest before I came.

Aubrey waits behind him, wide-eyed and worried. "I can't believe she would speak to you like that!" She shakes her head, clearly stunned by this bullshit. "I'm going to call Lauren. We'll...My gosh. The dress. We'll go sit with Claire together."

She leaves the room after a quick kiss from Dalton, and I follow him into the kitchen. He paces, unable to sit, but I drop into a chair and track him.

"What the *hell* is going on?" I demand. Straight to the point.

He mentioned a little bit before, but I'm impatient to hear all the damn details now.

"Why does Claire not have access to the money that is rightfully hers?"

He hangs his head and grips the back of a chair, ceasing the pacing. "I've been looking into it. Caleb, too. It took a while to get her to open up about it, but once she did, we were on it."

I don't doubt it. Both of them are good men who look after their own. I've come to see Claire as mine, though, and I'll be damned if I can't help her, too.

"Claire was left an inheritance by her father, and she's been living on that since she is his heir. I didn't realize she was only seeing the money in terms of allowances that Adelaide permitted, but that money was left to her by my uncle."

"What's the catch?"

"Adelaide." He deadpans. "She's remarried and divorced several times, but she's smart about it all. She has excellent lawyers, and with their help, she was able to change the terms of the estate to show that Claire wouldn't have access to it unless she married."

"Married to anyone?" I ask. The vapid woman's declaration rings in my ears. She said it as I entered Claire's cabin, and I can't get the words out of my mind. *Who said anything about* love? *You will marry the man I arrange for you, and that is final.*

She can't be right. Arranged marriages are illegal, aren't they?

"No." Dalton shakes his head. "I don't think so, no."

I exhale a huge breath of relief.

"I think Adelaide realizes that Claire will always push back. That she'll argue about marrying everyone she thrusts in her face, and so long as Claire remains unmarried, Adelaide will have total control of the estate."

And here I thought I couldn't hate that woman any more.

"She's using it as a way to further the rift between them just so she can maintain her hold on the money she married into."

The front door opens, and I turn to see Caleb rushing in. He looks from Dalton to me. His expression is grim. "Lauren just told me what happened. She and Aubrey are going to take Claire to Vail for the weekend to try to calm her down."

I sigh and nod. "That's a good move. She's very upset."

"That woman..." He glowers and looks between us again. "Can I do anything? Can I help?" He runs his hand through his hair and exhales a long, hard breath. "I've had my legal team assisting yours," he tells Dalton. "But is there anything else I can do?"

I understand his eagerness to help. It's all I can focus on, fixing this. Claire won't be alone, not with me in her corner, nor with these two couples and even Marian.

I'll be damned if Claire goes to New York, and I'll be double damned if Adelaide ruins another fraction of her life.

Dalton shakes his head. "My hands are tied. *I* can't do much other than stand up for Claire and tell my aunt to get the hell out of here."

I drag my thumb over my lip, mulling it over. I appreciate both men sticking up for her. With their lawyers looking into it, giving her a place to stay—or hide, and giving Claire a job to work on.

My mind keeps rolling over the memories of the afternoon, stuck in a loop seasoned with anger, shock, and despair. My thoughts keep cycling back to one thing, and I consider it with an open mind. I challenge myself not to view it as a far-fetched *what-if*, but a viable option.

It's a risk. A daring thought to suggest, but I can't stop revolving back to how it could play out.

Dalton might not be able to help Claire, but I could.

Caleb leaves, asking to be updated about this. He heads out to return to the bed-and-breakfast to help Marian figure out how they'll hold down the fort while Lauren goes to comfort Claire.

Alone with Dalton again in this quiet kitchen, where I have the freedom to think and truly analyze my idea, I try to think of the best way to word my thoughts on this. He could be angry, thinking I'm taking advantage. He might be elated, expecting too much hope. I don't know what he'll think, and I'm less sure of how to speak up.

He grabs a bottle of whiskey and brings it to the table. After he sets two glasses down and sits, he pours me one.

I bite my lip, debating if I'm being ridiculous or smarter than ever. It seems he's on to me, eyeing me suspiciously but not angrily or with any trace of accusation.

"I think..." He clears his throat. "I think we might have the same idea right now."

I hesitate, waiting to reply as he slides the drink to me.

CHAPTER 26

Claire

When Lauren and Aubrey showed up at the cabin, I burst into a whole new wave of tears. I got my crying under control before Sawyer headed out, but seeing my two new, *real* friends, I lost it all over again.

Lauren didn't give me a chance to explain. Somehow, they both knew. Why wouldn't they, anyway? Dalton saw the whole thing happen, and he wouldn't keep it a secret from Aubrey or their closest friends.

Like angels, they swept up to the cabin and corralled me into Lauren's car. Between the tears from what my mother did, the shame and worry for Lauren's reaction over her dress, and the confusion over what was going on, I followed what they said like a numb, lost sheep.

A chalet? In Vail? Just for me?

I was stunned.

As I sit here in the cozy space with them, an hour after they came to spring me from my misery at the cabin, sipping spiked hot beverages before a roaring fire under the mantle, I try to wrap my head around it all again.

They hadn't been heading out here and thought to ask me along. No, they did this all for me. To hear me out, to listen without interruption. These two sweethearts give me the freedom to let out all my anger and tears, and I know they're counting on finally piecing together all the details.

I don't hold back, telling them how this all came to be.

This is, without a doubt, a moment for the bitter truth.

"I know a little bit," Aubrey says, shaking her head. "I was there when your mom came over to yell at Dalton."

I sigh, hating that my cousin has faced her wrath on my behalf. "I'm sorry you had to deal with her like that."

Aubrey scoffs. "I sure hope she won't be invited to my wedding if he ever gets around to proposing."

I shake my head. "I don't blame you."

"I'm clueless," Lauren says. "Other than knowing she ruined the dress."

"Not any dress. *Your* dress." I sniffle, feeling another wave of tears coming.

She growls and scoots forward on her chair to grip my hand and squeeze hard. "No. Claire. You're not crying over my dress. Because whatever that woman ruined or broke or tore, I'm going to replace."

Aubrey giggles and elbows her. "Yeah, after what Dalt said about finally catching Jeremy in court, you'll be *loaded*!"

I blink, amazed she can have such hope. Financial freedom has sounded like a pipe dream for too long.

"Start from the beginning," Lauren prompts with no worry about her dress. I'm amazed she has such utter trust and faith in me like that.

"My mother has always been controlling. When I was a child, I wondered if it was because my father loved me so much. I was the apple of his eye, and he loved me so deeply. I was doted on, but never spoiled. Just being with him was a treasure, but he became ill, and by the time I was a teenager, he passed."

"I'm so sorry to hear that." Lauren frowns, pulling Aubrey in for a hug, too.

I pat her hand, knowing she can empathize with that much. Aubrey lost both of her parents as a teen as well. The difference between us, though, is that she had a pair of loving parents, whereas my mother has always been unloving.

"If not for my dad, I never would have been exposed to the idea of love. My mother has controlled who I see, who I interact with, what I do, and what I should never want to do. I was held to high expectations, required to be prim, proper, educated, and never lift a finger and 'work' because being an employee was a sign of weakness to the Rennard name." I roll my eyes, hating that I have to say this.

"She sounds awful." Lauren shakes her head.

"Yeah, you had to deal with that controlling crap, too," Aubrey says.

"I grew up with no love and heavy expectations on my shoulders. I've become used to never feeling like I would have an opportunity to escape her. I've all but given in to thinking I'll never get out from under her control."

Aubrey narrows her eyes. "Because she manages the estate?"

I nod. "And my trust is tied up in it. The only way I can get it is if I'm married."

Both woman curse and react with outrage, pissed on my behalf that I've been treated like this. "That can't be right." Lauren smacks her hand to her thigh. "That's the same crap Jeremy did with me."

I shrug. "Dalton's looked into it. I imagine Caleb has done just as much now. She's too smart and employs even smarter lawyers. My mother is determined to keep her greedy hands on the money left to *me*. The only way I'll get it is if I marry, but she's only ever encouraged that with her explicit approval. She doesn't want me connected to someone she deems unworthy, someone beneath our family name. Because if I marry 'beneath my status' it will bring her down, too."

"What is this, the eighteen hundreds?" Aubrey scoffs.

"I tried to get around her. I asked the man I was dating in Paris to elope simply so I could be married and get my funds." I hold my hand up, not wanting them to assume the worst. "I don't *want* the money. I won't even touch the majority of those billions. All I want is the capital to start my shop. I only need the funds to open my bridal shop." I can't help the smile on my face. Despite my mother's awfulness, I won't lose sight of my passion and my dream. "I just want the money to open my shop so I can do what I love. What I've always wished I could do."

"You're going to open up a shop?" Aubrey brightens, smiling wide.

"Here?" Lauren adds with equal excitement.

"Well..." I sigh and sip my warm drink, relishing the soothing burn of its heat as it travels down my throat. "I guess."

"Gee." Aubrey swats at my knee. "Don't blow us away with your enthusiasm."

I smile. "When I came here, I had loose plans to do an apprenticeship in Paris. It would give me real-life experience for my portfolio, but since you asked me to design your dress,"—I say as I glance at Lauren—"that's the same thing and even better. I..." I sigh, almost not believing I'm going to admit this out loud. "I'm going to do my best and open up my shop somewhere. Wherever I can afford it. I refuse to let my mother hold me back. I'm not sure this area will have the greatest opportunities for a shop to succeed, so maybe I *am* better off returning to Paris. Or New York. The way she holds my funds puts me in such a bind, but I'm determined to work hard, save up, and hopefully, one day, I'll have my shop."

"Stay!" They say it in unison, then giggle.

"Seriously. You complete our trio," Lauren tells me.

"I mean, you've got Marian, too. She's the mother we've all been needing in our lives."

Lauren makes a face at Aubrey. "No. I've told you, she's my fairy godmother."

"Whatever. She'll adopt you, too, Claire, like she did with us. Then we'll all have each other!"

"And..." Lauren glances at me before grinning at Aubrey, who nods with a knowing smirk. "And Sawyer is here..."

I pull my lips in and bite down on them, unwilling to speak up there. It's on the tip of my tongue to admit I'm falling for him, but I can't say that. No matter how sweet he was standing up for me with my mother, it still seems like I'm the only one who feels this deeply. I tuck that thought away and shrug. "Yeah, Sawyer is here, and I don't see him leaving."

They share a look and sigh, perhaps realizing they won't get more out of me about him. We move on, though, after that talk. They pamper me all night, feeding me and keeping my drinks flowing. It's a night of girl time I didn't realize I needed, and by the time I lie down to sleep that night, I feel slightly better.

***

Lauren and Aubrey bring me back to my cabin late the next evening. It was nice to break away with them and just talk. It was a release and the venting process I needed, but I'm eager to get "home" and start all over again on Lauren's dress. If not for her project, I fear I would be so lost and directionless that I'd beg to stick with them.

After more goodbyes, I head inside the cabin and drop my bag.

Shock slams into me with a tidal force. My jaw drops, and I gawk, staring wide-eyed at the person in my living room. I hadn't even looked for his truck as Lauren pulled up. We were too busy chatting, and he must have parked it off to the side, not right out front.

"Sawyer?"

He pauses but doesn't stop with the unboxing. His sweet smile threatens to melt me into a puddle, and the sight of what he's setting up floors me.

"Is that…" I approach him, almost frantic to rush closer and make sure I'm not imagining things. Because I very well could be. If I'm not mistaken, he's taking off the protective cover and guards for a brand-new sewing machine. Not just any old thing, like the one I'd found when I came here. It's a Brother Stellaire model, something I didn't even have at school. They're insanely expensive, able to last forever, and perform a variety of stitches, including embroidery. The last time I fell under a spell of wistful thinking, I looked them up and daydreamed about where I would find fifteen thousand dollars to afford the top-of-the-line piece of equipment.

"Sawyer." I swallow, becoming frantic at the thought of something like this here. "What are you doing?"

"Helping you set up something in your work area."

I gape at him and shake my head. "No. No way. I mean. Sawyer, I can't afford that!"

"I don't care." He stands and shrugs. "It's a gift. From me to you."

I know Kevin explained that Sawyer holds all of their dad's construction company now, but still!

I blink at him, too shocked to reply, but as I try to let this discovery sink into my brain, I notice how clean the whole place is. He reorganized the entire living room, going so far as to put up proper shelving while I was gone.

"Sawyer…" I lick my lips, feeling the burn of tears again, but this time, they would be tears of joy.

Before I can ask what exactly he's up to, he takes my hand. "I need to show you something."

I huff out a weak laugh, already so thrown off by his amazing and generous gestures.

He leads me outside, heading toward his truck, and I feel so very confused. And stupid. If I want to think he doesn't care for me, I might have to seriously reconsider. Buying me *that* sewing machine and putting this much effort into perfecting my workspace, he's practically showing me that he adores me. I watch his back as he guides me to his truck, and without a word, I take a leap of faith to just trust him and go with it.

If he's not careful, I'll be hopelessly, utterly in love with him and stare at him like he just hung the moon for me.

He seems to be in a trance as he drives, tense and nervous. We leave Dalton's property, and I do my best to tamp down all the questions running through my mind as he heads to Breckenridge.

Why?

How?

When?

What?

But mostly, *why*? Why would he go so far to make this happen for me like this if he's cool with diminishing what we have as a mere hookup?

He stops at a storefront on the main drag. It's full of tourists here for the summer season and retail shopping. Unlike the smaller town near the Goldfinch Bed and Breakfast, plenty of activity is going on here.

"Sit tight." He exits the truck and rounds it to open my door, and helps me out.

I step out and hold his hand, unsure what's coming next as he leads me toward the building. The specific place we're in front of is empty, maybe abandoned. Windows are covered up, and some peeling paint shows on the outer walls.

I shield my eyes and squint to look up, but no name reads on the awning, and no sign flaps in the slight breeze. My surprise is extended even further when he reaches into his pocket and pulls out a key that he slides into the door. He leads me inside to the empty space, and I furrow my brow.

"I own this building. My father purchased it, and he left it to me. The tenants recently retired and moved out."

My heart races as he tells me this, and I can't stay still. I walk around with him, confused but starting to catch on to what I think he's showing me. He points out a showroom, a huge back room, and an attached office.

Back in the center of the space, he faces me. "I spoke with Dalton, Claire. If we get engaged, it will give Dalton and Caleb's lawyers time to sort out the mess with your mother. It might be enough to convince Adelaide to drop the issue with your trust fund, or we can take the case to court and properly press charges against her."

I open my mouth, but he doesn't let me speak, holding up his hand.

"If it doesn't work, if your mother refuses to let go, you can have this place. It would be yours. All yours, for free. I can do the work to make it into the bridal shop of your dreams."

Holy shit. "Whoa." I suck in another quick breath as the start of a panic attack hits me. He's going so far with this and dropping one bombshell after another...I can't catch my breath. I'm excited. I'm stunned. I'm overwhelmed, and even though this is Sawyer, and I trust him, old fears of wondering what he'll expect from me rise to the surface. "Why are you doing this for me?"

He shakes his head, glancing at the floor. "I...I want to."

"But you don't want to marry me?"

He frowns. "I never said that."

All I can manage is a stare. I gaze at him, trying to make sense of it all, of him.

"Would you try, at least? Will you let me help you?"

Why? Why *do you want to help me so badly?* "By being engaged?"

"It wouldn't mean anything unless—" He hesitates. "If we did have to get married so you could access the estate that is rightfully yours, I'd give you a divorce right after that was settled. I wouldn't expect any money from you, nothing like that."

My heart feels like it's about to crack. *Nothing like that? Is he joking and trying to be cruel here?* "You don't want this."

"I want *you*, Claire. I think that's pretty clear."

A tense moment follows his blunt confession, but I fear a lifetime of trying to process this won't be enough.

He steps closer, raising his brows in a silent question.

I nod, agreeing, and hate how guilty I feel. I can't let this offer—or him—pass me by.

He exhales and pulls a beautiful ring from his pocket. He really means this. He came prepared. "This was my mother's," he says.

That makes me feel even worse. He shouldn't be wasting an heirloom, a family ring, on a sham with me. I almost backtrack, regretting this "game," but he slips it on my finger before I can move back.

"Dalton will handle the rest."

I stare at him, blinking quickly. I want nothing more than to lay my heart open for him, to tell him how I feel about him, but it's so clear he doesn't feel the same. If he did, he wouldn't safeguard his offer with backup plans and easy outs. He can't feel the same, but for whatever reason, he feels obligated to help me.

As he gazes into my eyes, I sense that he doubts this, or maybe he's unsure of himself.

He snaps, though, robbing me of a chance to ask, and he kisses me deeply.

I hold onto him, pressing up to match his desire, and as he dips me back, I can't help but imagine this is real, that I'm a bride in this future space of a shop, choosing my gown for *our* wedding, should he ever feel the same.

Chapter 27

Claire

For most of the next week, I do my best not to stare at the ring on my finger. It's not a showy, gaudy bauble of a piece. The diamond is bright and glittery but a smaller stone. As I dive right into the hustle of starting over on Lauren's dress, I appreciate its modest size. If I wore a larger rock or had to suffer with a sharp-edged setting, I would fear the ring snagging on the fabric and thread. It doesn't, and before long, it becomes second nature to trust that this ring is undoubtedly a perfect fit for a woman who works with her hands and deals with delicate materials prone to tears.

With the new sewing machine and the upgraded storage solutions for my things at the cabin, I'm able to work faster on the gown. I have a zest in my life. My dreams and goals aren't as distant now. Guilt pricks at me when I remember that Sawyer is offering me the shop space out of some obligation he feels toward me, maybe a sense of wanting to be a hero for the sake of playing that role. I don't know why he would go so far as to pretend to have an engagement with me, but I suppose it's not costing him anything. It's just a fake role. It can't mean anything to him, but still, a sliver of hope burns inside my heart as I wish this were a real thing, that he wasn't making this grand gesture out of pity to spare me from my mother's wishes.

He doesn't pull away like he did before, but we're both so busy that I don't have the time to focus on him. I am determined to sit down and talk with him, to truly communicate about where he's coming from with all of these plans to help me, but he's busy with work. One of his crew leaders was injured, and he's putting more hours in than usual. And I'm not available or idle, investing double the time to make Lauren's dress a complete garment on time after my mother's destruction of the first one.

The one night we managed to find a few hours together, we fell into bed, sleeping with each other with a rabid need to come close, but he snuck out in the middle of the night, alerted to one of his crews needing help super early at the construction warehouse where he stored his equipment. Sooner or later, we will have to sit down and really talk, because the longer this fake engagement drags on with my emotions in limbo, I feel like I might combust.

Lauren and Aubrey stop over to check on my progress on the dress, and it seems all they want to talk about is precisely what I wish I could chat about with Sawyer.

"It's beautiful!" Lauren gushes, wiping tears from her eyes.

Aubrey drapes her arms around both of our shoulders as we stand in a line facing the dress. "It really is." Then she claps my back and wheels

Lauren to face me. "Now. *What* is the meaning of *this*." She takes my hand, and they both stare at the ring Sawyer gave me.

"I, uh…" I smile, but I hold back on joining in their enthusiasm. "Sawyer came up with an idea to help me out." I knew I would have to spill the beans to them, but I have yet to know what to say.

"Sawyer actually proposed?" Aubrey gawks at me and shakes her head.

"I knew he would!" Lauren giggles.

Aubrey and I both frown at her. "You knew?" I ask.

"No, I mean it like a figure of speech. I figured he would," Lauren replies. "I've seen the way he looks at you."

"As…?"

"The woman he loves!" She hugs me. "Oh, how exciting!"

"But they *just* met," Aubrey argues.

"And he didn't actually propose," I add.

They deadpan at me. "I think we need more details," Aubrey says.

I fill them in on what I came home to after they took me to the chalet in Vail. The sewing machine, which I point out, then the shelving and how he tidied up.

"Then he drove me downtown to this building he owns on the main street."

"Oh, yeah." Aubrey squints in concentration. "I think I remember Kevin mentioning that one building before. That their dad bought it a long time ago."

"Kevin didn't want it?" I'm suddenly curious. He doesn't have that same interest in construction like Jason and Sawyer do, but that downtown building could serve many purposes.

"No. I think he didn't want the hassle of being a landlord or anything."

"Well, he gave me the storefront for a shop. If my mother balks at us being engaged and refuses to give me my funds, then I'll at least have the shop. One day, I'll save up enough to make it the place of my dreams."

"And..." Aubrey furrows her brow at my ring. "And he's willing to go so far with this fake thing just to help you?"

I nod, wishing I felt more confident about it.

"You're not actually going to get married?" Lauren asks.

"If we need to, to get my mother off my back, then we will."

Aubrey snorts. "If you *need to*? That's no way to consider marriage!"

"She means with the money." Lauren glances at me. "Unless you two really do want to marry?"

I rub my hands down my face. "I don't know!"

We sit, and they both wait for me to figure out how to explain it.

"I'm falling in love with him. I think."

Aubrey raises her brows. "You don't know?"

"I haven't experienced much love in my life to know. I think I am. I'm falling for him." *If I haven't already.* "But I don't understand his behavior. He kisses me, then pulls away. He sleeps with me, then gets all distant."

"Hot and cold, huh?" Aubrey rolls her eyes.

"Maybe," Lauren says without Aubrey's snark, "you should tell him how you really feel."

I pick at the pins for her dress, unable to sit and be idle when I could work on the dress.

"But then she's putting herself out in the open, being vulnerable," Aubrey argues.

"No, she would be honest." Lauren points around the room. "And maybe he's already beaten her to it. He's made himself vulnerable first, not telling her how he feels about her but showing her. He did all the cleanup. He installed the shelving. He bought that fancy sewing machine..."

"That's worth nearly fifteen grand," I admit sheepishly while stroking the top of it.

Aubrey's eyes go wide, and Lauren whistles.

Everything she says makes sense, but still, I glance at Aubrey and wonder if she's right to be protective and skeptical. I always have been, but Sawyer's affection challenges my way of thinking.

"Maybe Sawyer's way of telling you how much he cares about you is by acts of service instead of words," Lauren concludes.

Aubrey shrugs. "Hell, he did buy you an expensive piece of equipment after your mother ruined your first dress design."

Lauren snaps her fingers and points at me. "And he bought you shoes so you wouldn't keep tripping in the gravel."

"And," Aubrey says with a smile as she lifts my hand, "he's not afraid to *not* propose with his mother's ring, something I bet all three men in that family value highly..."

I sigh and consider their wisdom, wishing I could draw strength from them.

Clearly, they've found their happiness after some struggles.

I wish I could rely on their advice and know I could have my own happily ever after, too.

A real one, not a sham to spare me from my mother's control.

CHAPTER 28

Sawyer

At the end of the workday on Friday, one week after Claire sobbed on the floor with the ruined dress, I hold on to the hope we'll finally have a chance to sit down and talk. Every day and night has been busy for both of us. Me with work and Tom getting injured on the work site. Her with her dress and making use of the new machine I bought her.

Thank goodness I noticed her circling that specific machine in that catalog she left lying out on the coffee table. I never would've known what to get if I hadn't spotted that hint.

Before I can go home to shower and surprise her with a bouquet of flowers and a suggestion that I make her dinner at her place before we talk, I check my phone and see a voicemail from Dalton. It's not a long one, but the message is clear.

We need to talk. I fear it's bad news. Adelaide has to know about my engagement to Claire by now. Dalton spread the word. So, what is the witch trying to do now? It's got to be about her somehow.

I drive to meet Dalton at the coffee shop where he's talking with the owner about buying the place and making it a bigger, combined retail space.

He comes over to sit with me at a table, shaking his head. "Bad news."

"I feared as much." I tap my finger on the table, worried about what he'll share.

"Adelaide has been notified of the engagement, but it doesn't seem like it's enough."

I slant my brows at him. "How so?"

"Now, Adelaide is trying to get the trust out of Claire's name entirely, which means Claire doesn't have a lot of time to beat her at this game. She has *no* time to try to figure this out."

I'm crushed, beaten down by a wave of defeat. I wanted to help her, to save her. It isn't about impressing her anymore or winning her heart with things that matter to her and would help her succeed with her goals. It's not enough.

"Right now..." Dalton clears his throat. "All you could do is get married. If Claire marries, the estate would transfer to her name immediately."

I sink back in the old booth. Defeated. I stare at him, hopeless and frustrated that I—Claire and I—can't win.

I know Claire doesn't want to do this. Part of me fears she might be annoyed deep down that we're playacting and faking an engagement like this. I saw the pain in her eyes when I told her how I could help. She was uneasy and suspicious, and knowing she was so instantly averse to the idea of even a pretend commitment to me wounded my pride. She doesn't feel as deeply about me, and it's a lesson I wish I could make stick.

When will I ever learn?

But I'm stuck all over again. I'm damned if I put myself out there to help her, but I'm also damned if I don't. Now, she'll lose everything, and that's just not fair at all.

"Couldn't you..." Dalton shakes his head. "Never mind."

I don't want to ask him what he has in mind. If he's suggesting I go ahead and ask Claire to marry me for real, I'll have to explain how she doesn't want it. Dalton's a good friend. I know he wouldn't want me to suffer unnecessarily, but I can't know for sure if he values my friendship more than he values his cousin's happiness and security.

I push to my feet and leave, suddenly too awkward to sit there with the hard truth that I'll never be good enough for Claire, not even when pretending it all.

Outside, I shake my head and glower at the sidewalk, heading back to my truck in a dejected daze.

I bump into someone, and as I look up to apologize for not paying attention and looking where I was going, I snort in surprise.

It's Kevin. We never talk much, already distant because of how Dad never favored him and how we couldn't ever connect with mutual interests, but our differences over Gina back in high school served as the final nail in the coffin of our brotherhood.

"Sawyer?" He frowns at me. "What's wrong?"

I'm annoyed he can so easily tell something is wrong. I shake my head, too exhausted with life and heartache to explain.

Why can't she just love me? Why?

"Nothing." I move to pass him, but he dodges my escape, blocking me.

"Whoa. No. Even *I* can tell something's not right." We seldom cross paths, and when we do speak, it's in limited, dry and curt exchanges. But he's quick to be alert *now,* of all times.

"It's..." I groan. I want to say it's *nothing*, but he'll persist.

"Something happened with Claire?" he guesses.

I furrow my brow. "How did you know I was seeing her?"

"You mean engaged to her?" He laughs. "Aubrey. At work. Besides, I met her at the bar when they all went out a while back."

I hang my head and sigh.

"Come on." He pats my back and tips his head. "Come over, and we'll talk. After all, this isn't the first time I've seen you like this."

I narrow my eyes at the back of his head and follow. "What's that supposed to mean?"

He smirks at me. "Uh, Gina? Back in high school?"

I roll my eyes and walk with him. "We were dumb back then."

"Of course. Who isn't? But I know what I said back then still hits you now."

I don't reply, not wanting to have former hurts mixed with the current.

"I gave you shit about Gina. She was two-timing us, and I took advantage of it when she complained about you sometimes. She was a fancier girl, higher maintenance, and I tried to win her over by being the opposite of the outdoorsy guy you were."

"I don't need a reminder."

"But maybe you do," he says as we reach his apartment door and head up the steps. "Because if I'm not mistaken, Claire seems like another high-maintenance girl."

"Yeah," I grouse. "Another beautiful woman out of my league who will see me as a convenient man to sleep with for fun but never to get serious with."

He lets me into his apartment, laughing, and I debate hitting him.

"If we're being serious, you're already engaged."

Not for real. And even that fake crap won't be for long.

"People change, Sawyer, and wherever Gina ended up is the best for us. Claire, though..." He pulls out a chair at his kitchen table for me and sits in another. "She's not Gina."

"No shit." I slump into the chair.

"I only spoke with her a little bit, but she seemed very offended when I suggested you were simple-minded."

I lift my face and glower at him.

"She seemed so curious and excited to learn about you."

I sigh, looking down again.

"Genuinely interested, Sawyer. Maybe you two do seem like opposites, but maybe that's why you work so well. Well enough to get engaged."

I growl and drop my head back to stare at the ceiling. "We're not engaged. Not for real."

He stands and returns with two beers.

I look at his offering, then him, and wonder if we've finally let enough years pass to bury the hatchet.

"Talk to me, Sawyer. It's about time we act like brothers. And I *know* you're struggling with something, so try me. Lay it on me and see if we can't figure it out."

I sigh and take the bottle, draining a good third of it.

And then I tell him everything. How Claire and I met. The way she reminded me of Gina and how I was so untrusting of her interest because she seemed like a repeat of Gina, out of my league and no one would want to stick with a common worker like me. Then I summed up Claire's troubles about her mom and the idea to pretend we're engaged.

"But now her mom's moving faster. She's going to change it all."

Kevin shakes his head. "That can't be legal."

"You'd think. Dalton and Caleb both have their lawyers looking into it. It's twisted and messed up, but I know I can trust his word. It's not a bluff. Somehow, in some way, that woman will prevent Claire from ever seeing a penny of the money her father wanted her to have. And Kev, she needs it. She doesn't *want* it. She just needs the investment to make her business take off. I wouldn't be surprised if she let it all sit, only using what she needs to get afloat and start up her dream shop."

"What are the options now?"

I scoff. "Dalton says if Claire is married *now*, sooner than later, the estate will transfer to her."

"Married to anyone, right?" Kevin lifts his brows. "Anyone like...the man she's already 'engaged' to?"

"You weren't there." I shake my head and set aside the bottle of beer I drank. "She looked mortified and crestfallen."

"Fancy adjectives."

I kick his chair lightly. "She was *not* on board with the idea of marrying and divorcing for the sake of getting her money. I saw the pain in her eyes, like it would be the worst thing she'd put up with."

Kevin laughs, rolling his eyes. "And you assume it's because she doesn't want you?"

"What the hell else am I supposed to think?"

"Maybe that you asking her to go through this like it's a business transaction could be the opposite of what she really wants?"

I'm scared to let his suggestion settle into my mind, but my heart leaps with dumb hope.

"What if she wants the real thing and has to accept that *you* don't seem to?"

I shake my head, thinking back to how she categorized what we had as a hookup.

"What's the risk of telling her how you feel about her? About her, not this crappy situation she's stuck in."

I lick my lips and shrug. "I'd get my heart stomped on if she still isn't interested."

"And I bet you'd still survive. What's the risk if you don't tell her how you feel?"

I can't say it.

"You'd lose her. If you don't act, you'll lose her. Her mother will win, Sawyer, and that will be the end of it."

I stare at him, knowing without a doubt that he's right. I *hate* that he's right, and as I sit here and let that truth sink in, I smirk. "You know, I didn't count on this occasion happening today. I didn't set out to reconcile and make long overdue amends with you *and* have to suck it up and admit you're right about her, about this."

He smiles wide and splays his hands out as he shrugs. "It is what it is."

I narrow my eyes. "When'd you go back to school and learn to become a shrink?"

His chuckles don't piss me off for once. "Well, working with kids and volunteering at the high school, I hear a lot of sappy sob stories about love gone wrong."

"For kids? Teenagers?"

He exaggerates rolling his eyes. "There's *always* drama there."

"I'm not a teenager!"

He guffaws. "Then stop acting like one. Be a man about this and *tell* her, idiot, before you lose her."

I point at him and try to look stern. "Don't call me an idiot."

He rolls his eyes. "Then don't act like one."

I stand up, smiling at the wise guy who's most unexpectedly shown me the way.

I won't.

I'm still intimidated by the chance *I'm* right, that I'm correct in guessing Claire won't want me for real and for good, but I damn well will have an answer.

Because after a lifetime of never getting along with Kevin, I really, *really* hope he's right about this. Of all people, I never would've thought he'd be the one to kick some sense into me, but as I leave his apartment and jog toward my truck, I'm simply glad that he did.

My heart may not survive her rejection, but at least I've got my head on straight enough now to be able to tell her that she has my heart—and to beg her not to break it.

CHAPTER 29

Claire

I glance at the calendar, double-checking the mental countdown I've been sticking with for wrapping up Lauren's dress. The designing and thinking part of it all takes more time than the autopilot tasks of actually *making* the dress. With the new machine Sawyer bought me, I work even faster.

I laugh at myself, still stuck in the old timeline. I had a different countdown to the completion date, but when my mother knocked over the dress and forced me back a few steps, I had to re-calculate the dress being completed. Going back and making it for a second time has helped me to improve on my original design with the help of the amazing new sewing machine Sawyer gave me. The dress is nearly there. All I need to do is put the finishing touches on it, and I grin at the calendar.

It still feels silly, but I put a smiley face on the day after Lauren and Aubrey brought me back from Vail. The day Sawyer gave me his mother's ring. It seems like a lie to say he "proposed" that day, and it's easier not to think about it when I wish he really had.

It stings that he didn't just ask me for real, but I refuse to give up all hope on him. If he's willing to go so far as giving me that shop space and pretending to be engaged, he has to care about me to some extent. I don't know what holds him back. If we had a chance to sit and talk, I imagine I would have my answers, but we haven't. We've been too busy, and like before, I grow convinced that he's resorting to the habit of ignoring me and pulling away. I've hardly seen him over the last few days.

While it pains me to know he would rather stay away, I have to admit it's half my fault. I should have been honest with him at the shop space. I should have owned up to my feelings and been open about how I want him.

As soon as we can both sit down and talk... I vow to do it. Hiding my true feelings won't help either of us in the long run, and that's where I see us. Long term. For good. If not as an official couple, then as friends?

I grimace at the idea of being friend-zoned. It doesn't sound right.

Shoving my worries aside, I concentrate on tending to the final details the gown needs.

I don't get far, distracted by Sawyer striding in.

Speak of the devil, huh?

I smile but lose the courage to look so light and happy to see him. He seems tense, worried even. He's not rushing up to me with the intention to hold me or kiss me. A greeting doesn't come either.

All serious and somber, he stalks inside and stares at me. I tense up, expecting him to tell me something bad. If he's stuck in that seriousness, something *has* to be wrong. Before I can ask or say anything, he clears his throat and rubs the back of his neck.

"We need to talk."

I blink, trying to think of how to reply. Yeah. Hell, yeah, we do. I was just thinking that and kicking myself for the way we either avoid communicating or simply have lacked the time to do so. Hearing him declare it intimidates me. Why does *he* want to speak with me so urgently all of a sudden?

As I stand there and watch him, my heart constricts in a bad way. My stomach knots up, and I brace myself for something awful. I don't know how many more hits I can take, but it seems something bad is in store for me tonight.

"I love you."

I hold my breath, replaying his words again in my mind. Did I hear him right? I raise my brows, mute and too stunned to reply. Of all the things he could have blurted out first, I hadn't been prepared for that.

His simple, direct words pummel into me, and I almost knock the dress form over in reaction. I'm not going to faint. I'm not that kind of girl. I stumble, though, clumsy in body and mind as I try to accept what he has just told me.

I hurry to catch the mannequin shape and steady the dress. I use it as an anchor, too, keeping myself upright as I rely on it to stand.

"I'm sorry for being a dick."

I open and close my mouth, shocked even more with his apology. Again, not at all what I was expecting to hear from his lips today.

"I..." He rubs the back of his neck again but doesn't waver in maintaining eye contact with me. "I've never been in love before. Not real love like this. and I never want to be in love with anyone but you. Only you, Claire." He licks his lips before adding, "The idea of losing you has been eating me alive for weeks, and I can't stand the fact that it could happen."

I smile, choking on a sob. I'm so close to bursting into tears, so near an overwhelming level of joy and relief.

Sawyer loves me.

He loves me*!*

For so long, I wished it could be true, and now, the wait and anxiety is over. I don't have any doubt he's speaking the full truth. He looks at me with such raw and real emotion, I don't consider the possibility that he could be lying. It's been hard enough to dissect and try to decipher what he really wants from me. One minute, he's trying to save me from my mother, showering me with gifts and resources to go forward in my desired career. The next, he's walking back an almost proposal to something that seems like a business agreement for show. I've wondered every night since that day—how he could bounce back and forth between such extremes, and since Lauren and Aubrey put the idea in my head that he's trying to show me how much he cares for me, I've been letting this seedling of hope take root in my mind.

I sniffle and set the dress form up so I can step away from it. "I love you, too."

Each step I take toward him feels like a new beginning. For the first time, I *do* chase a man. This man. And as I hurry across the room to him, I'm propelled with an urgency that I hope will never fade. I run to him, assured after this moment that I will always be confident that I can overcome any threat of losing him.

He clutches me to him, catching me with those thick, strong arms I've come to rely on. He'll hold me when I need comfort; he'll hug me when I seek his affection. In his embrace, I never need to question my worth or the depth of our connection ever again.

"Claire," he utters my name with such elation and excitement, I can tell he was worrying about how I would take this news. I loathe the possibility that he was afraid I wouldn't reciprocate and give him my heart, too, but no more. We only have the future to remind each other as often as we please just how much we matter to each other.

"I love you, Sawyer," I repeat before he crushes his lips to mine.

I stand up on my toes, eager to push back up against him and prove with my actions how badly I need this kiss and want him with all my soul.

He breaks away, breathing hard before me as he smiles with such a sweet contentment I want to make it my daily promise. That with each morning that rises and before every night falls, I'll put this amazing smile on his face.

"And I love you." He seals it with another tender brush of his soft lips over mine, and I sigh into his kiss.

"But..." He sighs, heaving his chest against me. I cling to him, draping my arms over his shoulders as they slump.

"No." I shake my head. "No *buts*."

He sobers, losing the smile. I hold on fast to the fact that he doesn't release me. If anything, he hugs me closer, like preparing to brace me for a hit and wishing he could shield me from it coming near us at all.

I shake my head harder, wanting to pout. "No. Uh-huh. You can't be serious. You're not allowed to tell me you love me and then say *but*." I refuse to accept it. He cannot be planning to declare his love and follow with an ultimatum or threat! It's impossible to think I can go from such a sweet high and sink to this deep low of whatever has him so stressed out.

He nods, then kisses my nose. "I have bad news."

"About what?" I grip his shirt and shake my fist once.

"The estate. *Your* estate."

I go still as I understand. Something about my mother. I should have known. With all the trouble she's caused in my life, and all the strife she's stirred up recently, my mind should've gone there first.

"Oh." I deflate, but not in a bad way. Knowing he's merely concerned about the drama with my mother allows me to lose some of the tension that set in when he said that damned *but*.

"She's determined to change the documents. Dalton just informed me. She's hurrying her lawyers to change it all, so you'll never see a cent of your inheritance."

I open my lips, but he plows on, "The only way you can secure it is to be married *now*. Being engaged is nothing but anteing up the stakes for her, and it seems she's determined not to lose."

I snort. "Well, I could have told you that." I frown. "I did. I did tell you that she's driven to keep control of the money."

"Which means us being engaged won't pack much of a punch anymore."

I shrug. Honestly, I don't give a damn. I don't care what my mother does. To hell with the money. I've faced a convoluted way to get here and know this, but I've found love. I gave up on the idea of marrying for love, let alone seeking it anywhere, and it's exactly what I've found in Sawyer.

"I...I don't care." I shake my head to back up what I say.

For so long, I've focused on getting my funds so I could have the means to start my business. Sawyer has seen to that now, and even if he didn't, if he didn't have that shop space to give me or own that building, I still would have found my own way. I would make dresses and scrimp and save. With his love, I feel like I can do anything, and I'm no stranger to working hard for what I want.

"It doesn't matter to me. That trust, the money my mother wants to keep out of my reach and control, it's not important to me."

"No," he argues quickly. "That's not right, Claire. You can't give in and just let her win."

I smile, leaning up to kiss him and reveling in the way his hands hold my sides in a possessive, strong embrace. "*Love* wins. We win with each other."

He growls against my lips, fisting the back of my shirt as he kisses me deeply. Against my lips, he sighs and says, "No. I want you to be treated fairly. If we need to get married to beat her at this stupid, manipulative game she wants to play, so be it." He rears back to look at me seriously. "I meant it when I said I'd give you a divorce, but I want you to know that's something I will never want."

I roll my eyes and thread my fingers through his hair to pull him back down to me. "Didn't you hear me? I *love* you. A divorce would be the very last thing on my mind."

He gathers me closer in a firm hug. "I love you, too."

"I don't want to marry you because you feel like you have to." That would be the lousiest start of a marriage.

"I want to marry you because I don't want to lose you. Ever."

I beam up at him, rejoicing in his words.

"We can deal with whatever happens next—together," he adds.

"Then it's settled." I lurch up to kiss his full lips with excitement and awe.

"We're getting married," he agrees with a wide, cocky grin.

I nod. *Even if the shock hasn't sunk in yet.*

CHAPTER 30

Claire

"Is doing everything impulsively a French thing, or...?" Aubrey widens her eyes as we gather at the kitchen table.

"Oh, it's sweet." Marian bustles behind us as we frantically try to make sense of how to hold a wedding in a rush. Like less than a day, rush. Make that *hours*. In hours, I will be Sawyer's wife. Tomorrow is the big day, and I am suspended between a giddiness for it to happen and a panic that we can't pull it off on time.

Dalton was our saving grace, insisting that Sawyer and I both file for a license to marry when Sawyer presented me with his mother's ring. My cousin's reasoning was that my mother would doubt I was engaged just because he said so. As he expected, she sent her assistants and lawyers to look into the validity of Sawyer and I being betrothed. Having those legal documents ready helped us to hurry with this ceremony, but still. Less than a day?

I whimper and slump with my elbow on the table and my chin in hand. "I don't even have a dress."

Aubrey points at me and smirks. "Now *that's* the definition of irony."

Lauren swats a hand at her. "Nothing about this is ironic."

I shrug. "It's madness trying to hurry like this."

"You could elope," Aubrey suggests before she takes another bite of the pancakes Marian made.

I shake my head. I tried that with Owen, and it didn't stick. Although rushed, I want a real ceremony with Sawyer. This will be my first and only time to marry, and I don't want to skip it for the sake of sticking it to my mother.

My riches don't matter. I'm wealthier than any other billionaire if I have Sawyer's true love.

"No eloping. That feels like a crummy way to do this. I'd feel rotten about it afterward."

I want to walk down the aisle to him and see him as happy as I feel about it.

Marian gasps, dropping the skillet on the burner. We all freeze, looking up from the drawing Lauren has sketched of the Goldfinch's large dining room that we'll convert into a small wedding venue.

"Marian?" I ask carefully.

Lauren's eyes are wide, and Aubrey furrows her brow.

"That's it!" The B&B guru snaps her fingers and pivots to grin at us. "That's it!"

"Uh, what's what?" I ask, lost and wondering if she's losing her marbles.

"Rotten!"

I lick my lips. "Marian, I know we haven't had much time to hang out and get to know each other, but if you're speaking in some kind of code, I'm lost."

"Jason was telling me that the tomatoes will go rotten in the old garden we've abandoned behind the cottage out there." She points her spatula toward the window. "But the *new* garden."

Lauren catches on with a squeal. "Near the gazebo Jason just built for you! Yes!" She whips toward me. "An outdoor wedding, Claire! What do you think?"

"Oooh, I like it," Aubrey says, crumpling up the paper sketch of the dining room. "Fresh air. Lots of room."

"The lilies are in bloom," Marian adds.

"The daisies, too." Lauren nods. "That would be gorgeous."

I nod, smiling. "Sure. That's fine with me." I giggle, though, squinting at Marian. "He *built* you a gazebo?"

Marian rolls her eyes and dismisses me with a wave.

We laugh together at her blushing.

"Sounds serious," I tease.

"Ha!" Marian points the spatula at me. "*You're* the one getting as serious as can be with one of those Cameron men!"

I shrug. "True." Accepting that as my new reality is a marvel each time I hear it. This time tomorrow, I won't be Claire Rennard, but Claire Cameron. "Mrs. Sawyer Cameron. Mrs. Cameron. Mrs. Claire Cameron."

Aubrey laughs at me, testing it out. "You could hyphenate."

Lauren scrunches her face. "Rennard-Cameron? That's a mouthful."

"Mrs. Claire Cameron," I settle on with a dreamy sigh.

"Not unless we tell the boys about the change in plans first," Marian says. She leans toward the doorway to the dining room, calling out to Jason and Caleb, who are busy rearranging the furniture in there. She turns to Lauren. "You could mow out there again, lower the blades so it's nice and short."

"I bet we could find a rug to stretch out," Aubrey adds.

"I'm not sure when I can mow," Lauren says. "We're going to the spa later."

"Oh, that's right." Marian shrugs. "Well, I'll mow then."

"Wait, aren't you coming to the spa day too?" Aubrey asks.

"Nah. I'm too old."

"You are not too old to go to a spa," I protest. If anything, she's too old to be mowing. Guilt hits me. "Marian, I know you mean well, but are you sure you want us to have the wedding *here*?"

"I told you, Claire. I won't take no for an answer. It'll be here. I can't wait!"

I sigh, giving in to her excitement even though I worry about putting her on the spot like this. She doesn't have many guests in the B&B right now. She's not worried about them. We, all six of us, converged here for breakfast, and Marian latched on to the possibility of turning the Goldfinch into an impromptu wedding site.

If this is what makes her happy, I'm fine with it.

"All right." Lauren taps the pencil on her lip, viewing her list. "We can still do the fairy lights and string them outside. The candles could line up along the ledge of the gazebo..." She grins. "All that lace we found in your attic, Marian. That would look pretty draped on the wooden beams."

"Oooh. It'll be so magical." Marian squeals. "I am so dang excited!"

I laugh, glad to have entertained her. But we don't have time to pick at the preparations. We are heading out later. The guys are driving to Denver for tuxes, and the girls want to go to Copper Mountain for a last-minute spa day.

Then tomorrow, the wedding!

"What do you think, Claire?" Lauren asks me as she points toward her list.

"I think I'm still stunned this is happening."

Aubrey smiles. "What about a dress?"

I wince. That is an important detail. "When are we going to the spa?"

"Four o'clock," Lauren answers. "And you *are* coming, Marian."

"Then Jason can mow out there." Marian nods and wipes her hands on her apron. She sets the last pancake on a plate and turns off the stove. "Come on, let's go look at the gazebo and garden so Claire can have a better idea of the area."

Gazebo and garden or a narrow dining room, it doesn't matter to me, but as we walk through the grounds, I draw in deep breaths of fresh air and smile.

"It's gorgeous out here." It really is like something out of a fairytale. Flowers are blossoming, bees buzz in the distance, and everything smells so sweet and natural.

"Is it anything like what you've dreamed of?" Aubrey asks.

I give her a lopsided smile. "No."

Lauren and Marian shrink, pouting.

"Because I've never dreamed about my wedding. I never thought about it, knowing early on that it wouldn't be a love match with the way my mother treated it."

"That's so sad," Marian says as she takes my hand. She squeezes it, then pats it, nodding firmly. "She's wrong."

"You got that right," I reply cheerfully. As the hours tick down to the day, I feel more confident. Everyone is so happy for us and eager to stop what they're doing to help prepare. And with the surrounding support and excitement, I let myself fall under the spell of being thrilled for this to happen, more confident in Sawyer's feelings for me now.

"Doing this last minute like this is perfect, actually." I smile at the women as we head back inside. "I don't have to worry about trying to live up to any biases or standards. Just going with the flow."

"More like starting from scratch and making the best of what we have on hand," Aubrey says.

I nod, glancing at the time in the kitchen. "That's true. So maybe I should try to whip up a dress for this before we go to the spa."

Marian laughs. "Whip up?" She gestures at the room where she insists upon a "system" to make her delicious meals. It's nothing more than a dominance of the kitchen, shooing anyone out when they don't do things exactly as she wants. "You whip up a salad or a snack. Not a dress."

I wink at her. "I'll leave the food to you," I tell her, knowing she's probably most excited to prepare the cake. "I'll leave the decorations to you and you," I tell Lauren and Aubrey. "But *I* will work *my* magic and figure out a dress."

In five hours. I shake my head, realizing this is utter insanity, but I've never felt more alive.

Lauren drives me back to my cabin, and when she drops me off, my mind is racing with possibilities. I have enough samples of fabric that I can make do. With some extra lace that Marian stored up in the attic that Lauren just aired out, I can see a simple but elegant design shaping up in my head. Even though I'm working on the fly, rushing my way through an entire garment in the nick of time, I stick to it and don't take a break. I'll have lots of time to relax at the spa later, and tomorrow, I can't see anyone expecting me to do anything but walk down the aisle to Sawyer.

Oh, Sawyer. I smile in the privacy of the cabin, so excited to hurl myself into this whirlwind of a marriage with him. It's sudden and hectic, but I wouldn't trade it for anything.

The sooner I'm his wife, the more complete I think we'll both feel, and it has nothing to do with my money.

It's just us. How we click and have ever since the moment we saw each other.

My fingers ache by the time I'm done, and I grin at the final product. With moments to spare, I try it on carefully and blink away the tears that come to my eyes as I stare at my reflection in the mirror. I've created a simple dress of white satin with a fitted bodice and a flowing lace overlay; I love the way it flows around me, and I'm happy I could incorporate Marian's attic find in my wedding dress.

I hear the girls come in, but I don't leave the privacy of my bedroom yet. "I'm in here."

"Are you ready to go?" Aubrey asks, yelling to be heard over the music I left playing in the living room.

"Yeah. Just uh, want to get your opinion on this little something I 'whipped' together."

I exit, walking slowly to make sure I can catch each of their expressions. Like my whirlwind relationship with Sawyer, these women represent instantaneous bonds of friendship. It doesn't matter that we haven't known each other for long. I see it in the awe on their faces. I hear it in the gasps as I show them the dress. And Marian, the sweet woman, bursts into tears. She smiles through them—happy tears—and holds her arms out to hug me.

"You are a beautiful, darling bride, Claire. I'm so happy I found that lace for you."

I lean in for her to press a kiss to my cheek and savor the love she showers on me. It's a form of affection I've never received from my mother, and I want to savor this moment forever.

Creating a bridal gown for myself in the span of hours is a miracle.

Gaining these girls as true friends is another.

But tomorrow, I'll have the best blessing in walking through that garden to make my vows to Sawyer.

CHAPTER 31

Sawyer

I stand outside the fitting rooms and check out the tux. It feels strange, like it's not my reflection in the mirror that I'm staring at. I feel like I'm on the outside looking in, that it's not *me* getting married tomorrow to the one and only Claire Rennard, but some other lucky man who's deluded enough to think he deserves her.

She's mine. With or without this wedding, Claire is irrefutably my woman, the only person I want to go home to. She's the one, without a doubt. I want to wake up every morning seeing her smiling face and go to sleep with her cozying up against me.

We haven't shared many nights together. She hasn't even seen my freaking home yet. While it's all so rushed and fast, I'm not scared about my connection to her.

But what if she has second thoughts? It's just happening so fast that I can't help but be nervous. This isn't a case of being antsy or impatient.

I'm not struggling inside with this worrying and fussing about if this is the right thing to do.

I face deep, gripping nerves that make my stomach tense and knot. I swallow, wishing I could loosen the tie, but I don't want to annoy the tailor again. He gave me a stern look when I tugged at the strap around my neck in this monkey suit the first time. As he's now sticking pins near my crotch as he figures out how to adjust the seams, I want him to be very careful and focused on where those sharp points are aimed.

"You look like you're going to throw up," Kevin remarks as he exits the dressing room in a similar tux.

The tailor flinches, causing me to go extremely still with those pins. Then, with a slow, deliberate glance up at us, as if checking for impending vomit to fall near him, he sighs and shakes his head. "Please stand still."

I am. I shoot my brother a wry look. "I am not on the verge of puking."

"Well, you look uneasy," Jason says as he strides out confidently. He fusses with his tie as he steps onto the dais to my left while Kevin stands to my right.

How come you can mess with that tie and get away with it?

"I'm nervous," I admit.

"That's an understatement," Jason quips. "You *do* look off."

I look down at the tailor again and shake my head. "I'm fine," I tell him, or all of them. As I stare back at myself, I sigh. "I just want everything to be perfect for Claire."

"Not a lot of time to ensure perfection," Jason teases.

"I know, but still." I shrug, earning a growl of annoyance from the tailor.

"I want everything to be perfect for her, especially when this day is only happening because of the rush with her mother trying to screw her over."

"You mean this day wouldn't be happening otherwise?" Kevin arches a brow at me.

"No." I doubt I can answer that reliably. I can't tell the future. "Yes." It seems inevitable, though, that Claire and I would be destined to crash and burn together like we have. "I think we would have reached this point without her mother meddling in her life." But now that the hours are counting down to our wedding, I can't wait for it to come. "I'm not sure I'd be patient for a longer engagement."

Jason laughs. "Not like a week is long to begin with."

Kevin gives me a knowing look, aware from our talk yesterday that the actual agreement to marry with our feelings shared was only a day old.

He doesn't pipe up or poke fun at me. After a moment of us being measured and having our tuxes adjusted, Jason smiles wide. "And who cares about the timing. Time is all relative anyway, isn't it? We're here to live our one life, however long fate decides that can be, and we can only do the best as we can with the time we have."

"Nicely put, philosopher," Kevin says.

Jason chuckles. "Look at you two, for example. I know we didn't have the most conventional childhood, with me so much older by the time you guys came along, then our parents passing and such. There were many days over the years that I wanted to give up hope of you two reconciling and getting over the petty nonsense that kept you distant, like rivals or enemies. And here we are. It took years, but we're standing here together, not growling or glaring at anyone. It took time for you two to make up and figure out how to be civil, but there's no point in complaining it took too long or that it is too soon to claim a truce. It happened. And we should be grateful for it. I am." He rolls his eyes. "It was getting really old, keeping you apart."

I nod at him.

"You can thank our new sister-in-law for that," Kevin says. "She didn't say much when I met her in Frisco, but I saw how much she cared. Her slight ways of defending you challenged me to rethink how I've treated you, and I'm a bit ashamed to admit that if it weren't for her opening my eyes, I might never have thought about talking with you like we have." Kevin thumps me on my back, pissing off the tailor's assistant hurrying to perfect his tux. "Sorry, sorry!"

"And the same thing goes for Claire," Jason advised. "Don't look at it as happening too sudden or too fast. Don't worry about the details and making sure the ceremony and day is perfect or not. Be glad and appreciate that you did meet, that you did develop feelings for each other, and count on the gift of having her in your life and sharing her time with you every day that will come."

I nod at Jason, glad he can impart such logical and comforting advice. He's right.

"In case it slips my mind to tell you later, I'm happy for you, Sawyer. This is the real deal with Claire, and I'm glad you've found her."

The real deal? Yeah, that is a good view to have of Claire.

And tomorrow, she'll *really* be mine.

Back near Breckenridge, we drop off our tuxes before we prepare to head out for a tame bachelor's night. My brothers, as well as Dalton and Caleb, want to take me out for a night of drinking beer at the nearby bar. The girls are expected to head off to Copper Mountain for a last-minute spa treatment. I have a suspicion that my brothers and friends are trying their hardest to pull off a traditional day of separation, so Claire and I won't see each other, but I'm pleasantly surprised to see them at the Goldfinch. Lauren forgot her phone, and they doubled back here to grab it.

I sneak away from the guys and run over to steal Claire aside for a moment. All day, I've been fretting about her. If she's excited or scared. If she's happy with our plans or wishing we could take time to plan a whole production of a wedding package to get through.

She giggles, stepping aside with me. As I secret her away in a room off the main hallway at the massive B&B, I lower my head to hers and kiss her hard.

"I missed you," I whisper as everyone starts asking where we are.

"Claire!" Aubrey shouts.

"I *just* saw Sawyer over here a second ago," Jason says.

Claire bites her lip, whispering back to me, "Missed me? You just saw me this morning when you dropped me off here."

"That was hours ago."

She hums against my lips as I steal another kiss. "Well, after tomorrow evening, you won't be able to get rid of me."

"Damn right," I promise.

"We're really doing this," she whispers with elation. Her eyes are wide, glimmering with excitement.

"We are. And it's the real deal," I tell her, borrowing Kevin's words. "This is so very real for me."

She nods, sighing as she hugs me closer. "Me too. No *ifs, ands, or buts* about it. I'm not just doing this for any other reason than the way I love you and want to spend the rest of my life getting to know you."

"Not because of the estate?" I tease, knowing it's the last thing on her mind. She's been so used to living with scraps of an allowance that I know she can't be missing a formerly affluent life.

She blows a raspberry and rolls her eyes. "No. I don't care about that money anymore."

I kiss her, loving the feel of her smiling lips under mine.

"But hey, if this does work out with that trust fund, I'll treat you."

"Oh?" I lower my lids to give her a seductive look. "I thought I would always be the one to treat *you*," I argue playfully as I nudge my leg between hers.

"Hmmm." She arches toward me and kisses me, her tongue dancing with mine. It turns me on, and I dread having to walk away. "I'll...treat you with a gift. I'll buy you a brand-new truck."

"Is that so?" I tease back.

"Uh-huh." She traces her finger down my shirt, jumping up and passing each button as she moves. "And maybe some new shoes. You know, so you don't fall."

I kiss her and chuckle. "Your fall was the way we met."

"And now," she says sweetly as our friends call out for us down the hall still. "Now, I can trust that we'll always be there to catch each other when we fall."

I can't help but peck one more kiss on her lips. I've never felt this confident before, and with her sweet gaze, as she beams up at me, I know I'm set and focused on my decision, too.

"Sawyer!" Dalton finds us, and he chuckles as he pulls on the back of my shirt to yank me out of the small room with Claire.

"See you tomorrow, baby." I look back at her, unable to wipe the grin off my face while she fixes her lipstick.

I feel like I'm on top of the world, but I'm glad to head out with the guys. If I didn't, I'd cave to this need to see Claire tonight and hold her until my heart is imprinted with the beat from hers.

Tomorrow.

Disregarding Jason's sage words from earlier, I sigh and know every minute that stands between now and the moment when she'll see me at the end of the aisle will feel like eternity.

Tomorrow cannot come soon enough.

Claire is my future, and I want the rest of my life to start *now*.

CHAPTER 32

Claire

That evening, I pace in the small parlor on the first floor of the bed-and-breakfast, unsure what exactly I'm feeling, much less how I can go about it. Nerves fill me, but that's to be expected. I'm a bride. This is a new day, the mark of a date that will change me from a single woman to half of a married couple. Every year, from here on out, this will be my anniversary with Sawyer, signaling when we both took a chance on each other.

Hope is a close second. I rub my hand over my stomach, trying to quell the tension there. I'm optimistic that this is the right thing to do. *I* know where my heart lies, and with each minute that passes until I'm beckoned to head outside, I feel more and more convinced Sawyer meant it when he said this is real for him. We're not marrying to beat my mother to my trust fund. We're uniting in marriage because we love each other.

The door opens and closes behind me. I hold my breath, realizing the moment has come for me to exit and walk toward Sawyer.

It's Marian, though. Dressed in a simple but elegant silvery-teal summer dress, she presses her back against the door. Her smile is sweet and encouraging, and I'm grateful she isn't on the brink of tears this time. Her devotion to Lauren and Aubrey is clear. They are the daughters she wished she could always have. And yesterday, when she eyed me at my cabin when I showed them my hastily made dress, she proved that she considers me the same, crying tears of joy.

I'm not her daughter. My mother is in New York, racing to ruin my life. Little does my only parent know that her nefarious actions have pushed me to find my real love, but she doesn't *care* either. Marian does. She's present. And she somehow knew that I needed advice. Gentle encouragement. Something. I'm not hesitant to walk down the aisle to Sawyer, but...I'm overwhelmed with so many emotions I don't know what to think, and I want a level head as I go to my groom.

"Nervous?"

I nod, then shrug.

"Excited."

I give a firmer nod.

"Second thoughts?" She sits in a chair as I approach her.

"No." I sit and sigh. "It's just that it's here. The moment is *here*." I bite my lip and smile at her. "I'm just struggling to accept that this is really happening. I'm actually doing it."

"And you're okay with how it is?" She tilts her head to the side.

I shrug again. "I never thought I'd get to this point." It's all so rushed, but that's not what's bothering me. I lick my lips and lean forward. "It's just that this will be it. This will be my wedding story. It's what I'll tell my clients when they're nervous on their big days, if any of the brides I make a dress for are nervous and feeling so raw before they walk down the aisle. What if they ask me how I handled it? What if they ask me for advice on how I did it?"

Marian pulls out a slim flask from her pocket. "Ah. Then allow me to fill that role." She's considerate of my mother not being here, of *none* of my family or acquaintances here, other than Dalton. If this were a wedding my mother arranged, I would be readying myself to walk through a congregation of hundreds of guests.

"You'll do this," she says as she hands me the flask, "knowing that man is the man you love, who loves you, and both of you will never lose sight of that connection. It's as simple as that."

I arch a brow at her offering.

She shrugs. "I was scared to marry. It's such a *big* day. My mother and mother-in-law did that, too." She points at the alcohol. "Liquid courage. To stop *thinking* and just feel." She winks, and I giggle, tipping it to my mouth for a quick shot.

"My John and I married quickly, too," she shares. "We were friends, and we'd known each other for a while, but we didn't date for long. It was a whirlwind, and when it was my wedding day, I kept thinking, 'but I hardly know him!'"

I shake my head. "I haven't even seen Sawyer's house yet!"

"John and I hadn't done the deed, and I was obsessed with worrying if he snored!"

We both giggle, and between her honesty and the shot, I feel warmer and lighter. I don't feel as alone with this woman standing in as the mother I've always wished for.

"But that doesn't matter. None of it matters. You and Sawyer will learn about each other and get to know each other over the years. You have a lifetime to learn and both of you will change over time and you will relearn with each other." She pats my knee. "The biggest part is done. You love each other. And with that, the rest will fall into place."

We stand together, and I pull her into a hug. "Will you...will you walk me down the aisle?"

Her eyes go wide before she smiles. "*Me*?"

I nod. She's acted more like a loving parent than my mother ever has.

"Of course," she promises and presses a kiss to my cheek. "I'm honored."

And that's how I arrive to this spontaneous wedding that was pulled together in less than a day by these wonderful people I feel so blessed to have found. With everyone's help, the backyard and gazebo have been turned into something from a fairy tale. The twinkling fairy lights and flickering candles lend a hint of magic to the impromptu wedding venue.

Marian rubs the top of my hand as we reach the back door. She pats it before I reach for the bouquet Lauren tied of blooms from the garden. A little girl has been holding them for me. She's a guest with her aunt at the B&B, and she was thrilled to be included with this big role of handing me the bouquet. Her aunt is up ahead, snapping pictures. She's a commercial photographer, here on a vacation with her adorable niece. Upon realizing we were arranging a hasty wedding, she insisted on making herself our photographer. I'm sure Dalton's paying her plenty, but I'm grateful she happened to be here to pull off that role.

With Marian at my side, I walk down the aisle.

This is it. This is the day.

I don't trip once, deciding to wear my most sensible sandals over the grass. The lace skirt of my wedding dress trails behind me as I near the flickering lights of the gazebo. Marian squeezes my hand as we walk the short distance from the house.

I'm doing this. I'm really, really doing this.

My heart swells, and there's no doubt in my mind this is where I'm meant to be.

An older man from town plays a gentle, sweet melody on his guitar. He looks like a doppelgänger of Kenny Rodgers, but I think Aubrey said his name is Earl. Another local, I believe a former police officer, is the officiant up ahead, and his name actually *is* Ken. I don't care. I'll ask later. I'm simply happy both of them are here and willing to help make this wedding complete.

I don't need an orchestra with a proper wedding march. I don't want a fusty old priest asking me to recite long vows.

This is perfect.

Seeing the wide, smug smile on Sawyer's handsome face ensures it. He looks like the embodiment of love, of being in love with me, and this is all I could ever want. With the birds singing in the distance, surrounded by the few friends who matter to us, I reach Sawyer at the gazebo.

Only then do I trip.

Sawyer catches me, and I roll my eyes at his chuckles.

"Full circle, huh?" he teases and pulls me in for a quick kiss.

"Hey, hey," Kevin says, at the front with Jason next to him. "You missed a few parts before the kiss."

Everyone laughs lightly as I hold Sawyer's hand tightly.

Jason and Kevin had put their heads together to find vows for Sawyer, and Lauren, already surrounded with all things to do with weddings, located a simple vow for me to say.

It's short, but no less sweet, and after we slide rings onto each other's fingers, I gaze up at Sawyer and get lost in the love swirling in his eyes. All for me.

He mouths, *I love you*, as Ken tells our small crowd that we're husband and wife. I mouth it back to him the second before he pulls me close and slowly dips me back, pressing his lips against mine and stealing my breath. This is the defining moment that makes us more than two people arguing over noise and swapping teases. With his soft, warm lips on mine, I sigh and welcome in this sweet sense of belonging.

I'm married. I have a *husband*. And as he helps me to stand after that dip with the kiss, I giggle and lean against his side.

"We did it!" I tell him as they clap and cheer.

He lifts our joined hands and grins at me. "We did. And I couldn't be happier."

Every minute leading up to our simple ceremony felt like a drag of time, but following it, they pass in a blur. We head toward the cake Marian made, and with a small outdoor setting, we dance and chat with our friends. It's a toned-down affair, but still the actual thing. Aubrey catches my bouquet. The guest-slash-photographer snaps pictures of Sawyer and my first dance, and before I can realize it, hours have passed.

We leave in Sawyer's truck, but before Sawyer closes the passenger door for me, I hold my hand out and point at Lauren. "Don't forget. Your dress fitting tomorrow..."

She laughs. "I think we can delay it a day or two, newlywed!"

Once we leave, I sink into the cushion and sigh. I roll my head on the headrest and smile at Sawyer.

"Happy?" he asks me. He takes my hand and kisses my knuckles.

"Very." I take a good, long look at him, checking him out.

"The way you're looking at me, *wife*, is going to make me pull over, and I'll never show you our home."

A shiver traces over my skin. *Wife*. "I like the sound of that."

He arches his brows, giving me just as hot of a look. "Pulling over?"

"No. The other part." I unbuckle my seatbelt and crawl toward him to cup his face and kiss his cheek without making him look away from the road.

He grins, growling in need. "Wife?"

I sigh and slide my hand over his chest. "Say it again."

He stops at a stop sign and turns to grab me closer and kiss me hard. "My wife," he whispers against my lips. He pulls back and looks at me with a grin. "Buckle up that middle seatbelt if you're going to be sitting so close. That way, I can kiss you again at the next stop sign."

I shiver again and smile.

"We'll never get there," he says as he drives again.

"Ha." I kiss along his neck, unable to keep my hands or mouth off him as I snuggle against his side. "That's not *us*. We rush forward, too impatient to get what we want."

"You got that right."

"And now, I want *you*, husband." I lower my hand to grip him through his pants.

"Is it the tux? Seeing me all dressed up and proper that's making you wild?" he teases.

"Just you." I tug at his tie. "And knowing you're all mine forever."

He swerves a couple of times on the road, but he speeds us all the way to an elegant and modern condo.

It's not what I was expecting, but with how turned on I am, I don't care. All I can focus on is getting inside and having him inside me, filling and stretching me with that delicious burn of friction.

I kiss him as he picks me up out of the truck, and I giggle as he carries me over the threshold. "We'll move. We'll get something bigger. I'll build you anything you want, Claire."

I silence him with a kiss. We're married, and like Marian advised, we'll learn about each other and make our home wherever we want.

"And now, the moment I've been waiting for," he says as he sets me down in the bedroom. The lights are dimmed, and I can't look away from him. All the details can be seen later. Right now, he's my whole focus, and I sure like the way he's slowly taking off his tux.

"Now, I get to see the first and original Claire Cameron creation." He twirls his finger to prompt me to spin, and I smile wide. He's so sweet, so considerate, to know the dress I'm wearing is important to me. No matter how quickly I made it, I will treasure it forever.

He's down to his boxers, shoving them off as he stares at me, moving close.

"Wanna know the best part?" I ask, breathing hard as desire consumes me.

He growls, reaching forward as he steps out of his boxers. His fingers slip under my hair. He holds the back of my neck and kisses me hard. "What?"

I pant after that drugging kiss and turn, giving him my back. "One zipper. Easy to take off."

He takes the tab and drags it along the track. The dress peels off me, parting as it flutters to pool at my feet, and the feel of cool air on my body chills and excites me. He chases away the chill as he spreads his hot hands over my sides and across my stomach, hugging my back to his chest until his heat radiates through me.

"I love you, my wife." His hand cups my breast as he leans me back to him.

I turn around, kissing him deeply. "And I love you, my sexy husband."

He maneuvers us, bringing me down onto his bed. I don't take my lips off him once, and with the wetness so sticky at my core and the hardness of his erection pushing against my stomach, I know neither of us will last for foreplay. The entire evening of seeing him in his tux has been a tease that had me hot and bothered all night, and now, as he hovers over me and gazes into my eyes, I smile at knowing he's *mine*.

"I love you," I tell him again. I can't get enough of saying it, and as I part my legs to get him closer to where I need him, he groans and kisses me soundly.

"I love you, too," he swears as he slides in.

I shudder around him, hugging him close and arching my back up as he fills me fully. It's perfect, the same intense connection I know I'll never tire of. But different, too. Not only is this the first time we're making love as a married couple, but it's also the first time he's entered me without a condom.

"And I will never stop being in love with you, Claire," he gets out around hard, mind-numbing thrusts. His words are all I need. I come, gripping him tight and crying out.

After he finds his release and we lay together in a sweaty tangle of tired limbs, I smile and stroke my finger along the muscles of his bare back.

"And I will always be in love with you, Sawyer," I whisper gently before we ease off into sleep.

CHAPTER 33

Claire

A few weeks later

When it was *my* wedding day, I wondered how my "story" would come together. On Lauren and Caleb's wedding day, I get a firsthand look of how every bride will have a unique journey to their day. Especially this woman. This isn't Lauren's first time. She's set foot on the aisle twice before, and those experiences both blew up colossally.

Maybe that's why she's so calm. Practice making perfect and all.

Or not. As Aubrey and I help Lauren into the dress I've labored over and perfected the best I could at the cabin, Lauren shares some sobering, good news.

"It's *officially* over," she says with a sure and confident smile.

"What, your days of being single?" I tease. It's easier and easier to joke and tease with these two, and I will never lose sight of how I've found the best present in their friendships.

"Jeremy."

Aubrey laughs, a gritty and snark-filled sound. "Hell, yeah."

Lauren smiles at her reflection as I work on adjusting the dress over her. "He's done. My trust fund is fully in my hands. Every penny of it, and Caleb has arranged for my father to have to pay back interest on everything he's taken out if it."

Damn. Caleb's always been sharp like that, but... "Your dad isn't out there, right?"

She shakes her head. "No. Marian will walk me down the aisle." She smiles at me. "I saw how much she loved it at your wedding, and it makes sense."

It's traditional for the father to walk his girl down the aisle, but I feel certain our romances are far from traditional or conventional.

"When we met and were struggling to stay together, Caleb pulled out of investing in my father's vineyards. That was a blow. But now, he'll need to pay me back."

"And Jeremy will never get a penny either," Aubrey says with a happy sigh.

"He'll never hold onto a penny," Lauren says boldly. "Dalton's legal team reamed him for what he did to you, too. Libel, slander, all of it. He's looking at doing serious time for all of his combined crimes. He'll forever regret the day he made you lose your job because you helped me escape from marrying him."

I whistle. "We are quite a bunch of sloppy relationships," I tease.

"Only in getting there," Lauren argues. "Now we have our happily ever afters."

My fund is in my hands, too, and like Lauren, I feel like everything is falling into place as it should. I haven't spoken to my mother yet. I don't plan to. Her lawyers are hounding after me, and Sawyer has stood up for me, blocking them from communications. The best was when a pair of snobby legal eagles flew out here and tried to harass me while we were down in town. Ken and Earl were more than just helpers at a wedding. Those usually cranky, old chess players really care about the locals here, and I now belong in that category.

Dalton found out that my mother fled to Europe after the devastating blow of losing my portion of the Renard estate. She has never been one to deal with the fallout of her own actions. I'm happy to have an ocean between us.

Being surrounded by loving and friendly people who want to support me and not tear me down is a greater wealth to have come into than the billions in my account.

I have yet to touch it; I've been too busy with planning my shop.

"Oh." Lauren lifts her hand to her mouth and her eyes go glossy.

Now, *this*, I've had practice with in Paris.

"Look up. Blink. Up at the ceiling and blink. Press your fingers under your eyes and breathe steadily," I order gently.

Aubrey giggles. "You'll be coaching that often, huh?" She's no better, tearing up at the sight of Lauren in her gown. I'm misty-eyed, too. The blonde is absolutely beautiful in this dress, but I look deeper, seeing the gorgeous product for my first design job ever.

"Well, with the time and care and money brides will be putting into makeup, yeah." I laugh lightly, fussing over fluffing out the dress more. Aubrey's right. I bet I will soon be an expert in advising women not to cry.

"It's beautiful. It's perfect." Lauren steps off the dais and gathers us both in a hug and holds us tight. She releases us, but not before pressing a kiss to my cheek. "It's everything I ever could have wanted."

Aubrey, ever the smartass, sniffles and fights with her tears. "Let's do a recap. No shoulder pads." She holds up a finger. "No Madonna-esque lace from the eighties." She lifts another finger, and we laugh.

"No weird strips of tight plasticky fabric under my boobs," Lauren adds.

"And no layers of tulle and pouf with enough volume to rival a freaking storm cloud," Aubrey says.

I grin, loving their humor and inclusion, but it's time to move this along. "Nope. None of that. Just the dress of your dreams."

I hug them both again before urging them to get a move on, and I escape and hurry through the venue to find Sawyer in his seat.

"Everything went well?" he asks as I slip in next to him. He leans over to kiss me and holds my hand.

I nod. "She's beautiful."

He leans closer to whisper. "The ladies behind us said that guy over there," he says as he tips his chin toward the side where some stand, "is a—"

I gasp, my eyes going wide. "A well-known fashion vlogger!" He'll see my dress. Caleb's always been the one to attract publicity, but until now, I hadn't considered that the dress I designed for Lauren would also be getting so much attention.

Sawyer winks at me, and I try to contain my excitement as I look around the whole place. Caleb has pulled out all the stops for Lauren. He funded the dress of her dreams, and he's spared no expense in making sure she has the wedding of a lifetime. Third time's the charm, after all. This wedding and this groom will be her last, and it's absolutely lovely in here. With the flowers, lights, and small touches I suggested way back when, it's a stunning vista of wedding perfection.

When the music comes on, Sawyer and I go quiet, giving the bride our attention. As Lauren and Marian pass, I struggle not to be overly critical in inspecting the dress. Lauren is radiant, though, capturing my eye, as well as everyone else's.

She glides down the aisle and reaches Caleb, standing tall and smiling wide at the altar. Sawyer and I are seated a ways back, but from this distance, I see that he's struggling not to cry at the sight of his bride.

Holding hands and clinging to every minute of the ceremony, Sawyer and I sit together and enjoy witnessing our friends exchanging vows.

As we sit through it all, Sawyer reaches over and plays with my wedding ring. The diamonds sparkle in the light, and I glance down at the band he had made for me.

"Do you regret how we got married?"

I shake my head and smile up at him. "No," I whisper back.

Caleb's made this a grand affair, showing up and catering to anything Lauren's asked for. It's still a very intimate and romantic setting, though, not over the top. "Never," I tell my husband. It wouldn't have mattered if I walked down a long, elaborate aisle in a fancy old building or if we'd asked hundreds of people to come. The only thing that was important to me was that I married him, no one else. All the other details ceased to matter.

He kisses me and drapes his arm around my shoulders to pull me closer.

Later at the reception, I'm even more convinced the way Sawyer and I went about our wedding was the better route to go. We kept it short and sweet, with plenty of freedom to head back home and relax with each other in bed. And we stayed in bed, enjoying each other several times throughout the night.

Here, we are staying for it all. So many dances. All the toasts. The food. The drinks. Mingling. We barely have a chance to be alone, but as we dance on the floor toward the end of the night, I sigh and rest my cheek against his chest, loving his hard, hot body that never fails to anchor me.

"I'm in pain." He groans good-naturedly, and I giggle. "I ate way too much."

"It was all too delicious."

He smirks down at me. "I can't believe Marian said it was better than anything she's ever cooked."

I grin, loving that of one of the many things we've learned about each other, *neither* of us can hold our own in the kitchen. We're both hopeless at cooking, but trying and failing together has been so much fun.

"I doubt that. I still don't understand what her 'system' is in the kitchen, but she's a mastermind." I thought for so long that it was because she provided honest-to-goodness home-cooked meals, but we've sampled others' cooking, and hers is simply the best.

"That's why," he whispers, leaning in close, "Kevin and I started a bet on how long Jason will wait to marry her."

I snort a laugh. "Just for her food?"

He chuckles, shaking his head. "Nah. It's a whole host of things that he loves about her. And they're great together. A good fit."

I frame his face and kiss him tenderly. "Just like we are."

A good fit and a perfect match.

It's all I've truly needed to be complete.

CHAPTER 34

Sawyer

A few months later...

When I married Claire, I was nervous. I wanted everything to be perfect for her that big day. But today, as I guide her into my truck, I chew on my lip and experience, and even worse case of anxiety. As odd as it may sound, today has me more nervous than our rushed wedding day. I wanted our wedding to be one she'd always remember. After all, in her line of work, she'll be exposed to *many* weddings and numerous brides.

In the months since we've been a Mr. and Mrs., I know she's content with how we got hitched. Even though she is a participant in the wedding industry, she seems to rely on a sage piece of advice that she heard at Lauren's wedding.

Better to have a solid, wonderful duration of a marriage than a perfect single moment of one wedding day.

Since our marriage started, we've both kept that in the forefront of our minds. Each and every day, we strive to help each other be the best version of ourselves that we can be, and today is a huge example of that.

"I don't understand why I need to be blindfolded," she complains in the passenger seat as I drive away from my condo. The construction on our house will start in a few months, and I'm excited about the next phase of our lives. This current upcoming change in *her* life will keep her preoccupied from the house-planning part.

"To keep it a surprise."

She crosses her arms and smiles. "But I'll figure it out. There are only so many roads to turn on, and I'll follow it with the mental map in my head."

"What mental map?"

She swats at me playfully. "You're never going to let me forget how I got lost that first time I drove here."

I chuckle, smiling at the memory of her buying an SUV and promptly getting lost *with* the help of navigation. "It's just the big-city girl in you," I tease.

"I think you're doing a fine job of converting me into an outdoorsy one."

"Yeah," I joke back, "you've only worn heels on walks a few times lately."

This easygoing banter between us helps me forget about how nervous I am, and as we joke and tease each other like always, I start to feel smug. It won't be a complete surprise. I showed her that shop space months ago when I sort-of proposed. That day, I told her the retail place in Breckenridge could be hers, no matter what.

Since then, she's asked about when she can move things into it. I stayed consistent, hedging her questions and stalling her curiosity about how the space would be turned into her dream bridal shop. All winter long, I worked on renovating it into what she needed. Many times, she pointed out pictures of what she'd like, and I arranged for help from Marian, Lauren, and Aubrey.

Marian and Jason did get married, the day after Christmas. It was a quick, small thing at the B&B, more a formality than a ceremony, but we paid for her to go to Denver and tour a shop. Marian knew what dress she wanted, *not* a bridal gown; otherwise she would have gone with Claire. Instead, they used the trip as a ploy to tour a shop and take pictures for me. I worked off them and relied on the notes they jotted on their phones when that dress owner asked Claire what she thought of her space.

Claire hasn't been idle, either. Since the vlogger at Lauren's wedding reached out for the designer details, Claire got busy setting up her LLC for her business and letting her internship in Paris know she wasn't going to be there. With her receiving the money from her trust fund, she was able to go about it properly, making a real business before she moved into the space. So many steps were completed from home, all those behind-the-scenes details like formatting a website, structuring her bookkeeping, and even interviewing employees she might bring on board to help her.

While she's been aware I've been working on her shop, she has yet to see the finished product. Until today. She's impatient to start filling the orders she'll have to concentrate on. Much of her work was done by talking with clients on video calls and sketching. She explained that the majority of the design process happens before any needles are used to sew. Once the image is finalized, it's a quick process of *making* the dress.

I park at the curb, thrilled I can do this for her. "Do you know where we are?"

She pouts, blindfolded and with her arms crossed. "No."

I laugh and she gives into a giggle, too. "Oh, I'm hopeless. I'll just have to rely on navigation forever."

I exit the truck and open her door. "Nah. You can rely on me," I say as I guide her to the sidewalk.

She leans into me, kissing me, but since she can't see, she misses her mark of my face and smacks her lips on my bicep.

"Okay, ready?" I take her hand and lead her inside the shop space. Inside, I see that everyone is set up like we've planned. Without their help, I would have really struggled to keep my nosy wife out of here while I got it all ready. Lauren and Aubrey helped to distract her. Kevin helped pick up deliveries and bring them over. Dalton and Caleb got their hands dirty, too, cleaning and building alongside me and Jason. It's been a team effort, and I'm so proud to call them our friends.

We enter, and at the entrance, I take the blindfold off Claire's face.

She gasps and gazes with a wide-eyed expression as she takes it all in.

"Oh, my goodness." She swallows hard and walks around, clutching my hand so tight. "This is... This is..." She lunges back to hug me. "This is amazing!" She frames my face and kisses me hard as our friends cheer and welcome her in.

Dalton pops a bottle of champagne, and we all join in celebrating. Claire can't get enough of it all. She goes to each of us, hugging and thanking us for making the place sparkle like this.

"Look." Lauren leads us toward the front, where the tall windows will allow plenty of light in. "Just think of all this space you can decorate."

"Dress forms there." I point out.

"And shelving here to display more layers," Lauren adds. She was instrumental in this design, too.

"You can do seasonal rotations," Aubrey says.

"And in both windows!" Claire exclaims, eyeing the other side. When I brought her in here before, a wall was blocking the floor-to-ceiling window to the left. Now, both sides of the front door have windows for people to see inside.

We sip champagne and go through the main room, eyeing all the racks we've bought for her to hold dresses.

"I can't wait to fill them all up," Claire says. "Bridal and bridesmaid gowns..."

"And mother-of-the-bride gowns," Marian says with a wink at Aubrey.

I frown, wondering about that angle of teasing, but Claire doesn't stay still. She has yet to let go of my hand, and she leads me back through the store.

"I could have two counters for checking out," Claire says as she sets her champagne flute down and runs her hand over the smooth marble countertop.

"I've got a couple of part-timers at the school who would love some more work," Aubrey says.

"And right in town, too," Kevin adds.

"You did this for me?" Claire asks as we move to the far back, where her extensive studio awaits.

"We all helped," I say, not wanting to downplay or disregard everyone's efforts.

She smiles at me, and I feel like a king with the love shining in her eyes. "*This* is where you were all those times you claimed to have a random poker evening, wasn't it?" she accuses sweetly.

Jason laughs. "And the 'boys' night' at the pub."

Caleb joins in, patting my back. "And those times we called him and needed help with a leak or whatnot." He winks at Claire, and she rests her cheek on my shoulder.

"And here is where you can work," I say with a dramatic lift of my arm as I gesture at the wide-open area. All her sewing things are set away, thanks to Lauren helping me arrange them. And thanks to Aubrey for telling Claire she needed help at the school with an after-hour craft club. It kept Claire occupied while Lauren and I could transport her things from home to here. Marian drove with Jason to Denver to get the last of the fabrics, too. Not only are the sewing machines and accessories waiting for Claire's magic back here, but a beginning stock of fabrics are available, too.

"I'm stunned," Claire admits with tears in her eyes. "I...My gosh, this is my dream come true!"

I hold her close and kiss the top of her head as she wipes her eyes dry. I know they're happy tears, but still, I want to make sure this really is everything she's ever wanted.

"Did I do a good job?" I check as everyone checks out the final product of hard work.

"A good job?" Claire rolls her eyes and smiles before she pulls me down for a deep kiss. As she draws back from the kiss, she continues, "It's more than I ever imagined it could be. You've made the last of my dreams come true, Sawyer. Thank you."

I tilt my head to the side. "The last of your dreams?"

She nods and kisses me again.

"What was the first?"

"You." She leans up, staring at me with all the desire and compassion she gives me daily, and touches her lips to mine in a tender yet hard press. I grip her back, wishing we could *really* christen this place in another way.

"Finding you and knowing you love me as hard as I do you. You're a dream come true, Sawyer."

I sigh against her and hold her in my embrace, memorizing her words for the rest of my life. As long as I live, I'll never ever lose sight of the way it feels to know I've made her this happy. She will never have to wonder if I'll support her. I'll prove it to her, with love, every chance I get.

"So this is why you didn't want to talk about building our house for so long," she teases.

"We've got time."

"Yeah."

"And you said you like my condo."

She smiles sweetly. "I love it. But sooner or later," she says as she trails a finger down my shirt, "we might want to consider expanding."

A family. I feel like she's finally found one in all of us here, namely me, but I grin at what she really means. We've only talked about it a couple of times, but it seems we're in sync, both eager to start our own little family.

"A brand-new, family-friendly house is coming up next," I promise.

"I love you," she says as Dalton and Aubrey approach.

"I love you, too," I reply.

Dalton grins at us, and Aubrey sighs at the fairy lights interspersed within the gauzy lacework at the ceiling.

"This is remarkable," Claire says. "Thank you both. I know you've all helped, and I appreciate it so much."

"Now you can start having real customers here," Aubrey says.

"I can't wait!" Claire bounces on her feet. "I mean, I've already started talking with several brides, but I couldn't officially do anything until I had a workspace."

"Well, can I be your first official customer then?" She lifts her hand, showing us both a sparkling gemstone atop an engagement ring.

"Aubrey!" Claire lunges forward to hug her.

I grin, already in on the secret since Dalton told me he bought a ring over a year ago for her. He was waiting for the right moment, and it finally came.

"Another toast!" Marian calls out, hoisting the champagne in her hands.

We all congratulate Aubrey and Dalton, and carry on into the evening celebrating all the happiness and love we've managed to find.

Epilogue

Claire

Four years later...

"Grammy, Darren has more sprinkles than me!"

I sigh and shoot Marian a look. We've already filled both of Lauren and Caleb's twins' cups up with precisely equal amounts of edible decorations. Lauren was so tired of the bickering that she pulled out a food scale and proved that the digital numbers were the same.

Even though both boys were three and very smart, I doubted they knew what those numbers meant. And honestly, I have to side with Darren. Matthew's cup of snowflake-shaped sprinkles *does* look fuller.

"Aha." I dip my fingers in and snag the gumdrop he put in there. "That's why it looks uneven." I pop that candy in my mouth and smile.

"Aunt Claire!" Darren cackles in laughter. "No candy before dinner."

"That's right," Marian scolds playfully.

I've never seen her smile so much as when she's surrounded by us all here. We've all moved as close as we could to the Goldfinch. It's the mothership, as Kevin jokes, moving out here himself since he's taken a remote tutoring job instead of teaching at the local school. Lauren and Caleb live next door to the bed-and-breakfast with their adorable and hyper toddler twins. Jason moved in with Marian here once they married. Dalton and Aubrey aren't far, and Sawyer and I built our forever home just on the other side of the property.

We're all close here, keeping our de-facto "mom" happy. Marian's "Grammy" as well, doting on the twins, and hopefully any day now, Aubrey and Dalton's baby girl.

She waddles through the kitchen again.

"No snacking before Christmas dinner, Aunt Aubrey," Matthew nags in his little voice as she goes for another bottle of ginger ale.

"I'm pregnant. *Over*-pregnant. I can do what I want," she grouses playfully.

"I'm telling you, the stairs," Marian says. "Have Dalton walk you up and down those stairs again."

"It's not working," Aubrey whines. "That hasn't worked for days now."

"Only three days," Lauren amends as she helps me teach the twins the fine art of decorating gingerbread houses.

Aubrey shoots her a dirty, narrowed-eye look.

"Okay. Okay." Lauren holds up her hands. "I will not comment on how past due you are again."

Aubrey huffs. "Better you don't, Miss I-gave-birth-a-day-before-my-due-date."

Lauren mimes zipping her lips shut.

Aubrey pouts. "How'd *you* evict them on time?" She points her bottle of ginger ale at the boys.

Lauren giggles. "Easy. I tried Claire's attempt of enchiladas, and *Ta-da*!"

I laugh so hard I snort. "Oh, man. That time I put like four times the amount of pepper in by accident?"

Aubrey huffs and waddles to leave the kitchen. "That does it. Claire, I want my Christmas gift to be the spiciest freaking dish you can make a mess of."

I giggle, and I'm happy as a lark until the boys fight over the candy. Marian can handle this one. Lauren referees, but Grammy knows best, distracting the toddlers with a suggestion that they should count the gifts under the tree again.

I slip out, not an ideal candidate to help with Marian's system in the kitchen. Lauren has graduated to being trusted, though, so I leave her to help with the finishing touches on our traditional Christmas Eve dinner. It's always crowded and chaotic, loud and fun, but I wouldn't have it any other way.

I find my husband talking with Caleb about work. Sawyer often falls into discussions about projects, but when he sees me, I tip my head toward the living room.

After he excuses himself, he joins me on the couch. Darren is done counting his presents, but Matthew is trying to tally them on a paper.

It's relatively quiet in here, though, so I snuggle into Sawyer's side to enjoy the peace.

Soon enough, we won't have any.

"Before we eat," he whispers, "I want to give you a gift."

I grin. "Another one?"

He nods and shrugs sheepishly. "Can't help myself."

Since we both have money, more than we need, we've made a rule early on to never splurge on each other. Material things aren't the answer for happiness, and it's easy to keep ourselves in check, buying smaller, functional things, sometimes gag gifts.

He hands me a slim package, and I smile as I open it. "It's not, uh, another *adult* gift, is it?" I nod my head toward the twins.

He shakes his head. "Nah, but they shouldn't touch them."

I agree. I smile at the fancy scissors I've had my eyes on for a long while. They've been out of stock, so he really must have searched for these. "Ooooh, thank you, Sawyer. You know me so well." I lean in to kiss him.

"And I also know, to never, ever, under any circumstances, to borrow your fabric scissors."

I grin. "Hmm-mmm. That's right, mister. Especially not to cut *paper*!"

He smirks and kisses me again.

"I got you a gift, too."

He gives me a stern look. "You already got me a new saw."

I shrug.

"And another one of those insulated coffee cups."

I smile. "Because they are *not* as sturdy as they claim they are."

"You don't need to get me anything else." He kisses my cheek. "You don't need to get me anything at all. *You* are my gift."

I lick my lips.

"Can you take it back?"

I bite my lip and smile as I shake my head. "Trust me. I think you'll like it."

Leaning in, I whisper in his ear.

He goes still, tightening his hold on my hand. His eyes go wide, and a smile begins to spread wide across his face.

"Uncle Sawyer!" Matthew bounds up close and jumps in his lap. Darren tackles me.

"Grammy says it's dinner time!" Matthew squeals.

"Hurry and eat. Cuz then we can open presents!" Darren shouts.

I giggle and lead a bewildered Sawyer into the dining room, thrilled he's so shocked and happy about my *gift* that I can't claim credit for on my own.

This dinner is no different than any other that we've had here for holidays at the Goldfinch, but it does feel crazier with the twins' excitement for the presents later. We pass food around and eat. Glasses are filled, and treats are shared. With a liveliness I never want to lose, we eat and drink, and we prove that the more, the merrier.

Kevin shows up with more armfuls of gifts, and it threatens to derail the boys' interest in the meal. Jason and Marian tempt them to eat a little more, promising the mashed potatoes are the best ever.

"It's about time," Dalton says of the road repairs slated to begin soon. Meadow Lane has been a rocky, rough path to the bed-and-breakfast, but with all the business Marian gets here, it's a road-maintenance project long overdue.

"Wait." Aubrey holds up her hand. "I could have you drive me up and down that bumpy road. Maybe that will get this little girl to come out."

Marian rolls her eyes. "Oh, just ask Claire to make those enchiladas tomorrow."

Sawyer laughs so hard that I pound him on the back as he coughs.

"But what were you saying, Lauren?" Aubrey asks. "About Jeremy?"

We often have so many conversations at the same time, and it makes following along and keeping up a game.

"Jeremy's in court again. For more fraud cases, and slander not only toward you but another woman." Lauren shakes her head.

"And my lawyers called me this morning, confirming your parents are losing *again* in suing us about your trust fund," Caleb adds. They've gotten Lauren's money, but they've faced repeated battles with her parents suing and trying to cause trouble to get it back. I'm convinced they never will.

Finished with setting the gifts under the tree, Kevin joins us at the table. He sits between Sawyer and Jason, and Lauren grins. "A brotherly picture."

They all crowd in together and smile, then again for a second shot, but Matthew photo-bombs, jumping up to smirk behind them as Darren gives Jason bunny ears.

"You boys just have so much energy," Kevin teases as he loads his plate. "I was so worried I'd be late wrapping up a lesson that you'd gobble it all up before I'd get here."

"I saved you my green beans!" Darren tries to slide the vegetable casserole onto his plate.

"Have you had *any* vegetables today, young man?" Caleb asks.

Darren sighs and leaves the blob on his plate.

Sawyer leans around me to stage-whisper to him. "I don't like them either, buddy." But he's a good sport, taking a bite.

"I could use a little of that energy," Aubrey jokes. She holds her arm out to Matthew. "Here, rub some off on me."

Matthew laughs, rubbing his hand on her arm. "Why? Is the baby stealing your energy, Aunt Aubrey?"

She groans and nods. "For months! Can you believe it? And when she's born, I doubt I'll have any leftover, at all!"

"I'll babysit!" Darren offers.

"Uh-huh." She eyes me, though, narrowing her eyes. "I'll be calling on Aunt Claire over there to help. She'll have plenty of sleep and rest to help keep me sane."

"Sure did when the boys were born," Lauren says and smiles at me.

"Well..."

Sawyer stands up. "I'm not sure how long that'll be true." He holds up his glass and beams at me.

"Oh!" Marian gasps and covers her mouth. "You mean..."

Already, she's about to cry with joy.

I giggle and smile up at my husband.

"Claire's pregnant," he announces.

Cheers rise up from the table immediately, competing with Bing Crosby's tunes in the background. Sawyer leans down to kiss me. Lauren takes a picture of us, then comes around the table to hug me.

"Oh, I can't wait!" she gushes.

"Another baby!" Marian cheers as she hugs me next.

"Another baby girl?" Matthew asks as the men congratulate Sawyer with pats on his back.

"No!" Darren argues. "I want a baby boy! We'll be outnumbered soon!"

"Oh, Claire," Aubrey says with tears in her eyes. "I'm so happy for you!"

I lean around the corner of the table to hug her, but as she gets to her feet, she goes still.

Her smile drops, and her face goes blank.

"Uh, Aubrey?" I ask, gripping her forearm.

Her fingers tighten on my wrist and her eyes go wide.

"Eww!" Darren moves from his chair. "Someone spilled on this seat."

Lauren drops her jaw. Marian squeals with excitement. And Dalton curses. Caleb slaps his hands over Matthew's ears. "Language, dude."

"My water just broke!" Aubrey exclaims.

And chaos breaks over the room again.

Life's never dull here at the Goldfinch, and I doubt it ever will be, but that's okay. Every single moment brings love and fortune, and I wouldn't have it any other way.

The end.

Made in the USA
Las Vegas, NV
05 February 2025